PRAISE FOR THE NOVELS OF OPAL CAREW

"With deft attention to det ... bid-
den . . . this pleasing love ... *Weekly*

"A must-read . . . Carew definitely knows how to turn up the heat."

—*RT Book Reviews*

"Carew brings erotic romance to a whole new level. . . . She sets
your senses on fire!"

—*Reader to Reader*

"You might find yourself needing to turn on the air conditioner
because this book is HOT! Ms. Carew just keeps getting
better."

—*Romance Junkies*

"A dip in an icy pool in the winter is what I needed just to cool off
a little once I finished this yummy tale!"

—*Night Owl Reviews* (5 stars)

"Whew! A curl-your-toes, hot and sweaty erotic romance. I didn't
put this book down until I read it from cover to cover. . . . I highly
recommend this one."

—*Fresh Fiction*

"Carew is truly a goddess of sensuality in her writing."

—*Dark Angel Reviews*

"Carew pulls off another scorcher. . . . She knows how to write a
love scene that takes her reader to dizzying heights of pleasure."

—*Romance Story*

X
MARKS
THE
SPOT

OPAL CAREW

ST. MARTIN'S GRIFFIN ⚞ NEW YORK

X MARKS THE SPOT. Copyright © 2018 by Opal Carew. All rights reserved. Printed in the United States of America. For information, address St. Martin's Press, 175 Fifth Avenue, New York, N.Y. 10010.

www.stmartins.com

Designed by Omar Chapa

The Library of Congress Cataloging-in-Publication Data is available upon request.

ISBN 978-1-250-11680-2 (trade paperback)
ISBN 978-1-250-11681-9 (ebook)

Our books may be purchased in bulk for promotional, educational, or business use. Please contact your local bookseller or the Macmillan Corporate and Premium Sales Department at 1-800-221-7945, extension 5442, or by email at Macmillan SpecialMarkets@macmillan.com.

33614080580474

First Edition: April 2018

10 9 8 7 6 5 4 3 2 1

To Mark, Matt, and Jason
with all my love!

ACKNOWLEDGMENTS

Thank you to my wonderful ex-editor, Rose, who I miss but will always be a helpful voice in my ear. Thank you to my new editor, Eileen, for being so patient and helpful in our transition. And thank you to my agent, Emily, who I can depend on to always help forge the path forward. Also, thank you to my husband and sons for their unending support and love.

X
MARKS
THE
SPOT

CHAPTER ONE

Abi ran her finger over the embossed wedding invitation. The feel of the raised flowers, smooth under her fingertip, made her think of white satin.

She stared at the silver letters . . . *Join us* . . . and her mind drifted off, imagining herself walking down the aisle, wearing a beautiful white satin and lace dress adorned with delicate pearls and white sequins. In her daydream, her gaze locked on her groom, standing at the altar watching her approach with eyes filled with joy, his beaming smile melting her heart.

Del.

"Hey, earth to Abi," Jaime, her older sister, said. "You know we've got to get all these done this evening, right?"

Claire, Abi's other sister, laughed. "Don't worry about it, Jaime. If our little sister wants to daydream a little, that's okay. She's already stuffed more invitations than both of us combined. What were you thinking about, Abi?"

This time Jaime laughed. "Isn't it obvious? She's thinking about Del."

Ignoring her sisters, Abi slipped an RSVP and the invitation into an envelope, then turned it over and ran her dampened sponge over the glue on the flap and sealed it. Then she flipped it back and wrote Del's name and address on the front.

He was the next guest on the list.

She sighed, wishing this was her wedding coming up instead of her brother Kurt's. But despite the intense attraction between her and Del, he seemed more than happy to be just friends. Which she couldn't really blame him for after their false start in college.

But she'd do anything to turn things around. To finally find her happily-ever-after in his arms.

Jaime plucked the completed invitation from Abi and placed it in the box with the others. Claire added the one she'd just finished. Doing the invitations had been Kurt's task, but of course he'd left them to the last minute, then got pulled into something at work, so he'd called on his three sisters to help out.

Abi sipped her wine and realized Jaime was staring at her.

"What?" Abi asked.

"You know you'll be seeing Del at the wedding. You should make a move."

Abi's lips compressed. "I don't have a move."

"You're a woman. The only move you need is to get naked in his bed," Jaime said.

Abi's mouth dropped open. It wasn't like Jaime to say something so brash.

Claire's eyebrow arched. "You're suggesting our little sister march into a man's room, strip down, and climb into bed with him?"

Jaime shrugged. "I suggest a little more finesse than that but, yeah, essentially. And the point is, this isn't any man. It's Del, the man she's been mooning over for years."

"Forget it," Abi interrupted. "That is *not* going to happen."

"Come on, Abi," Jaime said. "You've been out of sorts ever

since you heard that Scruff was getting married." Scruff was the nickname her older sisters had for Kurt.

Claire placed her hand on Abi's, staring at her with concern. "What is it, honey? Why is Scruff getting married bothering you?"

Abi shook her head. "It's not. I'm thrilled for him. Suzanne is wonderful and I know they'll be very happy together." She squeezed Claire's hand. "I really want that for him."

Claire stroked her shoulder. "Of course you do. We all do."

"It's not really about Scruff," Jaime said, leaning back in her chair. "Is it?"

Abi shook her head. She'd been thinking about it a lot lately, confused by her own reaction to her brother's fabulous news. And she'd finally figured it out. "It's because after this, I'll be the only one in the family who's not married."

"But, honey, you are married," Claire said.

Abi sighed, pain flaring through her.

"Technically, yes. But I was married for barely a year before we separated and we've been apart for over two years now. I don't really think that counts."

Her chest constricted at the thought of Liam. The whole ordeal around their separation—her hands tightened into fists—around their marriage . . . was still difficult for her to think about. It brought up memories that were too agonizing to relive.

Claire slid her arm around Abi's shoulders and squeezed.

"I know it's been tough on you. But I still think you and Liam have a chance to make it work. I think the fact that he hasn't signed the divorce papers yet means he's not ready to let you go."

"No," Jaime said, "it means the jerk's a son of a bitch who just wants to prolong Abi's suffering. She belongs with someone who'll make her happy. Del will do that."

Abi glanced at Jaime who sat in the chair opposite the couch, sipping her wine. "I always thought you liked Liam."

The severe expression on Jaime's face softened.

"I did. Until he hurt my little sister."

When Abi got home, she slumped into her bed and stared at the ceiling. Both her sisters were home with their husbands now. Jaime with her two boys in the next room. Claire didn't have kids yet, but Abi knew she and her husband, Bill, were thinking about it.

Her sisters had everything Abi had ever wanted. A life partner who loved them. A family, or the opportunity to have one soon. And now Kurt did, too. In a month's time, he would be married and working on his family.

Where was Abi's happily-ever-after?

She closed her eyes, but sleep wouldn't come. All she could think of was Del and what might have been.

Abi had met Del at college, the day she'd moved into her dorm room. She'd received a scholarship to pursue her master's in Early Childhood Education at Brahm's University in Eldridge, New Hampshire. The same place her brother, Kurt, had gone for his graduate studies.

It was the first time she'd been away from her family, since she'd done her undergraduate degree close to home, and she'd been feeling a little lost.

Then Del had shown up at her door. He was a friend of her brother's, and Kurt had asked him to look out for her.

She still remembered glancing up to see the gorgeous man standing in her doorway.

He'd smiled, his straight, white teeth and the warmth glowing from his eyes making his whole face light up in a way that dug into her heart and tugged at her most intense feminine needs.

When she'd shaken his hand, electricity had sparked up her arm, firing every nerve ending along the way. His hand had been so big and warm and . . . comforting. In his warm olive-green eyes, flecked with what looked like golden stardust, she'd been sure she'd seen a reflection of the same intense attraction.

He'd shown her around town and helped her integrate into the social life on campus.

But because of his friendship with her brother, he'd insisted they remain just friends.

She'd kept hoping. Her face flushed with embarrassment as she remembered when she'd practically thrown herself at him one evening, kissing him and telling him she wanted more from him than friendship.

Despite the sexual tension between them, their friendship continued to grow. He was always there when she needed someone to talk to. And he looked out for her. He even introduced her to his best friend, Liam, clearly hoping she'd turn her attention to him instead.

The moment she'd met Liam, she'd fallen hard. It would be easy to tell herself that she'd only needed someone to distract her from her feelings for Del, but it wasn't that simple. The chemistry between her and Liam was spectacular, burning brighter than anything she'd ever experienced before. And both of them had mistaken that for love.

Her gut clenched as her mind started along a path that would take her on a rapid downward spiral. Tears prickled at her eyes, and she brushed them away. She pulled herself from the painful memories, refusing to relive them right now.

Over the long, dismal year when her marriage was falling apart, Del had been there for her. Encouraging her. Trying to help her keep it together with Liam, who had sunk into his own man cave of despair.

After she'd finally ended it with Liam, Del had been the one holding her hand. He had been the shoulder she'd cried on.

And he'd helped her get herself back on her feet and focused on getting her degree. Despite the fact that all she'd wanted to do was curl into a ball.

He'd known how vulnerable she was, and he'd been a true friend, never making a move on her. Even though she'd wanted him to.

Then she'd graduated and moved back home, hoping to get a position teaching. And needing to be near her family. She and Del kept in touch, but they continued to stay firmly entrenched in the friendship zone. She was sure that he had feelings for her and now that time had passed, it was time to do something about it.

Del grabbed the mail from his box and headed up to his apartment, then dropped onto the couch and sorted through it. He spotted the invitation to Kurt's wedding. He knew that's what it was before he opened it. Kurt had asked Del to be a groomsman and, of course, he'd accepted. The invitation was a formality.

He recognized the handwriting on the front of the envelope. Abi had addressed it.

He ran his finger over the inked lines, picturing her fingers gliding the pen over the paper. Imagining reaching for her hand and taking it in his, then bringing it to his mouth. Brushing his lips against the soft skin on the back of her hand.

Del couldn't help remembering the first time he'd met Abi almost four years ago.

He'd been attracted to her the instant he'd seen her. He'd heard a lot about her from Kurt, so he'd already known what kind of person she was. Loving, sweet, and giving, with a strong sense of family. And intelligent.

He hadn't realized how stunning she was, however. He'd seen pictures of her, but none of them did her justice. Her long, wavy, chestnut-brown hair that tumbled around her shoulders had glistened in the sunlight from the window. Her figure was slim, but well-rounded in all the right places. And when she'd gazed at him with her luminous blue eyes, his pulse had skipped a beat.

Damn, his friend's little sister should not have been so fuckably attractive. She'd been totally off-limits.

Even now, the memory of how she'd looked at him still sent liquid fire racing through his veins.

He stood up and walked into the kitchen, then grabbed a water bottle from the fridge. He returned to the couch and sat down again.

When he'd taken her out to dinner that first day, despite his best efforts, he'd forgotten he was with the sister of a friend, seeing instead a fascinating, vibrant, sexy woman he wanted to get to know better.

Much better.

When they'd stood outside her door, her wide, blue eyes gazing up at him, his intense desire for her had urged him to take her up on the invitation glowing in her eyes, and follow her to her bedroom.

But he had a sister. He glanced at the graduation photo of Cara on his bookshelf. One he cared about very much. And when Kurt had asked Del to look out for Abi, he'd taken that promise very seriously.

So he'd forced himself to resist the temptation of her lips. Of her incredible body. A feat that had become increasingly difficult the more time he'd spent around her.

He took a sip of his water, then slumped back on the couch.

Especially the day she'd made it clear she wanted more. He'd walked her to her door, and seen the desire in her eyes. She'd wanted him to kiss her. When he didn't make a move, she'd rested her hand on his shoulder and pushed herself up onto her tiptoes, then their lips had met.

Oh, God, he could still feel the gut-wrenching need that had swelled within him at the feel of her soft lips. His arms were around her before he knew what he was doing, pulling her tight to him. His cock swelling in response to her soft curves. His tongue had delved inside her, her sweetness becoming like an aphrodisiac. He'd pulled her tighter and she'd murmured softly against his lips.

When their mouths parted, she'd smiled up at him and invited him inside.

He raked his hair from his face.

That's when he'd come to his senses. He'd explained to her that he couldn't pursue the attraction between them. That he wanted to be her friend.

He'd been a complete fool. If he had only allowed them to pursue the intense attraction that crackled between them . . . allowed their romance to blossom . . . then he would have prevented the tragic events that followed.

And the limbo they both found themselves in now.

Fuck, he wanted her in his life. And not as a friend. Desire had turned to something more years ago.

The fact that she was his friend's younger sister didn't matter anymore. Not after so much had happened.

But she was married. To his best friend.

The marriage had failed, however. He'd seen it crumble before his eyes, despite Abi trying to keep it together.

Liam was resisting signing the papers, but Abi wanted the divorce. And they'd been separated for two years.

His lips compressed as he opened the envelope and pulled out the RSVP. He grabbed a pen and filled out the small card—no plus-one—then slipped it into the small pre-addressed, stamped envelope.

It was high time he stopped playing by the rules and did whatever it took to win her heart.

Abi stepped from the car and stood gazing at the lovely country inn with a beautiful garden of bright-colored flowers adorning the sides of the stone path leading to the front entrance, as Claire's husband, Bill, started pulling their luggage from the trunk of the car. There was a sparkling lake beyond the building, the shoreline spotted with tall trees.

Claire stepped beside her and drew in a deep breath.

"Mmm. The flowers smell lovely," Claire said. "Scruff and Suzanne definitely picked a beautiful spot for their wedding."

Claire hooked her arm with Abi's and they walked along the path toward the front door.

"Abi."

Abi's heart stuttered at the familiar male voice and she turned toward Del.

CHAPTER TWO

Del stood on the walkway leading around the side of the building. He must have come around the corner.

The sight of him took her breath away. He wore a casual light-blue striped shirt and navy jeans, accentuating his broad shoulders and slim waist. His wavy auburn hair was combed back from his face and his olive-green eyes, glittering with golden flecks, lit up as he smiled.

"Del. It's so nice to see you again," Abi said.

As he walked toward them, her heart stammered.

"Hi, Del," Claire said.

"Claire." Del held out his hand and Claire shook it. Then he turned to Abi. "I was out for a walk. It's a beautiful place."

"Yes, it is." But Abi only had eyes for him.

Bill joined them, pushing a cart full of luggage.

"Hey, Del. Nice to see you."

Abi watched as the two men shook hands.

"I bet you two have a lot to catch up on," Bill said as he turned his attention from Del to Abi. "Why don't Claire and I go check you in so you two can go and talk?"

"We can't check her in without a credit card," Claire protested.

"Of course we can," Bill said. "We'll put it on ours for now and Abi can change it later."

Abi knew that Claire held out hope that she and Liam would eventually wind up together again. That's why her sister was resisting Bill's attempts to push Abi together with Del. Claire insisted that the man still loved her. Abi couldn't seem to convince her that the marriage between her and Liam could never really work. He'd married her out of a sense of obligation. That's all.

Del smiled at Abi. "There's a lovely coffee shop overlooking the lake," he said. "Would you like to join me?"

"Yes, I would. Thank you."

Del stepped ahead of them and held the door open. Abi and Claire stepped inside, followed by Bill and the cart of luggage.

"It's this way," Del said, as Claire and Bill walked to the reception desk.

"It really is a lovely inn," Abi said. "Are the rooms nice?"

"I don't know. My room wasn't ready when I got here and then I got busy with the other groomsmen. We just finished dinner and I was going to take my luggage up there now but"—he smiled—"I'd rather spend the time catching up with you."

She smiled as she followed him up a curved staircase to the second floor, then to a door leading into a light, airy coffee shop. The hostess showed them to a table by the large windows.

A waitress showed up immediately.

"They have black currant tea here. I know you used to enjoy that. Or would you prefer a coffee?" Del asked Abi.

"I would love a tea."

Del ordered a coffee and the waitress went on her way.

"It is a beautiful view," she said, gazing out over the water.

"Yes, it is."

She realized he was staring at her, his eyes filled with a warm glow. Could it be that he was interested in her after all?

But then he shook his head. "Sorry, it's just . . . I haven't seen you since you graduated last summer. I've missed you. The talks we used to have. The close friendship."

Her hope faded.

"Yes. Our friendship."

Unfortunately, those words felt like a curse on her future happiness.

Except she knew he'd been attracted to her at one time. He'd admitted it to her . . . right before he'd told her they couldn't be together because she was his friend's sister.

She remembered that conversation all too well. And the sense of loss that had filled her. She had told him she was a grown woman who could make her own decisions, but he hadn't been swayed.

Then later, after her separation from Liam, when she'd most needed a friend, Del had been there for her. A strong shoulder to cry on. Warm arms to comfort her. A man she could depend on and know he would not take advantage of her vulnerability.

"Are you enjoying your position at Brahm's?" she asked.

"Yes, I am. Now that it's summer and classes are finished until the fall, I've got more time to work on my research. And how about you?"

"I've still been doing substitute teaching and hope to eventually get a full-time teaching position, but I'm off for the summer right now, too. I also do some work for some of my old professors developing online courses for the university. I love it because I work from home and set my own hours. It's a long-term project and they're very flexible about deadlines, knowing I do teaching, too."

"That's wonderful," Del said.

The waitress brought their drinks and they sipped them in silence for a few moments.

"So how's the divorce progressing?" he asked.

"You probably know better than I do since Liam keeps in

touch with you. All I know is that he still hasn't signed the papers."

Del nodded. "It must be rough on you."

She sighed. "I just want it to be over." She sipped her tea and shrugged. "Who knew *turning down* money would be a problem?"

Liam was a wealthy man. She hadn't signed a prenup, but she'd told Liam and his lawyers that she didn't want anything from him. He'd insisted on a sizeable settlement, though, which she'd refused. She knew he wanted her to have it because he felt an obligation to her, but she didn't want to take his money.

"Will he be at the wedding?"

Her gaze shot to his. "I hope not. Did he tell you he would?"

"No, but I know Kurt really likes him. And he's never given up hope that you two would get back together again."

She pursed her lips. "Claire, too." She shook her head. "But, no, I'm sure he won't be attending. I saw the guest list when I was helping with the invitations and he wasn't on it."

That was all she needed. For her ex to show up at her brother's wedding.

As the car whisked along the highway, Liam sat in the spacious backseat, settled into the leather, working on his laptop.

Liam had assumed he wouldn't be invited to Kurt's wedding, but had decided that even if he was, he wouldn't go. But Kurt had reached out personally to invite him. In fact, Kurt had badgered him until he'd finally agreed to go. It was clear Kurt still held out hope that Liam and Abi would get back together.

Liam, on the other hand, had finally given up hope.

He saved the document and closed the device, then set it in the case beside him. In the flap inside the lid, he could see the edge of the large brown envelope. Mocking him.

The key to freedom, his lawyer had told him. More like the key to complete and utter unhappiness. The final death knell to the only future he had ever, or would ever, care about.

A future with Abi.

She was the one love of his life. The only woman he wanted to be with. Yet somehow he'd blown it so completely and thoroughly that he didn't know how to fix it.

He pulled the envelope out of the flap and stared at it, then finally, his chest tight as a drum, opened it and stared at the stark white papers. He flipped to the page marked with a neon-green sticky note.

His gaze dropped to the signature lines on the bottom, each marked with an X.

A place for Abi to sign and a place for him to sign. Once they both did that, it would be done. Their marriage—the one thing in his life he'd ever truly wanted—would be over and Abi would be able to move on. To her true happiness.

His heart ached. He would be adrift. Lost in a storm of despair.

He could keep fighting for her, but then she'd only grow to hate him. She'd already made it clear she wanted nothing more to do with him.

The distance that had grown between them as their marriage had slowly faded was hard enough to bear. At least with this gesture of presenting her with the papers this weekend and giving her what she'd been wanting for so long—his signature—maybe she would at least think of him fondly in the future.

He stared at the page again.

X marked the spot.

When he signed there, he'd be signing away his happiness.

As Abi walked to the elevator, she texted Claire to arrange to pick up her room key.

Ran into Jaime while checking in. She's got your key. She's in room 714.

Abi took the elevator to the seventh floor, then knocked on Jaime's door.

"There you are," Jaime said when she opened the door. "Did you have a nice talk with Del?"

"Yes, it was nice seeing him again. You have my key?"

"Yeah, let me get it."

Abi stepped into the room behind her. "Where are Dave and the kids?"

Jaime grabbed a keycard folder from the dresser.

"At the pool. The kids weren't here five seconds before they were bugging me to go."

Abi laughed. "Like us when we were kids. The highlight of staying in a hotel was always the pool. We loved the water."

"It's fine by me. They'll be exhausted and sleep really well tonight. And this gives me time to sort everything out. Like getting you settled in your room."

Jaime had volunteered to manage the room assignments, making sure all the wedding guests got checked in all right, ensuring everyone's needs were met and managing any changes needed.

Abi held out her hand. "Okay. Well, hand over the keycard and you've got me all handled."

But Jaime held tight to the key. "I'm going to walk up with you."

Jaime headed to the door, Abi on her heels.

"I can find my own way to my room."

But Jaime continued out the door and once they were in the hallway, Jaime slid her hand around Abi's waist.

"So I want to walk with my sister and chat," Jaime said. "What's wrong with that?"

"You know I'm totally fine with the wedding, right?" Abi asked. "I'm not stressing or anything like that."

Jaime pushed the elevator button. "That's good, but that's not what I wanted to chat about."

"Then what?" The elevator doors opened. "And why are we taking an elevator? I thought this floor was reserved for all the guests."

"That's true, but they offered us an extra suite and that's two floors up."

"You're giving me the suite?"

"No. I'm giving it to Del. I asked the hotel to tell Del they made a mistake and need his room for a family member, so they're upgrading him."

"Okay." Abi shook her head, confused. "But why?"

Jaime grinned, her eyes sparkling. "Because I've set you up in the room next door. A *connecting* room." She leaned in close. "And I've ensured the dead bolt is unlocked. That way, you can easily slip into his bed without anyone knowing about it."

As Abi started to protest, the elevator doors opened and Jaime grabbed her hand and led her down the hallway. Another hotel guest was walking down the hall, so Abi kept her silence, until Jaime opened her hotel room door at the end of the hall and the two of them were inside.

"Jaime, I told you I wasn't going to seduce Del."

Jaime turned her no-nonsense, older-sister stare onto Abi. "And why not? You're crazy about the guy. And it's clear to everyone but you that he's crazy about you, too. But neither of you knows how to get past this friendship limbo you've gotten yourselves into."

Jaime took her hand and squeezed.

"So take control. Make this happen." Jaime tipped her head. "Or do you have a better idea?"

"Well, I . . . uh . . ."

"I thought not." Then Jaime pulled her into a hug. "Look, Abi, I just want you to be happy. And I believe Del is the man to make that happen. You're a smart girl. Don't let this opportunity slip away."

Abi slumped on the bed, staring at the door Jaime had exited. Del would be busy until about eight, Jaime had told her, because he was helping out with some last-minute errands. It was seven now, so she had plenty of time to psych herself up and slip into the other room before he got back. She could be waiting for him completely naked in his bed.

Maybe Jaime was right and that was the best way to break through this limbo they were in and move their relationship forward.

She did want that.

She nibbled her lower lip as her gaze slipped to the connecting door between the two rooms.

Could she really go through with such a blatant and desperate move?

Her heart quivered.

Jaime was right. She needed to move this relationship forward and that meant taking a chance.

She stood up and hesitantly walked to the connecting door. The thundering of her heart grew louder the closer she got and by the time she reached the door, she could barely catch her breath.

She stared at the doorknob, frozen to the spot.

If she just went in and looked around, that didn't commit her to the plan.

She sucked in a deep breath, then grabbed the knob and turned.

It had been a long trip and it was late. Liam wanted to get into his room and to bed. He pushed his keycard into the slot on the door of his suite and opened the door.

He'd run into Del and Kurt in the lobby, and they'd gone for a drink to catch up. Kurt had only been able to stay a few minutes, but Liam and Del had chatted for a couple of hours.

Liam had missed his old friend. He and Del had been close all through grad school, but finally Liam had graduated and started his business, while Del had remained in the academic world.

Distance made it difficult to keep a friendship going.

And then, of course, there was the breakup with Abi. Not that Del had ever taken sides . . . exactly . . . but he had been Abi's shoulder to cry on. And Liam knew that Del had a thing for Abi. It's the reason he had introduced Liam to her in the first place, since Del had had it in his head he couldn't date his other friend's sister.

And in his heart, Liam knew Abi had a thing for Del, too.

He stepped into the suite. It was much smaller than the ones he was used to, but it was elegant in its way and had a homey feel.

When he was talking to Del and Kurt, Del mentioned that he'd been bumped to a different floor because of a mix-up. That's when Liam found out that most of the guests were on the seventh floor—which would include Abi. Liam would have preferred to get a room on another floor so there'd be less likelihood he'd run into Abi in the hall. This was her brother's wedding and he didn't want to add undue stress. And running into him was bound to stress her.

When he mentioned that, Kurt suggested that he and Del switch rooms. Del was happy because he preferred to be on the same floor as the wedding party anyway since he was a groomsman.

Liam rolled his suitcase into the sitting room and glanced around. There was a fresh bouquet of flowers in a vase on the dining table, the fragrant blossoms filling the space with a delicate scent. He loosened his tie and headed for the bedroom door.

Then froze.

On the white, wooden surface was a note. Scrawled in Abi's handwriting.

Being away from you for so long has made me realize how much I want to be with you. The fact that we're drifting apart is breaking my heart. I don't want to lose you. I love you. If that scares you, I understand. But in my heart I think you feel the same way about me.

I'm waiting for you inside. If you're willing to take a chance on us, then join me.

If not, then tell me that it's over between us and I'll go.

Abi

CHAPTER THREE

Joy surged through Liam.

Abi loved him. She wanted to get back together.

But how had Abi known what room he was in?

Fuck, of course. Kurt must have told her. Kurt had told him several times over the past few weeks that Abi still had feelings for him, and clearly Kurt wanted them to reconcile. He must have told Abi where he was and arranged for her to have a key.

Liam sucked in a deep breath, his heart pounding. It didn't matter how she'd come to be here. All that mattered was that she wanted him back.

He opened the door and stepped into the bedroom. Pillar candles were set around the room and soft music was playing. A bottle of champagne stood on the dresser in a silver ice bucket, with two tall, slender glasses waiting to be filled.

A large king-sized bed dominated the room.

And lying on the bed was Abi.

A smile crept across his face. Her eyes were closed and her angelic features glowed in the candlelight. His heart ached at the sight of her beloved face.

He had spent a long time talking to Del—over two hours—and now Abi was fast asleep.

If he had known she was here waiting for him, he would have been up in a heartbeat.

His gaze glided over her. The long eyelashes fanning across her cheek. Her cute upturned nose and heart-shaped lips. The long waves of chestnut-brown hair cascading over the pillow, and the duvet covering her.

And her creamy-smooth, naked shoulders.

His cock lurched to attention at the realization that she was naked under that cover. If he pulled it away, he would see her ripe, round breasts. Her dusky-rose nipples. The delightful, delicate petals of her pussy.

He sucked in a breath, his cock straining painfully against his pants.

He walked across the room, shedding his jacket and tie, and dropped them on one of the armchairs by the fireplace. He unbuttoned his shirt, anticipating what was about to happen. He was going to be touching her soft skin soon.

He slipped off his shirt and shed his pants, being quiet so he wouldn't wake her. He liked the idea of kissing her from her slumber.

When he was totally naked, he slipped into the bed and glided close to her.

As much as his hormones insisted he touch her, he found himself staring at her sweet face. Remembering those early days when he'd wake up in the night and gaze at her just like this, knowing how lucky he was to have found her.

Finally, he couldn't hold back. He leaned in and pressed his lips to her shoulder then followed a fluttering path of butterfly kisses along her satin skin to her neck. He nuzzled at the base, which he knew she loved.

Abi felt tingles dancing along her skin and sighed at the delicate feel of lips nuzzling her neck. Liam often woke her like this when he worked late. She murmured softly and glided her arms around his neck, drawing him closer.

He chuckled softly and his arms slid around her, pulling her tight to him. The feel of his hard chest against her breasts made her nipples blossom to tight buds.

His body was so warm and welcome. Her hands glided down his back, then over his hard, muscular ass.

But as he continued to hold her close, his mouth now playing along the side of her neck, she remembered this wasn't Liam. Their relationship was over.

Her heart stuttered as she remembered this was Del. She'd stolen into his room and climbed into his bed to wait for him. She must have fallen asleep.

But he was holding her now, so that meant . . . her pulse quickened . . . that he must feel the same way about her.

She squeezed him, her fingers still curled over his ass. Oh, God, his butt was firm and hard. Like Liam, she knew Del worked out and kept his body in tip-top shape.

His mouth glided along her jaw then he captured her lips. His tongue nudged at the seam of her mouth until she parted it, welcoming him inside. He surged deep and explored her. Her heart pounded as his tongue curled and stroked, then undulated against hers. She glided her fingers through his hair, the passion of his kiss lighting a fire deep inside her.

She arched forward, wanting to be closer. Needing to feel the length of his naked body against hers. She ran her hand down his sculpted chest and over the well-delineated ridges of his abs.

Then she bumped against it. His marble-hard, impressively long cock. She wrapped her fingers around it, barely able to reach all the way around the thick shaft, and glided its length. Oh, God, he was every bit as big as Liam was, which was saying a lot.

He released her lips, pulling her to him in a tight embrace, as if he never wanted to let her go.

"Oh, I've dreamed of this for so long," she murmured against his shoulder. "You can't know how much I've wanted this."

"Fuck. Me too, kitten."

As soon as Liam used the endearment he'd called her ever since he'd met her in that sexy cat costume at the Halloween party, she stiffened in his arms. A feeling of dread filled him.

"Liam?" The shock in her voice totally killed his belief that she was here for him.

Her hands pressed flat against his chest and pushed. She was strong, but he was stronger. Unwilling to give up their closeness, he allowed her only a few inches. She gazed up at him, her blue eyes wide.

"My God. What are you doing here?"

"Isn't it me who should be asking that? You *are* in my bed."

Her eyes widened more. "What?" She shook her head. "No, this is . . ." Then she bit her lip.

But she didn't have to finish the sentence. He knew what she was going to say.

This is Del's room.

Fuck, she was here to be with Del.

But now that he'd tasted her lips again . . . felt her soft body against his . . . he couldn't give up. He loved her, and the way she'd responded to him . . .

In his heart, he believed she still loved him.

Even if he was wrong and it was just lust, that was enough for now. Given a chance, surely he could convince her to love him again.

He had to try.

"I have to go," she said, trying to wriggle away, but he wouldn't release her.

"I don't want you to go."

"Well, that's too bad," she huffed.

He smiled. "On the contrary. So far it's been *very* good." He curled his fingers around her head and drew her close, then captured her lips. Before she could protest, he plunged his tongue deep and swirled inside. His other hand stroked down her back to just above the curve of her luscious ass, and pulled her tighter to his body. His cock, rock hard and aching, pressed against her.

As he kissed her with fiery passion, the stiffness in her body ebbed and soon her soft curves were undulating against him as her mouth moved with his. As her sweet tongue slid inside his mouth, he moaned in delight.

"God, Abi, you can't imagine how much I've missed this."

Abi knew she shouldn't be doing this. That allowing herself to fall prey to their seething sexual attraction wouldn't do either of them any good.

Because having sex with him wouldn't magically solve the problems between them.

But as much as she knew this wasn't a good idea, she couldn't help herself. Their sexual chemistry was potent. And mind-numbing. When she was in his arms, she couldn't think straight.

Weakness drained her resolve and she arched against him, her arms gliding around his neck. He smiled, then found her lips again. Her pulse raced as his mouth moved on hers, blanking out rational thought.

His hands glided down her shoulders, then around her back and he pulled her closer. Her breasts crushed against him, her tight nipples practically drilling holes through his broad chest.

"Tell me you want me, kitten. I want to hear you say it."

"I do, Liam. I want you so badly."

It was no lie. She'd dreamed of being with him. When she lay in her bed in the darkness and couldn't fall asleep, which was more often than she liked, her thoughts turned to him and what it had been like to share a bed with him. To feel his comforting arms around her every night.

She found his mouth again. Pressing her tongue between his lips. Tasting fresh spearmint.

This was so familiar. So comforting. So intoxicatingly invigorating.

She slid her hand down his chest. His muscles rippled under her fingertips as he slid his arms around her back. She glided over his tight abs and found his cock again.

His long, hard, *familiar* cock.

As she stroked its length, he groaned. "Oh, baby, I could die and go to heaven right now."

He brushed her hair back from her face and their gazes caught.

Shock surged through her at the look of complete and utter love in his eyes. He smiled, his eyes glowing, and he kissed her again.

But this time she couldn't breathe. Panic washed through her as she realized that's what she wanted. For him to look at her like that. Love glowing in his eyes. Ready to admit his undying love for her.

But she was only seeing what she wanted to see.

His mouth consumed hers again. Sparks flashed around her nerve endings and she felt herself falling under his spell. Her heart aching with the need to be with him.

God, help her, she wanted this. She was too weak to pull away. To tell him they couldn't do this. It would wreck her in too many ways. Leave her a quivering mass of blistering emotions. How could she cope with that kind of pain again?

She felt her defenses fading fast. Her resolve seeping away as his heart beat against hers, his lips playing on hers with a mastery she knew all too well. And succumbed to every time.

She had only one chance. She drew her lips away, long enough to breathe the word, "Sunflower."

His lips stopped moving on hers instantly. Then he slowly drew away.

That had been their safe word when they'd done role playing. Liam had often become her Master in the bedroom and she loved submitting to him. Their agreement was that when she said that word, he would stop whatever he was doing.

He drew back and stared down at her. "Abi . . ."

"No." She surged back, slipping from his hold, and slid out of the bed, heedless of her nudity. She didn't want him to see her naked and would love to pull the covers around herself, but more, she needed to get away from him before he used his persuasive charisma and the fiery attraction between them to seduce her back into bed again.

When she was two steps from the bed, she heard his simple words.

"Abi. Please don't leave."

She could hear the pain in his voice. The haunting sadness.

She froze and, her pulse roaring in her ears, she turned around.

He sat on the bed, the duvet draped loosely around his waist, every bit of his chiseled body portraying a strong, dominant man.

But the vulnerability she saw in his eyes tore at her heart.

Without conscious thought, she turned and stepped back to the bed. She sat on the edge beside him and stroked his cheek. The roughness of his raspy whiskers made her feel femininely soft in contrast. And it brought out her nurturing instincts.

"Liam, I don't think we should—"

"That's right. Don't think." He took her hand and brought it to his lips, then nuzzled them against her palm. "Right now, I want you. And you want me. That's enough for now."

He squeezed her hand and she stared into his chocolate-brown eyes. The depth of feeling there took her breath away.

She'd lost the ability to believe he loved her, but they'd shared so much together. Lost so much together. The depth of their connection couldn't be denied.

He glided his arms around her and held her close to him, her ear tight to his chest. Hearing the thumping of his heartbeat.

"Give us this one night, my love. Will you do that?"

Before she could answer, Liam tipped up her chin and kissed her.

When she melted against him, he knew he'd won. He eased back and their gazes locked.

She nodded and his heart leapt in joy. He laughed and dragged her into another kiss, then drew her into bed with him, his lips never leaving hers. Her body, so warm and soft against him, sent heat flooding through his veins.

He wanted her physically, there was no doubt about that. But more, he wanted her heart. He wanted her to love him as much as he loved her.

Somehow he had to find a way.

CHAPTER FOUR

Abi woke up to darkness. She immediately knew she was in Liam's arms. Tight against his body. It was warm and comforting, and she wanted to snuggle against him.

But she was confused.

She'd been in his arms, ready and willing to make love. But he'd held her close to him, stroking her hair, his other hand gliding over her back in comforting strokes.

And she'd fallen asleep.

Oh, God, how had she wound up in this position?

If she was going to slip away from him, now was the time. But as soon as she made a move, his arms tightened around her.

"Where do you think you're going?" his deep masculine voice rumbled.

"I was . . . uh . . . just going to—"

"Slip away in the middle of the night? Is that any way to treat your husband?"

The smile on his lips and the delighted gleam in his eyes took her breath away. It was moments like this when she could believe that she was the only woman in the world for him.

He rolled her back and prowled over her body. His lips covered hers and his mouth moved on hers with a tenderness that melted her heart. At the same time, he slid her hands over her head and held them tight to the bed as if he owned her.

And right this instant, he did.

"You promised to stay the night," he murmured against her ear.

"I did?"

He chuckled, a deep rumble in his chest. "Yes, you most certainly did."

"I'm sorry, I—"

"That's good that you're sorry. But that doesn't mean you'll get out of your punishment."

Heat washed through her at the word.

When they'd first been together, they'd tried many things in the bedroom, including occasional role-playing where he'd taught her the pleasures of submitting to him without question. It had a potent effect on her, satisfying a pulsing need deep inside.

And it often involved being punished if she didn't follow his instructions to the letter. Sometimes she would defy him in small ways to earn herself a punishment.

It was something she'd never thought she'd be into. But that was before she'd met Liam and understood what it was like to be mastered by a man who could understand exactly what she wanted, when she wanted, even better than she did.

He was a Master in every sense of the word.

He rolled off her.

"Go and get my hairbrush from my suitcase. It's in the other room."

His authoritative tone triggered a powerful response. Her insides quivered with the desire to please him. To obey him. Anything he commanded her to do right now, she would do without question. "Yes, Master."

His eyes glittered and she knew she *had* pleased him.

She walked out the bedroom door to the large black suitcase sitting against the wall. She tipped it flat and unzipped it, then found his accessory bag. Inside, she found a rectangular wooden brush and she carried it back to him. He was sitting on the side of the bed.

"Very good, kitten. Now bend over my knee."

Obediently, she lay across his lap, presenting her naked ass to him.

"Are you ready for your punishment?"

"Yes, Master."

He stroked her ass with his fingers and goose bumps danced across her skin. Then the flat of the brush whacked against her. She whimpered at the burn.

"Thank you, Master."

He smacked again and her fingers tightened around the fabric of the duvet at the smarting sting.

"Thank you, Master."

"You can thank me at the end, kitten."

"Yes, Master."

This time, he dragged the wooden surface over her burning skin in light strokes. Back and forth across her cheeks. Then he bounced it up and down in light taps. Connecting again and again with her skin. Slowly, the strokes became harder. Her skin tingled with heat. Soon he was paddling her ass over and over. Her breathing was hard and euphoria filled her.

He smacked her ass a couple more times, then tossed the brush aside and gave her one loud smack with the flat of his hand. Then he stroked over her hot flesh, soothing it. She arched against his palm and he laughed.

"Do you want more punishment, my love?"

"Yes, Master, please."

He laughed.

"Since you want it so badly, my punishment will be to deny you more spanking."

She groaned, wanting to feel his hand crack against her reddened ass.

Instead, he rested his hand on her round buttocks and stroked. Around and around. Gliding over her. His hand strayed down toward her thighs, and he caressed lightly. When she felt his fingertips grazing her inner thighs, a mere inch from her pussy, she arched again.

She wanted to feel him touch her there.

She widened her legs and used her knees to push herself up higher toward him, inviting. "Please, Master. Stroke me there."

But she knew he wouldn't let her get away with that. Damn, she was out of practice. "Please, stroke my pussy, Master."

"I'd like to, kitten, but I think it's too soon for you to be making demands. Now kneel down on the floor."

She bit her lip, stopping herself from begging. It wouldn't work anyway.

She slipped from his lap and knelt on the carpet beside the bed. He lay back on the bed and tucked his hands behind his head. His cock stood straight up, like a rocket about to launch.

"Do you know what I'd like you to do now?" he asked, one eyebrow quirking up.

"I think so, Master. Would you like me to suck your cock?"

"Very good."

She reached out and wrapped her hand around his thick shaft. Oh, God, she'd missed this. Stroking the soft kid-leather skin, wrapped tight over solid steel. She glided up and down, watching the purple veins pulsing along the sides.

"May I join you on the bed, Sir?"

"Yes," he said simply.

She stood up and climbed onto the bed, then straddled his

legs and leaned forward. At the first brush of her lips on his cock-head, he sucked in a breath.

She subdued a grin. He was out of practice, too. In the old days, he could hold his reactions to her under strict control, maintaining the semblance of being oblivious to her touch.

Until he burst in her mouth in a spectacular orgasm, of course.

The games they'd played had been absolutely delicious, catapulting them to exhilarating heights and leaving them so intensely sated, she thought their wicked lust had been satisfied for good. But then it boiled back up again the next time they were together.

She wrapped her lips around him and swallowed the mushroom-shaped head. She swirled her tongue over his tip again and again. Spiraling down the sides, licking under the rim, then swirling to the tip again.

She glanced at his face, seeing the barely contained delight blazing in his eyes. She squeezed her hand snugly around his base and stroked while she suckled on his cockhead. He grunted in approval. Then she surged deep on him, taking him down her throat. She'd learned how to take him deep inside. How to squeeze him with her lips, and the rhythm that brought him so close to the edge he could barely hold back, even given his herculean restraint. He was an excellent Dom because he did maintain such excellent control.

But he was rusty and she pushed her edge. It was fun being a little more in control than usual, at least in drawing out his pleasure.

As she glided up and down, he rested his hand on her head. He coiled it around her hair and guided her faster, which surprised her. Usually, he insisted on slow. Prolonging the pleasure as long as he could.

She sensed he was getting close. She cupped his balls and stroked lightly, making him groan.

"Make me come, baby. Right now."

She squeezed around his hot, hard cock as it moved between her lips. He guided her in short, fast strokes. The sound of his rapid breathing resonated through the room. Then he stiffened and a fountain of heat filled her mouth. She kept moving as he continued spewing.

Finally, he grunted and fell back on the bed. She drew her lips from him, swallowing the salty semen, then she licked his shaft from top to bottom, ensuring every bit of it was shiny clean.

She climbed off him and knelt on the floor again. "Is there something else you'd like, Master?"

"Yes, I want to taste you. But I need a minute to rest."

She smiled. "Would you like some champagne to revive you?"

He smiled. "That's a great idea."

She started to stand.

"No, stay there." He got up and walked to the dresser, then pulled the bottle from the ice bucket. The bottle dripped from the melting ice and he wiped it with a cloth napkin by the glasses, then popped the cork. He carried the bottle and the two empty glasses with him as he walked to one of the big armchairs by the fire. He set the glasses on the side table and filled them, then set the bottle down.

"Come here," he said.

She walked to him and he handed her a glass.

"Sit on my lap."

She sat down, facing him, her naked thighs straddling his. She sipped the bubbly liquid, loving the feel of it gliding down her throat.

He took a deep drink of his own, finishing half the glass, then set it on the table again. He smiled, his focus on her naked breasts. Her nipples blossomed under his scrutiny.

When he cupped the bottom of her breast, then lightly dragged his thumb over the hard bud, she moaned softly. He leaned forward and took it into his mouth. The feel of his warmth around her sent her senses reeling. She hadn't been with a man since Liam and that was why this was affecting her so dramatically.

But she knew that wasn't true. Even if she had been fucked five times yesterday by the most passionate lover she could imagine, she would still feel this way when Liam touched her.

He lapped at her nipple with his tongue, then suckled again.

"Oh, that feels so good," she moaned.

He stroked her other breast then suckled that one. She glided forward, her wet folds rubbing against his semi-erect cock.

God, she wanted it hard again so it could thrust inside her. She desperately wanted him to fill her up right now.

But she knew he had something else in mind first. When he'd said he wanted to taste her, he hadn't meant her nipples.

She downed her champagne and filled her glass, then topped his up, too. Holding the bottle in her hand, she smiled at him. "You said you wanted to taste me."

"Yes, but I'm enjoying sitting here with you on my lap right now."

He would make her wait, knowing she wanted him to dive into her wet pussy right now. But she decided she would torture him a bit. "No problem, Master."

She pushed herself up, still kneeling over his lap and watched him as she lowered the green bottle and pressed the neck against her stomach. Then she glided it downward. His eyes widened as he watched its descent.

She glided it between their legs. His thighs widened at the feel of the cold glass. She rested the base of the bottle on the chair, then pressed the top against her folds. His breaths were slow and deep as he watched her lower herself onto the bottle.

It was cold and unyielding inside her. She squeezed the glass, thankful for something hard inside her, but wishing it was Liam's big cock.

Still, the sight of unbridled lust in his eyes was a delightful reward.

She slowly glided up and down a few strokes, then, when she saw the flickering heat in his eyes jolt up a notch and his hand wrap around his swelling cock, she pushed herself up until the bottle slipped free, and she lifted it. It glistened with her moisture.

She held it in front of her and glided her finger along the slickness on the glass. Then she held it close to his lips. He opened and captured her finger in his mouth, sucking it deep. Her heart pounded at the delectable sensation of being pulled into him.

Locking her gaze on his, she opened her mouth and licked her lips enticingly. Then she ran her tongue along the glass, tasting her own essence.

"Ah, fuck, Abi. You're driving me wild."

His arm clamped around her waist and he pulled her tight to him, then found her lips. His tongue drove deep, plunging into her like she wanted his cock to do inside her wet opening.

But when he released her mouth, he took the bottle from her hand and wrapped his lips around the opening, then tipped it back, taking a deep swig of the remaining champagne. After he swallowed, he glided his lips down the neck of the bottle as if it was a green cock. The sight made her wonder what it would be like to see him suck another man's cock. Her vagina ached as it clenched tight at the thought.

He glided up and down, then pulled the bottle free and licked his lips. "Absolutely fucking delicious."

Then he ran his hand down her stomach and his fingers glided over her slick folds and dipped inside her briefly. She sucked in a breath, lust coiling inside her, but he drew his hand back to the bottle and slathered the moisture on the tip of bottle, then sucked back what was left of the champagne. He tossed it aside.

"Stand up and turn around," he commanded.

She scurried to her feet and turned.

"Lean forward and spread your legs."

She obeyed, bending at the waist, knowing her pussy was

exposed to him. When she felt his tongue nudge her, she whimpered.

"You like that, baby?"

"Oh, yes, Master."

"Good." He pressed his face to her, his tongue gliding over her intimate folds.

He licked several times, then she felt his fingers opening her up. His tongue slid into her opening and thrust several times.

When she felt his tongue nudge against her clit, she moaned softly. But it had been so long, and she was so desperate for the orgasm she knew was only a few breaths away, her knees buckled. She slid to the floor and knelt forward.

"I'm sorry, Master, I—"

But he'd followed her down and pressed her flat to the floor, then flipped her over, stopping her words.

His face was buried in her softness as he licked her clit. His big fingers found her opening and two glided inside her. He pumped them into her and he licked her nub again, pummeling her with exquisite delight. When he began suckling, she moaned. Joy spiraled through her as she felt the rising storm carry her away. An orgasm surged through her and she exhaled in a deep, long moan.

As it rose and rose, she sucked in air, then exclaimed, "I'm coming."

The word faded into a reedy moan. He thrust deeper with his fingers and she squeezed around them.

"Oh, yessss," she breathed.

Somehow he drove her pleasure higher. Sent her flying off the edge to an unparalleled ecstasy, as she moaned louder, barely able to hold onto the here and now.

Finally, she felt herself floating back to earth, a deep glow warming her.

Then he rolled her over and tipped up her ass. She felt his hot tip press against her and excitement shot through her at the thought that his big cock would soon be inside her.

He drove forward, filling her in one deep thrust.

"Oh, God!" she cried.

She shot to heaven again as his cock glided into her over and over. His hefty girth stretched her and she moaned in delight. Her head spun as he rode her, his shaft driving in again and again.

"Oh, Liam! Oh, my God!"

"Ah, fuck, Abi!"

He thrust deep, pinning her hard to the floor, then he shuddered against her as his hot semen filled her deep inside.

Finally, he collapsed on top of her. The feel of his big body covering her touched her in a way she wasn't ready for. In her vulnerable state, she felt close to tears, wishing this was what it could be like for them all the time.

His lips played along the back of her neck as he shifted his weight slightly so he wasn't crushing her. Then he rolled sideways, taking her with him, and he held her tight to his body, her back to him.

He stroked her hair from her face and nuzzled her neck as they lay there on the floor. She blinked back the tears determined to escape.

After a few moments, he lifted her up and carried her to the bed. He snuggled her against him under the covers as if she was something he cherished.

She sighed deeply, then gave herself over to the moment. Allowing herself to enjoy the wonderful comfort of being in his arms.

As she felt the veil of sleep claim her, she knew she would regret this in the morning.

Liam held Abi close to him, wishing he never had to let go.

The first rays of the morning sun were shimmering in the window and he knew that meant the end of this loving interlude with his wife. When she woke up, he'd see the regret in her eyes. The fervent wish that she had not allowed herself to get swept up in the passion between them.

When he'd seen her note last night, he'd been filled with hope that she really wanted them to be together again. But the joy that had swelled inside him burst the moment her wide eyes had turned to him in surprise at the sound of his voice.

He knew at that instant that she wasn't there to be with him. She had wanted to be with another man.

Del.

He nuzzled his face in her hair and breathed in the sweet scent. Orange blossoms.

She stiffened slightly. She was awake now.

He didn't loosen his hold on her. He wasn't going to make it easy for her to slip away from him.

"Good morning," he murmured against her ear.

She drew in a deep breath. Instead of straining away from him as he'd anticipated, she rested back against him. His arm glided up her stomach, stopping when it brushed against the bottom of her naked breasts.

He shifted as she eased onto her back, gazing up at him. Her wide blue eyes were filled with caution.

"Good morning," she responded.

CHAPTER FIVE

As Abi gazed up at Liam's handsome face, her heart swelled, filling with both pleasure and pain. Being with him last night had been incredible. Toe-curling. Breathtaking passion and fireworks.

But it was always incredible with him.

Sex had never been a problem for them. But that wasn't enough to make a marriage work. The fact that he'd married her because she'd been carrying his baby . . . That wasn't good enough for her. He'd insisted he loved her, but then he'd known that was the only way to convince her to marry him. And it hadn't been hard to convince her, because she was so in love with him.

She didn't blame him for that. He'd been trying to do the right thing for her and the baby. And she was sure, deep down inside, that he'd believed it himself.

He stroked her hair behind her ear with such tenderness, her heart ached. Right now, gazing into his chocolate-brown eyes, filled with warmth, she could almost convince herself again that he loved her.

But believing that would only lead to despair.

When she'd lost the baby . . . when he'd pulled away from her so completely . . .

Her chest compressed so tightly she could barely breathe.

Despite all of that, she still wanted to be with him. Lying here with him, so close, his gaze on her filling with desire as he watched her . . .

The emotions flickering across Abi's features confused Liam. She hadn't run away yet, which was a good thing. And in her eyes, he saw pain, but it was mingled with so many other things.

"What are you thinking?" he asked.

Her voice trembled as she said, "I'm trying not to think at all."

Then her arms came around him and she pulled him close. Her lips found his as she arched forward, her luscious breasts brushing against him. He leaned closer, consuming her sweet mouth. Her tongue nudged his lips and he opened, then delighted at the feel of it sweeping inside.

He prowled over her, his cock swelling to a rigid column of hot need. As soon as it fell on her belly, she grasped it with her hand and squeezed.

"You want me," she murmured as she stroked him, driving his desire higher and higher.

"Of course I want you," he breathed. "I've never *stopped* wanting you."

"Make love to me, Liam," she whispered.

She dragged the tip of his cock over her slickness. Fuck, she was so wet.

"This is what you've done to me." Her voice was quivering with need. "Now I need you inside me."

"Whatever you want, my love." He eased forward.

Her hand, still gripping him, guided him inside as he moved. Then her fingers slipped away and her arm slid around his waist as he pushed deeper. He moved slowly, enjoying the feel of her passage tightening around him as she hugged him with her intimate muscles.

"Oh, fuck, baby, you feel so good around me. Every time I'm inside you it's like I've died and gone to heaven."

Her hands covered his ass and she pulled, trying to draw him all the way in, but he chuckled as he maintained his slow progress. Finally, the full length of him was inside her and the two of them were panting as he lay on top of her.

A tingle of delight danced through him as her lips pressed to his collarbone, then brushed along it in butterfly kisses. Then she pressed her tongue into the hollow and licked, swirling the tip over his flesh in that way she knew drove him wild. He rocked his pelvis forward, filling her a little deeper. She sucked in a breath and squeezed his ass, her fingers digging into the flesh.

"Ohhh, Liam. Please fuck me." Her voice, so full of need, sent a wild hunger flooding through him.

He drew back, then glided deep again. Her luminous blue eyes gleamed in the morning light, never leaving his face. He drew back and filled her again.

"Is this what you want, my love?" he asked, his breathing increasing.

She nodded, her eyes seeming to fill with moisture. "Yes. I need you. I want you to make me come. To fill me with your seed."

That's what he wanted to do, too. Especially filling her with his seed. God, he so much wanted a baby with her.

But that could never happen. The doctor had told them she'd never have children, so she'd never be the natural mother of his baby.

None of that mattered right now. All that mattered was that she wanted him. And that made him deliriously happy.

He pivoted his hips forward again, glorying in the feel of her swallowing him inside her warm, soft body. Then he drove in again.

"Oh, yes, Liam. Like that."

He nuzzled her neck and she tipped her head sideways, giving him full access. Her skin was so soft against his lips. He glided his tongue along her collarbone, tasting her sweetness, and she moaned.

His cock throbbed and desperate need overtook him. He began to thrust deep and hard. Driving into her again and again.

Abi clung to him, her hands cupping his hard, muscular ass as he pumped into her with his thick, hard cock. It stretched her with its girth and when he drove all the way inside, she felt like he filled her entire body.

"Oh, God, yes, Liam."

How had she lived without this man in her life?

He plunged into her again and again. He watched her, his brown eyes filled with warmth and . . . oh, God, how did he do that? Look at her as if he really loved her?

He thrust again and conscious thought slipped away. He drew back, stroking her sensitive passage with delight, then drove forward again. Pleasure quivered through her, building with each deep stroke of his cock. Building higher and higher.

"Oh, Liam . . ." Her tremulous voice faded to a soft moan.

"Are you close, kitten?" He sucked in a breath. "Because I'm going to explode any second."

She squeezed his ass tightly and he groaned.

"Yes . . . I'm . . . ohhh . . . so . . . close."

He rammed into her again and again. She arched against him, then felt it begin. A flush of heat. Her body tingled all over. Then the tight coil of tension inside her began to unravel.

"Oh, yes. Liam." She gasped as he drove in hard. "Ohhh, God." Her voice had gone an octave higher.

"Come for me, kitten. I want to see you come." His words were tight with restraint. He wouldn't let himself release until she was there.

The swell of pleasure washed over her and she moaned.

"Yessss! I'm coming." The word lingered on her lips as she rode the wave, curling under her . . . through her . . . then exploding in an exhilarating blast of pure, unadulterated joy.

Ecstasy claimed her and she clung to Liam as he filled her over and over again.

"Come . . . too . . ." she breathed, wanting him there with her.

He groaned and jerked against her, then shuddered. The spasms of his body against her sent her over the top once more. Oh, God, she loved knowing she had this effect on him!

Then he erupted inside her. She felt the heat filling her.

Intense emotion gripped her as she wished his semen could fill her with his baby. That she could bear him a child and the three of them be a family.

She knew how much he wanted that. His parents had died when he was a child, and he'd been raised by people who didn't love him. He wanted a family of his own . . . a sense of belonging . . . knowing someone loved him unconditionally. His child would love him that way. And he would love his child with an astounding depth.

He collapsed on top of her, then rolled them sideways, pulling her tight into his arms. She clung to him, never wanting this moment to end.

Knowing it had to all too soon.

Liam stroked Abi's hair, feeling so close to her his heart ached. She had given herself to him so completely. Both last night and again this morning.

He wanted to believe they had a chance. That maybe, somehow, they could make their marriage work.

But it hadn't been him she'd come to see last night.

He reached for the phone, never letting her go and dialed for room service. He ordered two breakfasts then hung up.

"Eggs Benedict? That's so rich," she murmured against his chest.

"Yes, and it's your absolute favorite. You're not going to deny it, are you?"

She brushed her cheek against his skin.

"I like a lot of things for breakfast. I think you've already given me my favorite this morning."

She nuzzled his nipple. When her tongue teased against it, he laughed.

"Are you trying to start something again?"

"No, if I were trying to start something, I'd do this."

She slid beneath the blanket, her hand gliding down his stomach. It wrapped around his cock and her mouth encircled the tip. As she suckled, he groaned.

"Ohhh, baby." He rested his hand on her head, his fingers gliding over her scalp. "That's incredible."

He was swelling in her mouth and when she glided deep on him, he grew so rigid he thought she'd choke around him. But she had mastered taking his cock long ago. She could take it deep into her throat, which thrilled him. And when she drew back, she'd squeeze him with her lips . . . ah, like she was doing now.

Then there was this thing she did that caused a deep suction that absolutely drove him wild. She had him halfway in her mouth and cradled his balls in her hands, then swallowed. The deep suction it caused made him groan loudly.

"God, kitten, if you keep doing that . . ."

Her mouth slipped away and she popped her head from under the covers. "Then you'll come?"

"Fuck, you know it."

She grinned. "Good."

Then she disappeared again.

She sucked and squeezed him, sending his blood boiling. Her gentle caresses on his balls made him ache for more. Within minutes he was throbbing in her mouth.

"That's it, baby. I'm going to come."

She suckled on his tip as she stroked his column with vigor. Then he felt it. The building heat. The tension in his groin. The surge in his heart rate. Then a release deep inside and he erupted in her mouth.

He groaned as he filled her. His cock nestled in the warmth of her mouth. Her gentle hands stroking him.

Once it was done, he ached knowing she would slip away, leaving his empty cock cold and wanting. But she lingered, not letting go yet. She still cradled his balls in one hand and gripped his cock in her other. Then her tongue swirled over him.

She eased her mouth away, but then her tongue lapped at him, like a kitten drinking milk. Tiny little licks over his shaft. Moving from the tip, down to the root.

Still holding his cock in her hand, she continued to his balls and lapped at them.

God, he wished this would never end.

Not just the fact that the sexual stimulation was exhilarating, but the fact that she was giving him such loving and intimate attention.

A knock sounded on the suite door.

"Ah, fuck. Room service," he said.

She slipped from his cock and popped up from under the covers. "Great. I'm starved."

Then it dawned on him. She was doing this to avoid talking. Because she knew he'd try to convince her to stay with him. To reconsider their divorce. And after last night, she couldn't convince him she didn't have feelings for him. At least, sexually.

Liam got out of bed and grabbed one of the hotel robes from the bedroom closet then went to get the door. A young woman with a room service trolley smiled when he opened it.

"Your breakfast, sir." She rolled the cart in and continued to the dining room, then set the table for them.

He signed the check, with a generous tip, and sent her on her way.

Abi appeared in the doorway wearing jeans and a soft, sky-blue sweater that draped nicely over her curves. He loved her in that color. It brought out the blue in her eyes.

"Oh, that's a lovely table," she said.

He glanced at it and realized she was right. From the glittering, stemmed juice glasses to the crystal vase of sunny bright, fresh flowers on the center of the table, the woman had done a nice job making it an inviting setting.

Abi walked to the table and leaned toward the flowers to breathe in their scent. Yellow roses, purple bearded irises, and hot pink asters. Right from the colors to the choice of flowers, they were perfect for Abi. The smile on her face set his heart alight. The bouquet could have been made to order for her.

And he wished he had thought to do just that.

She stood up, staring wistfully at the flowers, then she turned to him and sighed.

"You know, I didn't realize how late it is." She picked up one of the covered plates. "I think I'll take my breakfast back to my room. I have some things I have to do before the wedding and—"

But he stepped in front of her as she started to walk in the direction of the connecting door.

"I don't think so."

When faced with Liam's broad chest, Abi knew her escape plan had failed miserably. He was not going to let her slip away without talking about this.

She frowned as he took the plate from her and set it back on the table.

"Sit," he commanded.

She sank into the chair he pulled out for her.

"Liam, please. This is my brother's wedding day. I'm not up to a conversation like this."

He sat down across from her. "You mean a conversation about why I found you waiting in my bed naked? It wasn't *me* who started this sequence of events, now was it? I think you owe me the courtesy of discussing it."

She pursed her lips, not wanting to admit that she'd thought she was in Del's bed. Yet knowing she couldn't let Liam think she'd been after him. Oh, God, she didn't want to hurt him, but she didn't want to encourage him, either.

At her long hesitation, he said, "Abi, I did my best to give you space. I wasn't even going to come to the wedding because I didn't want to make it awkward for you, but Kurt specifically asked me to come."

"He did?" She shouldn't be surprised. Kurt had always thought Liam was perfect for her.

"I agreed, but I arranged a room on a different floor, so you wouldn't accidentally bump into me." A half grin spread across his face. "Yet bump into you I did." His smile grew wicked. "Several times, in fact."

Her cheeks heated.

"And all because *you* climbed into *my* bed." He reached out and took her hand. He held it tenderly, stroking the back lightly with his thumb. "My love, you know I would love nothing more than to reconcile with you."

"Liam, please . . ." she said, shaking her head. She didn't want to have this conversation with him again.

"Why won't you believe me when I tell you I love you?" The sincerity in his warm, brown eyes unnerved her.

She bit her lip, fighting back the swell of emotion that would have her eyes filling with moisture all too soon.

"There are so many reasons." She squeezed his hand. "I think you believe you love me, but as I've told you so many times, it's just a sense of obligation. You asked me to marry you because I was pregnant with your child, then after I lost the baby . . ."

But he was already shaking his head. "I told you then and I'll tell you now, I married you because I was in love with you. The baby was just a wonderful bonus."

"We'd only known each other a few months. We were both infatuated with each other, but true love?" She shook her head. "That takes longer. What you feel for me is a sense of obligation. Maybe a need to ensure you don't fail at something so important to you. Love and family." She drew her hand away. "But, Liam, you have to let me go."

Liam had heard this from her countless times before, and he couldn't seem to break her out of her tidy little belief system that explained why she couldn't be with him. He knew he'd hurt her after she'd lost the baby. By withdrawing into himself. By grieving so deeply he hadn't been able to help her with her own grief.

He'd do anything . . . *anything* . . . to make it up to her.

But she wouldn't give him the chance.

"So why did you climb into my bed last night?"

He already knew the answer. She'd meant to be with another man. And he was sure that man was Del.

But he had to hear her say it.

She stared down at her hands, her teeth nibbling at her lower lip in that adorable way she had.

"I mean," he continued, "what am I supposed to think when I find my estranged wife waiting for me naked in my bed?"

"That I made a mistake?"

"In judgment or location?"

Her gaze darted to his.

"Because if you hadn't meant to be in my bed, why did you make love to me two"—he rubbed his chin—"or was it three times? Do we count that delightful attention you gave me when we were waiting for room service to arrive?"

Her eyes flared with annoyance at the same time as her cheeks turned a deeper rose color.

"I thought it was Del's bed. Okay? Is that what you want to hear?" Then she bit her lip as if she wished she could take it back. "Oh, God, but don't tell him. He doesn't know I . . . I mean, he and I haven't been . . . he doesn't even know I think that way about him."

His eyebrow quirked up. "You really believe that?"

She stared at him in shock.

"You made it clear to him in college, before you met me, that you had a thing for him."

"But that was a long time ago," she said.

"You don't really think he's forgotten, do you?"

"Well, ever since you and I met, he's been a friend, and only that. Even after you and I separated."

"Yes, I know. He was your shoulder to cry on."

He couldn't help the resentment in his voice. Even though he was glad Del had been there for her so she hadn't felt so alone. Liam wished *he* had been the one she could have leaned on. But that didn't mean he was happy about the closeness between the woman he loved and his best friend.

"Please don't tell Del."

He sucked in a deep breath. "Tell another man that my wife waited in his bed to seduce him? Yeah, I don't think that's going to happen."

Liam took the cover off her breakfast and poured her a cup of coffee.

"Go ahead and eat before it gets cold."

Abi showered and dressed, then grabbed her makeup bag and went down to Claire's room where Abi, Jaime, and Claire were going to help each other with hair and makeup.

"Ah, this is great," Jaime said, settling back in one of the chairs at the round table. "With Dad and Sally taking care of the kids for me, maybe I'll actually be ready on time."

"That was the plan," Claire said as she picked up an empty

cloth tote bag and the ice bucket. "I'm going to grab some sodas from the machine. Any requests?"

"Surprise us," Jaime said.

As soon as the door closed behind Claire, Jaime grinned.

"So . . . ? How did it go last night?"

Damn, this was what Abi had been dreading.

"Fine," she said through gritted teeth, hoping Jaime would leave it at that.

But that was a hope doomed to failure.

Jaime leaned forward. "Honey, you know I'm going to need more than that. I bet he was thrilled to find you in his bed. Was it everything you'd hoped for?"

"Jaime, I'm not comfortable talking to you about this."

"Because I'm your older sister? Come on. I'm not asking you to tell me all the intimate details"—she grinned—"though if you want to, I'm all ears. I just want to know if you're happy."

As Abi stared at her fingers, Jaime tipped her head.

"And it's becoming very clear that you *aren't* happy." She reached out and took Abi's hand. "Tell me what happened."

"I'm not telling you what happened between Del and me. How would you like it if I asked what you and Dave did in bed last night?"

"Well . . . last night we had two munchkins in bed with us, so believe me, nothing exciting happened. But last Saturday, after the kids went to sleep . . ." She grinned. "Dave does this thing with his tongue that—"

"Oh, my God, stop right there. I do *not* want to know."

Jaime grinned. "You sure? Because if I tell you how he does it, then you could tell Del about it and—"

Abi covered her ears. "I said stop," she pleaded.

Jaime laughed. "Okay." Then her expression grew serious. "But really, Abi. I want to know. What went wrong?"

"I really don't want to talk about it."

"Talk about what?" Claire said as she stepped in the room

with cans clanking in the cloth bag and the ice bucket in her hand.

"Nothing," Abi said.

"Not nothing." Jaime turned to Claire. "As you know, I suggested that she make a move on Del. So yesterday I arranged to move Del to the ninth floor and I set Abi up in the connecting room. To make her decision a little easier."

"Really? So did you do it, Abi?"

Abi's hands clenched into fists.

"So what words did you not understand when I said I don't want to talk about it?" Her voice rose in frustration.

"I'm sorry, Abi," Claire said. "I'm just surprised, and a little confused."

"Because you didn't think I'd do something like that?" Abi asked, trying to calm her breathing.

"Well, that, too. But mostly because Kurt told me that Del and Liam switched rooms last night."

Jaime's head swiveled toward Abi, her eyes wide. "You *didn't*."

CHAPTER SIX

Abi wiped tears from her eyes. The bride was beautiful. The vows were beautiful. Everything was beautiful.

God, her life sucked.

But she watched her brother, his face beaming with joy, kiss his new wife. Abi was so happy Kurt had found Suzanne and that the two of them were starting a new life together.

After the ceremony, they all went outside to the garden where the photographer took pictures of the happy couple and the wedding party. Claire slid her arm around Abi's waist.

"Don't worry. You'll find your happiness, too. Sometimes it just takes time." Claire squeezed. "You know, maybe what happened between you and Liam last night was destiny. I really think you two are meant to be together."

"Claire, please. I'm mortified it happened and completely embarrassed. I don't want to think about it."

"But the two of you are so right together—"

"Claire, you don't know what it was like. You don't know how much it *hurt*. When I lost the baby and he abandoned me—"

Claire pulled her into a hug.

"He didn't abandon you, sweetie. He was hurting, too."

"I know that," Abi murmured. "And I feel for him. I do. But I was so alone."

Her heart ached at the memory of lying in bed by herself, the emptiness eating away at her. Wanting Liam to hold her. But Liam had spent night after night . . . month after month . . . avoiding his own pain by sitting in his den working long into the night.

"I know how important having a family of his own is to him. But . . . if he was really in love with me, he would have been there for me."

Abi drew away from the comfort of her sister's hug and plucked a tissue from her clutch bag, then wiped her eyes.

"As much as I wish it was otherwise," Abi continued, "he only married me because he wanted the baby. I'm sure he convinced himself he really did love me, but that doesn't make it true."

"Ah, sweetie, I wish you'd come back here to live after it happened. I mean, I know you were trying to make your marriage work after losing the baby, and that's really good, and it made sense going back to finish your master's. But we had no idea you were struggling with so much. We thought you and Liam were good and helping each other through the tough time." Claire squeezed Abi's hand. "I wish I'd been there for you."

"I know. I chose to stay away. I needed the time. And Del was there for support. He was wonderful. He held my hand through the emotional upheaval, always there when I needed a shoulder to cry on . . . which happened a lot. Especially after the doctor told me I'd never be able to conceive again."

Claire's eyes reflected Abi's own sadness.

"And he never took advantage of my vulnerable state."

Claire nodded. "Del is a wonderful man. There's no denying that."

Abi pursed her lips. "But you still think Liam is the man for me."

Claire shrugged. "Sorry, but yeah. I do."

Abi sat at the table with Claire, Bill, Jaime, Dave, her two nephews Sam and Ty, and her dad and his wife, Sally, who sat beside Abi. She didn't know Sally well, since Dad had moved to Denver after they got married to be near her family, but she seemed to be good for him. He was the happiest she'd seen him in the eight years since they'd lost Mom.

"So, are you seeing anyone?" Sally asked as they ate the main course.

"Uh . . . no, I'm not." Abi reached for a roll and buttered it, then took a bite.

"Kurt told me that Liam's here," her dad said. "How are you handling that?"

Her cheeks heated. "There's nothing to handle, Dad. Our separation is amicable."

His eyebrows quirked up as he cut through his prime rib. "Have the divorce papers been signed yet?"

Her stomach tightened. "Not yet."

He put down his knife, then turned his pointed gaze on her. "Then it's not amicable." He sipped his wine. "You know, sweetie, this has been going on for too long. Do you want me to talk to him for you?"

Oh, dear God, no.

"Thanks, Dad, but I'd rather leave it to the lawyers."

He spiked his fork through the bite of beef he'd cut off and waved it at her.

"Clearly the lawyers aren't helping, otherwise this wouldn't be dragging on so long. They're getting rich while they suck you dry."

Sally patted his hand. "Henry, I'm sure Abi knows what she's doing. Sometimes these things just take time."

"Like with your ex?" he asked. "If he'd had his way, your divorce would still be going on and you and I still wouldn't be married. He did everything he could to stop us from being together."

Sally squeezed has hand. "But we're together now."

Dad harrumphed, but he took Sally's hand and kissed it, then turned back to his dinner.

"And what's this I hear that Liam offered you a nice settlement—enough that you'd be set for life—and you turned it down?" he asked.

Abi's gaze jerked to Claire and she shrugged, with only the tiniest bit of remorse in her eyes.

"I don't want his money."

"I thought you said it was an amicable divorce," he said pointedly, being typical stubborn Dad.

"Dad . . ."

"What? Is it wrong for me to want my baby to be taken care of? And that son of a . . ." He bit back the rest of the sentence. "He's got more money than he knows what to do with. He can spare a little for you after hurting you the way he did."

"I don't want to be taken care of, and he didn't . . ." Ah, damn. She did not want to justify herself to her father, or to anyone else. "Look, forget it."

She pushed back her chair and stood up.

"Sweetie, wait. I didn't mean to upset you," he said, but she grabbed her clutch and turned away.

Jaime started to get up to follow her, but Abi shook her head and strode across the room, escaping out the double doors to the atrium. A few minutes later, she stepped outside into the courtyard. The sun was low on the horizon, casting long shadows on the slate patio and across the lovely gardens. She sat down on an ornate concrete bench and gazed across the glittering lake.

Why didn't everyone who wanted her to reconcile with Liam, or wanted her to push Liam to end it for good . . . why didn't they understand how painful this was for her? As much as she wanted

this whole divorce to be over . . . so they could both find clo-
sure . . . it wasn't because that's what she really wanted.

In fact, she wanted nothing more than for the two of them
to really have a chance at happiness. But wishing didn't make
it so and with Liam still living in a fantasy world, she had to
be the strong one.

Even though she was tired of being strong. For once, she
wished she could just let go and follow her desires. Forget the
consequences and do what felt right at the time.

Like she had last night.

She shuddered. *That* had been a complete disaster. It hadn't
been fair of her to give Liam hope.

But he was a big boy and he could take care of himself. And
their little transgression had given her something very special.
Being in his arms again had literally been a dream come true.
And would lead to many more steamy dreams to fill her lonely
nights.

"Hey, I saw you come out here. You looked upset."

She glanced around to see Liam standing a few feet away.

"I needed some air."

He walked toward her and sat on the bench beside her.

"It looked like you and your dad were having words. Did it
have anything to do with me?" he asked, ignoring her explanation.

She laughed, trying to lighten her mood.

"Not everything's about you, you know."

He settled back on the bench. "Except when it comes to your
unhappiness, it seems."

She tipped her head back and nodded. "Yeah, well, signing
the divorce papers would go a long way to fixing that."

"And so would your accepting the settlement I offered."

"Liam, I really don't want to—"

He waved his hand. "I'm sorry. Let's pretend I didn't bring it
up, okay?"

She smiled. "Okay." She glanced at her hands. "Really, though, if you signed those papers, you'd be helping yourself out, too. You know my dad wants to talk to you about what's taking so long."

"Uh-oh. He never liked me."

She laughed, knowing Liam wasn't in the least bit worried. "Well, you did get his baby girl pregnant."

He nodded. "So true."

But behind the smile on his face, she saw the wistfulness. The regret.

She had to remember. This had been hard on him, too. Maybe his not letting go of her was because of his inability to let go of what they'd lost. The baby had meant everything to him. He wanted so desperately to be part of a loving family.

Her heart ached for him.

And for the fact that even if they could make things work between them, she could never give him that family.

She rested her hand on his. "We did our best. But now it's time to let go."

The feel of Abi's hand on his tore at Liam's heart. This quiet interlude where they'd been able to talk about what had happened without the intense emotions had been a welcome respite from the constant pain of losing her. But now she was asking for something from him he still wasn't ready to give.

Even though the papers were sitting in his briefcase ready to be signed. Even though twenty-four hours ago he'd been all set to sign them. To give Abi her freedom.

But after last night . . . he couldn't.

He had to find a way to save his marriage. But he knew it wasn't going to happen this weekend.

"I still need time," he said.

"How much time?" The bite of frustration in her voice set him on edge.

He stood up. "I'll see you later. Maybe we can have a dance."

Then he strolled away.

Del had seen Abi leave the ballroom before dinner was done, clearly upset by something her father had said. Then he'd seen Liam leave moments later.

Del excused himself from the head table as soon as he could, then strolled toward the courtyard, knowing that was exactly the type of place Abi would go to collect herself. He glanced out the large glass window just in time to see Liam strolling across the courtyard to another door leading into the hotel.

Del opened the door and walked to where Abi was sitting.

"Hi. May I join you?" he asked.

She glanced up and smiled, but there was sadness shadowing her eyes.

"You look beautiful," he said.

In fact, she looked stunning in the royal-blue gown that wrapped at the waist, accentuating her slim waist.

"Thank you." A slight blush colored her cheeks. "And you look very handsome in your tux."

"I came out to see if you're okay. It looked like you were having an argument with your dad."

"Oh, God, does everyone know?"

"Don't worry about that. I don't think anyone else noticed. Not everyone keeps an eye on you like I do. And Liam, too, it seems. I saw he was out here with you."

She frowned and nodded.

"So what's going on?"

She shrugged. "Dad was expressing his opinion about how I'm handling the divorce. Spoiler: He thinks I'm doing it badly. And Liam . . . well, he says he still needs more time before he's ready to sign the papers."

"Do you want me to talk to him?"

She frowned. "Why do the men in my life all think they should talk to Liam for me?"

He laughed. "What, did Kurt offer to talk to him, too?"

"He didn't offer. He just did it. He called Liam to make sure he came to the wedding. Both Claire and Kurt seem determined to push me back into Liam's arms."

Del's stomach tightened. "And how's that working?"

She gazed at him, her luminous blue eyes clouded. "I can't go back to Liam. Nothing's changed."

He and Abi had talked about this many times. She believed Liam didn't love her. Liam, on the other hand, had repeatedly told Del that he *did* love her. Del didn't know what to believe, but he'd seen the pain Abi had suffered after losing the baby. He remembered the feel of her in his arms, her tears dampening his shirt when she'd desperately needed someone to talk to while Liam was cocooned in his own grief.

It seemed clear that Liam was not capable of being there for her the way she needed.

"So you're still in limbo. I know that must be hard."

She nodded, then her hand moved to his. The soft touch of her fingers on his set his heart pounding. He wanted so much to pull her into his arms and kiss her.

But what kind of friend would that make him?

As if reading his thoughts, she leaned in a little closer. He breathed in the delicate scent of her hair.

"Del, you and I have been friends for a long time now." Her gaze grew more intense. "Have you ever thought about us being . . . more than friends?"

CHAPTER SEVEN

Abi watched his face, trying to decipher his enigmatic expression.

Oh, God, she'd totally blown it.

He squeezed her hand. "Abi—"

"Hey, Del, there you are," Tony, one of the other groomsmen, called from the glass door leading out to the courtyard. "Kurt needs us. The toasts are about to begin."

His jaw clenched and for a moment she thought he was going to ignore Tony. Then he glanced over to the other man.

"Thanks. I'll be right there."

He turned back to Abi and squeezed her hand. "I have to go. We'll talk later, okay?"

Her stomach clenched. That would be when he'd let her down easy.

"Yeah, of course. I should go back in now, too."

As she walked back into the ballroom, Abi saw her dad standing off to the side of the bar gazing out the window. She drew in a breath and walked toward him.

He saw her coming and smiled.

"Hi, Dad."

"Hi, sweetie. Would you like me to get you a drink?"

She glanced at the long line and shook her head. "No, thanks. I just wanted to say that I'm sorry I disappeared like that. I'm a bit emotional right now."

His gaze dropped to her stomach and she was taken aback.

"Oh, for heaven's sake, Dad. I'm not pregnant."

His gaze jerked back to her face.

"No . . . of course not." He cleared his throat. "So why are you emotional?"

"It's just with Kurt's wedding and so many family and close friends coming together . . ." She shook her head. "Look, you and I don't see each other much and I don't want to ruin our time together."

"Me, either, sweetie. I'm sorry I came on so strong." He opened his arms and she stepped into them, loving the big bear hug he gave her. Like when she was little.

"I know you've got your life under control," he continued. "I hate to see my baby hurting, so sometimes I open my big mouth when I shouldn't."

An apology? From her father? That was new. Sally really was a good influence on him.

He kissed the top of her head, like he used to when she was a girl. "And when I thought there for a minute that you might be . . . you know . . ."

"Pregnant? No, I get it, Dad. It's not like I haven't done it before. And I know how disappointed you were in me. But you know I can't . . ." The words choked off.

He held her tighter. "I know, baby. It's just that for a split second there . . . I was hopeful."

She drew back and stared at him, her jaw dropping open.

"You were?"

He nodded, sadness in his eyes. "I know how much you want a baby. And . . . I'd love to be a granddad again." He shrugged. "I guess I still want to believe in miracles."

He reached for her hand and held it snug in his.

"And you never disappointed me," he continued. "All I've ever wanted is for you to be happy. And if I sometimes think your choices aren't leading you that way . . ." He squeezed her fingers in his grip. "I speak up. But you're a grown woman and I trust you'll find what you're looking for." He grinned. "After all, you're stubborn like me."

She laughed. "I am that."

"And like your old man, if life throws obstacles in your path, then you'll find a way around them and keep on going. Like when you went back to finish your master's."

"And when you went after Sally." She smiled and glanced to the table where Sally was watching them with a smile. "She's really great, Dad, and I'm glad to see you so happy."

She leaned in and gave him a kiss. "Now maybe we should both go sit with her," she said. "I heard that the toasts are going to start any minute."

"That's a great idea." Then he pulled her in for another hug. "You know, Abi, I'm really very proud of you."

Her heart flip-flopped. "Thanks, Dad."

Liam sipped his drink as he watched Abi sitting at the table, laughing with her father and stepmother. He wished that he and Abi could get past their problems as easily as she and her father had.

The music had started and the crowd was dancing. Liam stood near the back of the ballroom, feeling like an interloper at this family gathering. Kurt strolled to his side, having gotten a drink from the bar himself.

"Why don't you go ask her to dance?" Kurt asked. "Then you can talk to her."

Liam shrugged. "I've already talked to her this weekend. She's not really interested in anything I have to say."

"Hey, man, I know you're not a quitter. Surely you're going to try harder than that."

He turned to Kurt, glad to have him on his side, but knowing he understood Abi better in this than her brother did.

"We both know that Abi is stubborn," Liam said. "You like to challenge that stubbornness head-on, but in this, I think I need to give her some more time."

"Yeah? And how's that been working for you?"

Liam frowned.

"As for giving her time, I think you might be running out."

Liam turned to see Del walking toward Abi's table.

Abi glanced up as Del approached. Would he take her aside and have that chat with her now?

Her stomach clenched. She really wasn't up to having Del reject her, no matter how gently he did it. She had so hoped that this weekend would end in her turning things around between them. Convincing him that they could become much more than friends.

"Good evening, Frank. Sally," Del said, nodding to her dad and stepmother.

"Hello, Del. Good to see you." Dad stood up and shook Del's hand. "Are you going to join us?"

"Actually, I came to ask Abi to dance." He turned to her and held out his hand. "Abi, would you dance with me?"

She took his hand and stood up. "Yes, of course."

He led her to the dance floor, then he turned to her and slid his arm around her waist. The feel of his big, hard body close to hers, his heat melting through her, made her breath catch. He began to move to the music, guiding her around the floor in a gentle sway.

She kept her silence as they danced, not wanting to hear him actually say he didn't want her.

"It looks like you and your dad made up," he said.

"Yeah, you know how we are. He gets pushy. I get ticked off. Then we talk it through and everything's okay. We're getting it down to a science."

He chuckled. She liked the sound.

She rested her head against his shoulder, enjoying being in his arms.

"Are you enjoying the party?" he asked.

"I am now." Oh, God, why had she said that?

He laughed again and his arm tightened around her.

"I'm glad." He swirled her around a few more times. "We got interrupted at a most inopportune time earlier."

Here it comes.

"Yes. But it's okay. You don't have to let me down easy. I get it that—"

"No, Abi." His gaze caught hers. "What I wanted to say was . . . that I want to be more than friends, too. For so long I held myself back. First because I'd promised Kurt I'd look out for you, and that meant protecting you from me, too. Then because you needed a friend after you lost the baby and your marriage went into meltdown."

She realized that their dancing had slowed to a stop.

"Now I think it's time I stop worrying about what I need to do to satisfy other people, and worry about what I want." He tipped up her chin, his warm, green eyes shining. "And what you want. And I think that's the same thing."

She felt herself nodding, totally mesmerized by his eyes. Feeling herself drawn to his lips. She started to lean toward him. He seemed to be caught in the same spell.

She wanted to feel his lips on hers. To kiss him with all her heart. For him to possess her mouth, then make her his in every sense of the word.

A new song started, with a faster beat, breaking them out of the spell, their lips a whisper's breadth from touching.

"Let's go somewhere we can talk," he said. But the heat in his eyes told her he wanted to do more than talk.

She nodded and took his hand, then led him off the floor toward the door.

"Let's go to your room," he said as they left the ballroom. "It's on a different floor so people won't see us."

She hesitated at the thought that Liam was in the room right next door, but before she could answer, a ding sounded and the doors on one of the elevators opened. Del swept her inside and as the doors closed behind them, he drew her close.

"Are you sure about this?" he asked.

At the glow in his eyes, heat simmered through her in anticipation of what was to come.

She smiled. "I've never been more sure of anything in my life." She stroked his cheek. He'd been clean shaven for the wedding, but his cheek was a little raspy now. "You know how I felt about you in college. I've longed for this day."

He smiled and drew her into his arms. When his lips met hers, tingles danced through her body. Every part of her lit up with joy.

He wrapped his arm around her waist and drew her closer to his body. She slid her hands around his neck. His tongue glided between her lips and she stroked it, then suckled. He groaned into her mouth.

His hand moved to the small of her back and she could feel a bulge swelling under the fine wool of his tuxedo pants.

The thought that she was turning him on sent heat flooding through her. She wanted him. And *he* wanted *her*. What could be more perfect?

The elevator doors opened and she practically dragged him from the elevator and down the hall heading to her room.

Liam raced up the stairs, knowing he had to do something to stop what he knew was about to happen. As soon as he'd seen Abi leading Del from the ballroom, her hand a vise grip around his, he knew she was going to take him up to her room and give herself to him.

And he couldn't allow that.

His gut clenched at the thought of another man touching her.

As he raced out the door from the stairs and headed to his room, he heard the ding of the elevator arriving.

He heard their footsteps, then they turned the corner and came into view.

As soon as Abi saw him, she slowed. He could see her fingers tightening around Del's hand.

"Liam."

They kept walking toward her door as Liam leaned against his, only a few yards away.

"Are you calling it an evening?" she asked as they arrived at her door.

"Yes, I am. And you?"

She frowned. She opened her purse and pulled out the keycard. "You know, this isn't really any of your business."

"Really? My wife is about to take a man into her hotel room and that's not my business?"

"I'm not your wife. Not really."

"I have papers that prove otherwise."

"Hold up," Del interrupted. "Look, this is awkward. We can all agree on that. But, Liam, you have no real claim on Abi at this point."

"Really? And you have no problem with her jumping right from my bed into yours?"

CHAPTER EIGHT

"Liam . . ." Abi's pleading tone did nothing to diminish Liam's anger.

"Liam, you two have been separated for two years now," Del said.

"True, but we have connecting rooms and she climbed into my bed last night to wait for me."

Del's gaze snapped to Abi's.

"Is that true, Abi?"

"No. I mean . . . yes, it is, but—"

"Fuck!" Del spat out, then turned on his heel and strode down the hall.

The look Abi sent Liam would have disintegrated a lesser man, but Liam was satisfied that he'd blocked the only real competition he had for Abi's heart.

At least for now.

Abi opened her door, then slammed it behind her.

Abi tossed and turned in her bed that night. She had come so close to having Del in this bed with her. To finally taking their relationship to an intimate, romantic level.

To possibly find her happily-ever-after.

Then Liam had ruined it!

She rolled onto her back and stared at the moonlight reflected on the ceiling and bit her lip. Her chest ached. But it wasn't Liam who had ruined it. He'd only spoken the truth. She *had* climbed into his bed, and her defense that she thought it was Del's bed fell apart spectacularly when she'd *stayed* in bed with Liam. When she opened herself to him and made love not just once, but twice. When she surrendered to his will, loving every minute of it. Then, as Liam had pointed out that morning, when she again initiated sex, pleasing him one more time.

That last time was partly because she was stalling so they wouldn't have a conversation, but it was also because she knew she'd never be with him again and hadn't been ready for it to end.

She sighed. Liam may not really love her, but she had it bad for him.

She didn't believe there was only one person in the world who could be a soul mate. Otherwise, the world would be too sad a place. So although she loved Liam, she believed she could love Del, too, and that the two of them could be happy and have a future together.

She just didn't know how she could ever convince Del to consider being with her again.

She glanced at the connecting door.

It would be so easy to knock on that door right now. To tell Liam she would stay married to him. But the fact remained that she couldn't give him a baby. Her heart ached. Even if they adopted, she knew that in his heart, he wanted a child of his own. With his blood.

And she realized, that's what really stopped her. If Liam stayed with her, he'd be settling. She didn't want that for him, and she didn't want it for herself.

She rolled over and pulled the covers snug around her, tears swelling in her eyes.

Her life was like a story, somewhere in the middle. Full of what-ifs that had failed. Dead ends and wrong turns.

She'd failed at being a mother. She'd failed at being a wife. And she'd failed at becoming a lover with Del. She'd even failed at being his friend.

Now she had no idea what to do next. All she could hope for was a sign. Something that would tell her what direction to take her life now.

A knock sounded on the door and she blinked, bleary eyed. Sunlight shone in the window. She definitely hadn't gotten enough sleep last night.

She got up and pulled on her robe and walked to the door, but the knock sounded again and it was coming from the connecting door. She finished tying her robe and stared at the door.

What did Liam want now? He couldn't possibly think she'd talk to him after that stunt last night.

But what if he'd finally decided to let go of her and sign the papers?

She grasped the doorknob and pulled it open.

The sight of him in his snug-fitting jeans, his chest bare, his face freshly shaved, set her hormones on alert. She breathed in the musky scent of his aftershave and so many poignant memories, mostly of them in bed together, flooded through her. The two of them naked, her lips brushing over his neck, his arm around her, holding her tight to his solid body. His cock gliding inside her.

Her knees felt weak.

"Good morning. I ordered breakfast for the two of us. I thought it would give us a chance to talk."

"Why do you think I'd talk to you after last night?"

He smiled. "You answered the door. I wasn't even sure I'd get that far."

She frowned. "I thought maybe you might have signed the papers to make up for it."

"Hmm. There's a thought. But . . . no."

"Fine." She started to close the door, but he stopped it and pushed it open again.

"But speaking about the papers, I think we should sit down and talk about how we want to proceed."

"It's easy. You sign the papers. I sign the papers. Then we let the lawyers do the rest."

"Except that you clearly still have feelings for me."

"No, I don't," she said a tad too quickly.

He laughed. "I don't believe you." Then his smile faded. "But I do believe that you think I'll hurt you again. Give me a chance to prove that'll never happen. I know I abandoned you emotionally after . . ." His eyes grew haunted. "After we lost the baby, but I promise you, that won't happen again."

"Well, it can't really, can it?" Bitterness edged her voice.

"Ah, kitten. I'm so sorry." He pulled her into his arms, but she stiffened.

She wanted to succumb to the comfort he offered, but the pain inside her was too deep. It gripped her too tightly.

As much as Liam said he wanted her, *he* still had the option of finding a woman who could bear him a child. *She,* on the other hand, would never be able to have a child of her own.

She couldn't help resenting that a little bit.

Or maybe a lot.

His arms loosened, and as she drew in deep breaths trying to calm her roiling emotions, she realized he'd guided her into his room and toward the table.

"Sit and eat something. You'll feel better."

It was such a ridiculous statement—as if eating something could wipe away her despair at losing the ability to bear children—that she just accepted it and sank into the chair. He took the lid off a plate and presented her with eggs Benedict again. Because, of course, he knew her so well. She would never turn down eggs Benedict. It was her decadent guilty pleasure.

She picked up her knife and fork and cut through the layers of creamy sauce, egg, Canadian bacon, and English muffin. The first warm bite sent delight through her.

"I'm just eating breakfast," she said once she'd swallowed, "but not having a talk with you. I've said it all before already."

Liam watched the rapture on her face and smiled. He loved being the cause of her looking like that. Whether it was by providing her favorite breakfast, or making love to her, it made him happy.

Of course, making love to her made him even happier, as the swelling of his cock at the sight of her blissful expression proved. But making her happy in any way was his goal in life.

She might refuse to talk to him now, and he'd give her that, but he had been able to get her into his room again. He was sure that with persistence, and a little time, he could get her talking to him again, and he would find a way to convince her to give them another chance.

A knock sounded at the door and Liam stood up to answer it. When he opened it, he saw Del on the other side.

"Liam, I think we should talk about Abi and what happened between you. I have feelings for her and—"

Del's words had come rolling out in a rapid pace, then stopped cold as his gaze focused over Liam's shoulder. He'd seen Abi sitting at the table in her robe. In Liam's room.

"What the fuck!" Del turned and strode away.

Liam turned to see Abi rushing toward him, her eyes wide. She pressed past him and stared down the hall. But Del was gone.

She turned to Liam and sent him a laser stare, then stormed through the connecting door and slammed it behind her.

Abi rolled her luggage through her apartment door and closed it, then slumped on the couch. She should go unpack right now and get it over with, but she didn't have the energy.

She'd royally screwed things up with Del this weekend, and

her divorce had taken a giant step backward. How could she have been so stupid as to have slept with Liam? And then going back to the scene of the crime the very next day . . . and being caught by Del . . . ?

She rested her face in her hands.

She'd never be able to convince Del to give her another chance. And now Liam was saying that he wouldn't even consider signing the papers until she agreed to sit down with him and have a discussion about their feelings.

He'd texted her that she'd have to agree to come out to his summer house and spend the weekend together where they could hash everything out. Of course, she knew he meant to have sex be part of it because A, he was a man and B, it was his greatest weapon against her.

Because as soon as he touched her, she went up in flames.

Every time.

He intended to wield that weapon to wear her down and convince her they could make their marriage work. Maybe she should take him up on it, in hopes she could convince him they couldn't, and that no matter how much she melted in his arms, they could never be truly happy together.

But that reasoning was folly. It was her addled brain trying to give her permission to have what she wanted deep inside. To be in Liam's bed again.

And no matter what, convincing Liam of anything was an undertaking beyond her abilities.

Over the next month, Abi received a letter from Liam reminding her of his conditions and asking her again to set a weekend where they could talk.

She burned it.

Also, she sent an email to Del and apologized to him, and told him she still hoped they could be friends. She wanted them to be so much more, but she needed to know he was still her friend before she could try again to take the relationship further.

He took a week to respond and it was brief, saying only that he would always be her friend.

She was thankful for that. Not having Del in her life at all would be devastating. But she wasn't sure how and when to proceed with trying to build on that.

So here she sat . . . in limbo again.

Her phone rang and she picked it up. The call was from her doctor's office. She'd gone in for a physical the other day and to have a few things checked out.

"Hello?" Abi said.

"Abi, hi. It's Dr. McCallister."

"Oh, hi." Abi's voice was tight. The only reason her doctor would call was if she'd found something in Abi's tests. "Is everything all right?"

"Yes, nothing to worry about. I wanted to talk to you personally because I have good news for you."

"You do?" What possible news . . . then she remembered telling Dr. McCallister that her period had been late, which was unusual for her. Surely it couldn't be that . . .

"It seems, my dear, that you're pregnant."

CHAPTER NINE

Oh God oh God oh God. Abi clung to the phone, her heart pounding.

"Hello? Abi?"

"Yes, I'm here."

She must not have heard right. It couldn't be true.

"I know you must be surprised, given the diagnosis after you lost your first child. It is pretty amazing. You are happy about this, aren't you?"

"I don't know . . . I mean, I'm in shock."

A baby? She sank onto the couch. She was actually going to have a baby?

Happiness quivered through her. Then terror.

"How likely is it that I'll carry it to term?" Abi asked, dreading going through a pregnancy, especially as difficult as the last one, only to lose the baby again.

The physical issues she could deal with, but to go through the emotional trauma again . . . her gut twisted.

"I want you to come into my office and we'll discuss it. But to set your mind at ease, it was conceiving that was the difficult part for you. I know you're worried because of your last pregnancy, but we'll sit down and talk about what we can do to make this pregnancy successful. I think we have a very good chance of you having a healthy, happy baby."

Joy kept welling up inside her, but accompanied by a strong sense of dread. She didn't know how she would cope with the emotional roller coaster of not knowing.

And then she realized that either way, once Liam found out he was the father, he'd never give her the divorce.

Del opened the door to his modest house near campus, expecting to see the pizza delivery guy, but to his shock, Abi stood on his porch.

His heart lurched. She looked so good. The sundress she wore showed a hint of cleavage and hugged her body snugly to the waist, then flared over her hips. Her chestnut-brown hair flowed over her bare shoulders in cascading waves, shimmering in the late afternoon sunlight.

"Del, I'm sorry to show up unannounced but . . . I didn't know where else to go. I just got in the car and started driving and then wound up here."

The anxiety in her sky-blue eyes sent dread rushing through him. She'd driven two hours to get here. What the hell had happened to upset her so much?

"Come in, Abi." He took her arm and guided her into the house then closed the door.

"Tell me what's wrong."

"I . . ."

He watched as her eyes filled with moisture, her lip trembling. His chest clenched.

"I'm pregnant," she said.

Shock jolted through him.

Tears spilled from her eyes and she dashed them away. "I'm sorry, I'm sure you don't want to hear about my problems after

what happened. The fact that I'm carrying Liam's baby. Again.
I just—"

Fuck!

"Are you going back to him?" he asked, his jaw clenched.

She shook her head. "No. I can't."

Abi was sure that he'd send her away, but she really hadn't known
where to go. She didn't want to discuss this with her family. Not
until she knew what she was going to do. They all meant well, but
she didn't want to be pushed in a direction she didn't want to go.

To her total shock, Del stepped close and pulled her into his
arms, then took her lips. "I love you, Abi. Whatever you need, I'm
here for you."

Her eyes widened. "You love me?" Her words were a mere
breath.

"Ah, damn. I didn't mean to blurt it out. I—"

The doorbell rang and he drew back.

Her heart sank as he backpedaled. She wanted it so badly to
be true.

"I ordered pizza. Are you hungry?"

"Um . . . yeah."

"Okay, you go sit down and relax." He turned her toward the
couch, then walked to the door.

She fidgeted as he paid for the pizza then set it on the coffee
table. A moment later, he returned from the kitchen with plates
and cutlery, then made a second trip for glasses and a pitcher of
water.

He served her up a slice, then poured water for them both.

"Look, I didn't mean to—"

"Say you love me," she interjected, her chest tight. "It's okay."

He took her hand and drew it to his lips, then smiled before
he kissed the back of her hand. Tingles danced along her skin.

"Oh, no. I meant it when I said I love you. I have for a long
time."

Her eyes widened. Could it really be true? This was what she'd wanted for so long.

"What I meant was, I didn't mean to say it so soon and spook you." He squeezed her hand gently. "I know you want to explore where our relationship might go, but you probably need time. It's just that when I realized a baby is on the way—"

She surged forward, her arms flying around his neck and she kissed him, her lips pressed firmly on his as she held him tight.

Then his arms came around her and he deepened the kiss, his tongue gliding into her mouth, his lips moving on hers with passion.

When they finally separated, she gazed into his warm, olive-green eyes glittering with gold flecks.

She stroked her hand along his stubbly jaw. "I love you, too."

Ever since she'd met Del, she'd known he was special. Even though he hadn't allowed their relationship to go beyond friendship, she'd fallen for him. Not with the same white-hot flame she'd felt with Liam from the start, but with what she felt was a deeper, more reliable kind of love. His strong, steadfast presence had been her salvation during the most difficult time in her life after losing the baby and then the slow death of her marriage.

He was someone she could depend on.

She could trust his love.

He smiled. "Abi, I know we've never even gone out on a date, but we know each other better than most couples do. I've been by your side through joy and despair. I've been your friend, and I want to be your lover."

He shifted from the couch to the floor, resting on one knee. Her breath caught as he took her hand in his and brought it to his mouth, then kissed it lightly.

"And even more, I want to be your husband. And the father to your baby."

Then he gazed deeply into her eyes.

"Will you marry me?"

"I . . ." She sucked in a breath, then shook her head. "I can't."

All Del's hopes came crashing down around him. He thought he would finally be able to have what he'd been dreaming of. Abi. As his wife.

"Oh, no," she cried. "I don't mean because I don't want to. I mean because I'm still married."

She stroked his cheek, then her soft, velvet lips brushed against his, tempting and tender.

"I can't believe you asked me, and I love you so much," she said. "I want to marry you. But the divorce isn't done and I don't know when Liam will sign the papers."

"So if you were free right now, you'd say yes?" he asked, relieved.

But she didn't answer right away.

"Abi?"

"I . . ." She took his hand as she bit her lip. "Del, I love you. I really do, but I did that once before. Married a man because I was pregnant."

"This is different."

"No, it's not." Her hand fell to her stomach. "This might not be your baby, but you're still asking me because I'm pregnant. If I weren't, we'd start seeing each other, get to know what we're like as a couple. Get to know each other in a romantic relationship. Take one step at a time, instead of rushing straight into marriage."

"But if we're in love . . ."

"That's Liam's argument."

"But you're not in love with Liam." At the look in her eyes, he stopped short. "Are you?"

Then he realized that she'd never said she didn't love Liam. She'd only said that she believed Liam didn't love her.

"Del, I love you. That's all that matters. I want to be with *you*."

He drew in a deep breath. He didn't want her to love Liam.

And he was sure she didn't want to love Liam, either. But neither of them could change it.

She'd already decided her marriage to Liam wouldn't work, no matter how she felt about him. So Del would suck it up and do his best to help her get over Liam while he stood by her side. Supporting her however she needed him to.

They would find a way to make it work.

"So if not marriage, what next?" he asked. "We start dating? What about the long-distance thing? Would you at least consider moving in with me here?"

"I don't know. There's so much to think about and . . ." She shook her head. "I'm still getting used to the fact that I'm pregnant."

He stroked her hair behind her ear as he gazed into her blue eyes. "Are you happy about that?" he asked.

Her lips turned up in a smile and her face glowed with an ethereal beauty.

"I am. I didn't believe it would be possible for me to ever be a mother and now . . ."

She rested her hand on her stomach.

He rested his hand on top of hers. A life was growing inside her. A child that hopefully they would raise together.

She'd said she loved him, so it was just a matter of working through whatever she needed to finally accept his proposal.

"When are you going to tell Liam?"

She seemed to crumple. "Do I have to tell him?"

"He *is* the father. It wouldn't be right to keep it from him."

"But if he knows I'm carrying his child, he'll insist I move in with him and we become a family. He won't accept no for an answer."

Del knew that was true. If he found out she was carrying his baby, he would do everything in his power to win her back. Maybe even threaten to sue for custody of the child if she refused to stay with him. And with his money and resources, he'd probably win.

"You can't tell everyone it's my baby. Liam's good at math. He'll figure it out. Even if we lied and told him we actually hooked up the weekend of Kurt's wedding, he'd insist on a DNA test."

"I know. I have to tell him. Of course I do. It wouldn't be right. I'm just overwhelmed and worried he'll never sign the divorce papers." She leaned against him and he slid his arm around her. "I can't imagine how difficult he's going to make this for us."

"Whatever happens, we'll see it through together. I promise you, you and I will raise this child together."

She cupped his cheek and gazed lovingly into his eyes.

"You've always been there for me. I can't express how much that means to me." She smiled and moved in closer. "I'm so glad we're finally going to be together."

She ran her hand down his chest and rested it over his heart. The glitter in her eyes took his breath away.

"I've yearned to be with you for so long."

His mouth turned up in a wide smile. "I've wanted that, too."

He'd allowed too many things to get in the way in the past. The fact that her brother had asked him to look out for her had forced him to stomp down his growing feelings right from the beginning, but those feelings turned out to be more than lustful stirrings. They'd grown into a deep, heartrending love.

She may be carrying Liam's baby, but she didn't want to be married to Liam. And Del was done with being the good guy. She wanted Del, and he wasn't going to let anything get in the way of that now. Because they both finally had a chance at happiness.

She leaned forward and nuzzled his neck. A powerful flood of emotions surged through him.

He'd dreamed of this . . . of taking Abi in his arms and making her his. Completely and forever. But he wanted their first time to be special. Something they'd remember for a lifetime.

Not just pushing aside their pizza and having a quick one on the couch.

But, damn, with her lips brushing lightly against the base of his neck, her soft body pressing closer to his, and—God help him—her hand stroking down his chest heading straight for his rising cock . . .

"Oh, fuck, Abi," he said, grasping her wrist mid-stomach, "don't you want to wait until after dinner when we can put on some soft music, light some candles? Make it romantic? I want our first time to be special."

"There's only one thing I'm hungry for right now," she murmured, "and it's not pizza."

She curled her hands around his neck and slid onto his lap, facing him, her knees on either side of his thighs. The heat of her body on him, her private womanly parts resting on his rising bulge with only thin layers of fabric as a barrier, was driving him wild.

She kissed him, her lips soft and yielding.

"And every time will be special with you." She stroked back his hair in a gentle caress.

Then she captured his mouth again. Her tongue nudged against his lips and he opened. He groaned at the feel of her soft tongue exploring his mouth and he pulled her tighter to him, deepening the kiss.

His cock was so hard now she had to feel it against her body.

She rocked her hips, gliding over his shaft.

Oh, yeah, she felt it.

CHAPTER TEN

The feel of Del's rock-hard cock pressing against her intimate flesh as Abi glided back and forth was intensely arousing. Her panties were wet with her need.

She slid her hand down his stomach, feeling the well-defined ridges of his abs through his shirt, then she unzipped his jeans. When she reached inside his flap and wrapped her hand around his thick, hot shaft, she was delighted by how big it was. She pulled it free.

She sucked in a breath as she stroked him. God, this was happening. She'd ached for him and now she was going to feel him slide inside her.

"Sweetheart, we're going awfully fast," he murmured against her ear, his breath sending wisps of hair fluttering against her temple.

"I don't think four years is fast," she breathed, her pulse accelerating at the thought that they'd soon be joined.

"Why don't we head to the bedroom? Let me undress you and explore your lovely, naked body slowly."

"Later," she murmured against his ear. "Right now, I want you inside me."

She pulled the crotch of her panties aside, and pushed herself up on her knees. Locking gazes with him, she pressed his cock-head to her slick opening.

"Fuck, you're so wet."

She murmured softly as she lowered her body onto his thick shaft. His eyes glittered with heat as he filled her, slowly, stretching her as his cock went deeper and deeper.

Finally, he was all the way inside and they stared at one another, drawing in deep breaths.

It was so intense. So intimate.

She stroked his cheek.

"I love you, Del." Then she pressed her lips to his.

His arms tightened around her and his tongue plunged into her mouth. He thrust it deep, in and out, as his cock twitched inside her. She squeezed his shaft with intimate muscles, sending pleasure skittering through her.

Then he rocked his hips, pushing deeper inside her. Driving the pleasure higher.

She tore her lips from his. "Oh, God, Del, you feel so good inside me."

"And you feel fucking good around me, sweetheart."

She cupped his face in her hands, then lifted her body. She began moving. Up and down. His cock gliding along her passage, stroking her. Sending waves of delight through her.

"Fuck, Abi, I'm not going to last long."

"Me neither." She already felt the rising tide.

She kept riding him, taking his cock deep each time. He rocked, rising as she lowered onto him. His hands grasped her hips and he guided her faster.

"Oh, God. I'm so close," she cried.

She trembled with the intense joy swelling inside her.

"Oh, yeah. Fuck." His cock throbbed inside her.

She squeezed him and he groaned. Joy burst through her as she surged over the edge. She moaned, her hands gripping his shoulders tightly as she rode the wave.

"Fuck, sweetheart. You're coming."

She nodded, her whole body trembling with bliss. He kept guiding her up and down, stoking the pleasure as she shattered in ecstasy.

"Oh, yeah!" He pulled her tight to him, groaning in her ear.

The feel of his cock erupting inside her, filling her with his hot seed, sent her to new heights of euphoria. She clung to him, moaning at the intensity of the orgasm.

Finally, she collapsed against him. She rested her head on his shoulder as he slumped back on the couch, the two of them panting.

After a moment, he twitched inside her and she giggled.

"Do you find something funny?" he asked.

She gazed up into his glittering eyes, loving the warm glow she saw there. "No. I'm just deliriously happy."

After eating the pizza, which they reheated, they sat back on the couch and Abi snuggled into Del's arms.

On the drive here, her head had been swirling with chaotic thoughts and conflicting emotions. Delight at actually being pregnant. Worry because she was pregnant again while not in a stable marriage.

She wanted to just be able to feel the joy at regaining her dream of being a mother.

Her overriding concern was Liam. How would he react?

Of course, she knew the answer. He would double his efforts to win her back. He wanted a baby and he'd convinced himself he wanted her. Now he would believe he could have both. She was sure there was no way out.

But now, here in Del's arms, she relaxed. She wasn't in this alone. Del would stand by her side and together they would figure it out.

He kissed the top of her head. "What are you thinking?"

"I'm thinking I'm glad I'm here. I'm thinking that maybe, after everything that's happened, I can actually find my happily-ever-after." She gazed up at him and smiled. "With you."

He smiled. "If you keep talking like that, I'll start to get the idea that you might eventually accept my proposal."

"I'm just worried I'll never get out of this marriage with Liam. And if I do . . ." She gazed up at Del, into his warm, green eyes. "Oh, Del, do you think he'll take the baby away from me? If I convince him we can't be together . . . You know how much he wants a baby."

"Sweetheart, I won't let that happen."

She didn't know how Del could make that promise. Liam had the money and the will to get whatever he wanted.

Almost. He couldn't have her.

But he'd be a formidable enemy if he decided to go after custody of the baby.

"Come here, sweetheart," Del said, pulling her closer. "Don't stress about it. We'll figure it out."

She felt so protected in Del's arms. So loved.

A buzzing sounded from her purse, and she leaned over and grabbed it from the floor, then pulled out her phone. She glanced at the display and saw a text from her sister.

"It's from Jaime."

As she read the text, her heart rate accelerated.

"Oh, no. I was supposed to go to her place for dinner tonight. I was supposed to be there an hour ago and now she's worried sick."

She realized there were other texts. She dialed Jaime's number.

"Abi," Jaime said, as soon as she picked up. "Where are you?"

Jaime's voice was tight with concern.

"I'm so sorry," Abi said. "I totally forgot."

God, that sounds so lame.

"Something came up," she hurried on to say, "and it totally distracted me."

"Well, it's not a great excuse, but because I'm so relieved you're not dead in a ditch somewhere, I'll let it go. So head over now. I'll hold dinner."

"No, I can't. I made other plans that I can't break."

She could sense the tension on the other side of the line . . . imagine Jaime's knuckles turning white as her hand clenched around the phone.

"We made these plans over a week ago. Now you're blowing me off? And the kids? They were looking forward to spending time with their Auntie Abi."

Abi felt a swell of emotion overwhelm her and she knew tears would flow soon.

Was this because she was pregnant?

She opened her mouth but no words would come.

"Abi?"

"I . . ." The word came out a hoarse whisper, so Abi cleared her throat. "Jaime, I'm so sorry. I didn't mean to disappoint you and the boys, but . . ." Tears swelled from her eyes and her throat closed up.

Del took the phone from her hand.

"Jaime, it's Del." He pressed the button to put the phone on speaker.

"Del? Are you in Maryville?"

"No. Abi's here with me in Eldridge. She's going to be staying with me for a few days. Maybe more."

"Why? What's happened?"

Abi stared at Del and she shook her head. She didn't want her family to know about the pregnancy yet. Not until she'd had more time to get used to the idea.

"Nothing. She's fine. Something upset her this afternoon and threw her into a tailspin. She went out for a drive and wound up here."

"Del, what is it? What happened?"

"Jaime, Abi will tell you about it later. Don't worry. She just needs some time to get her bearings."

"Does it have something to do with that *husband* of hers?" The acid tone she used made it clear what she thought of Liam. "Is he still giving her grief about the divorce?"

"It's not my place to say."

"It must be pretty serious because it's not like Abi to forget plans with family."

Abi drew in a deep breath. She had to say something. She didn't want to leave her sister hanging like this.

"I have good news," Abi said, her voice a little shaky.

Del's gaze jerked to her, his eyebrows darting up.

"Yeah?" Jaime said. "Lay it on me."

"Del and I have talked, and we've decided we want to be together."

"What? Oh, honey, that's wonderful. I'm so happy for you. It's certainly taken the two of you long enough. Del, are you still on the line?"

"Yes," he answered, "we're on speaker."

"You look out for my little sister and take good care of her. Then send her home soon so I can find out what triggered all this."

"Will you forgive me for missing tonight?" Abi asked.

"Under the circumstances, I suppose so," she said grudgingly, but she used her big-sister I'm-not-letting-you-off-the-hook-that-easily tone. "But I want a full account of what happened when you get back."

"Of course," Abi said.

"And, Abi . . ." Jaime's voice had softened. "You know whatever caused you to rush up there . . ." She sighed. "Well, you know you can tell me anything, right? I'm always here for you."

"I know. Thanks, Jaime."

Abi hung up the phone and slid it back into her purse, guilt pulsing through her that she didn't go to Jaime first and tell her about the pregnancy. Her first inclination had been to run to Del, even though she knew her family would always be there for her.

But somehow, Del was there for her in a way that was more substantial. He was the one she wanted to spend her life with, so it made sense to go to him first.

Her heart ached and suddenly tears were flooding from her eyes. Del pulled her to him and stroked her hair. He kissed her head and held her as she sobbed. His shirt was damp with her tears and he handed her a tissue. When she wiped her eyes, he took the damp one, then handed her a new one.

Still the tears flowed.

"I feel like an idiot crying like this," she said between sobs.

"Don't. You're a pregnant lady. You can't help it."

She lifted her head and stared at him, her jaw dropping open. Was he really minimizing her feelings like that?

"You think that what I'm feeling is just hormones and—"

He laughed. "Of course not. I was trying to make you laugh."

"By making fun of me?"

He cupped her cheeks. "I'm not making fun of you, love. I know you're dealing with some pretty emotional issues, and I was trying to help." His lips turned up in a charming half grin. "Hopefully I'll get better at it."

The second he'd called her "love" her mood had flipped like a light switch.

She rested her hand on his shoulder, feeling her eyes tear up again, but this time from happiness.

"You're great at it," she said softly.

He wiped an errant tear that streamed down her cheek.

"I can see this is going to be an interesting journey. Tears when you're upset. Tears when you're happy. I'm going to go crazy trying to figure out whether to make a joke or hug you."

"Always hug. Then you can joke later."

"Yes, ma'am."

He tightened his embrace around her and she sighed against his shirt.

"It's okay that you didn't tell her," Del said.

She nodded. "Deep down, I wanted you to be the first to know. Hoping things would wind up like this. With us together."

She smiled and leaned back, gazing up at him.

"And now, here we are."

CHAPTER ELEVEN

Del grinned. Abi's emotional turmoil was unsettling, and he hoped he'd be able to be there for her in a way that helped her.

But now seeing her smile set his heart alight. And the gleam in her eyes reminded him that they still had a romantic interlude planned.

And there was no time like the present.

"Yes. We definitely are." He leaned in to kiss her, anticipating the feel of her soft lips against his.

Her phone buzzed.

He drew back, knowing she'd want to check it.

As she pulled it from her purse, he asked, "Is that Jaime again?"

She glanced at the display, then frowned.

"What is it?" Del asked.

"It's a text from Liam."

He raised an eyebrow. Why was her husband, or rather soon-to-be-ex-husband if Del had anything to do with it, texting her?

She sighed and put the phone back in her purse.

"It's related to the divorce."

"I assumed."

But he didn't like it all the same. It still stung that she'd had sex with Liam at the wedding.

"So what does he want?" Del asked.

She sighed. "At the wedding, he told me he wouldn't even consider signing the divorce papers until I agreed to meet with him and talk about our feelings."

"Did you talk to him about your feelings when you were in bed with him?"

Oh, shit! The moment the words were out, he wished he hadn't said them.

She stared at him, her brow furrowed, and he was afraid she'd start to cry again.

But she sucked in a breath, steadying her emotions.

She bit her lip. "Del . . . I didn't mean to sleep with him. Please believe me. I went into his room because I thought it was yours. Jaime set us up in connecting rooms so I could go in and wait for you, then tell you how I feel. But somehow things got switched and Liam wound up with the room."

"That doesn't explain why you had sex with him."

Her eyes clouded. "I . . . fell asleep in the bed and when I woke up, he was kissing me and . . ."

"And he's so irresistible to you, you couldn't help yourself."

Guilt clouded her eyes and she dropped her gaze to her hands.

Shit! That's exactly the way it was. He would always be second to Liam. If Liam ever convinced Abi she could really trust him again . . . his heart stuttered . . . Del was sure she'd run back to him in a heartbeat.

Not that it would be easy for Liam to do that. When their marriage had fallen apart, it had devastated Abi. Liam's withdrawal after losing the baby had wounded Abi too deeply. It would take something monumental to turn things around.

But whether that happened or not, Del knew he had to share a place in her heart alongside the man who had hurt her. Because she was never going to stop loving Liam.

And knowing he was second place made him feel like shit.

"I'm sorry, Del. If I could take it back, I would. And the next morning . . . breakfast . . . I was trying to push him to sign the papers."

He nodded. He was sure she probably was. But he didn't know if she'd spent the night with him or not. And he wasn't going to ask. The wrong answer would be too painful to hear.

But he had to get a grip on himself. For the first time, Abi and he had a chance to build a real, loving relationship together and he wasn't going to blow it.

"Look," Del said, "I can't really say anything. He's still legally your husband, and you and I . . . we were just friends."

"And I wanted us to be so much more. I didn't know then if you wanted me, but I was going to do my best to seduce you. To convince you we should start a romantic relationship."

He tipped up her chin and stared at her with solemn eyes. "I just wish you weren't still so attracted to him."

Abi's chest constricted as guilt flooded through her. She couldn't lie and tell him she wasn't still attracted to Liam. It was more than attraction. The man seemed to have a spell over her. He could mesmerize her with his voice. If he commanded her, she would obey.

"Del, Liam and I are over. You know that. I'm with you now." She stroked his cheek tenderly. "I want *you*."

His jaw twitched, but he nodded.

"I love you. Please believe me."

He sighed, then nodded. "I do."

But he looked pensive.

"What is it then? What are you thinking about?"

"Damn, it's just that I could kick myself. When Kurt suggested I switch rooms with Liam so I could be on the same floor as the rest of the wedding party, I didn't think anything of it. I wish I had known that your well-meaning sister had arranged things to get us together. If only I had said no to Kurt's suggestion."

He gazed at her with an intensity that gripped her.

"Then you and I would have been together that night . . . and you'd be carrying my baby right now instead of Liam's."

Her heart swelled at that thought. Everything would be so much better if that's what had happened.

"We can't do anything about the past, or the fact that I'm pregnant. But we're together now."

He smiled, the golden specks in his olive-green eyes glittering like stardust.

"Yes, we are."

He tightened his arm around her.

She stroked his cheek, then leaned in and dragged her teeth along the rough stubble on his chin. Then she glided her tongue over it. God, she loved the masculine feel of the whiskers against her lips.

His hand slid down her back, pulling her closer to his hard body.

"Mmm. Sweetheart, that's an invitation I'm not going to ignore."

He shifted his head and his lips found hers. His mouth moved on hers tenderly at first, then more passionately. His tongue slid into her mouth and he explored with confidence, swirling inside her depths. She stroked her tongue over his.

"Mmm, fuck, I want you so badly." His voice was a deep rumble.

She ran her hand down his chest, then rested it over his heart, her palm flat, feeling his heartbeat. He loved her. And she loved him. She couldn't wait to feel him inside her again.

"I want you, too," she murmured.

She started to move onto his lap, needing to feel their bodies pressed tight together.

"Oh, no, you don't. We're going to do it properly this time." He scooped her up into his arms and stood up.

She laughed as she wrapped her arms around his neck. "Really? I thought last time worked pretty well."

"It's going to be even better this time. Believe me." He carried her toward the bedroom.

"Oh, I do."

He set her on the bed. "Now you stay right there."

She watched his fine, tight butt as he walked from the room. A moment later, she heard soft music playing. Then he returned with a couple of pillar candles and a lighter.

"I would have brought wine, too, but in your condition . . ."

"I don't need wine. I only need you."

He finished lighting the candles and turned to her. He dimmed the lights and smiled.

Anticipation built inside her as he stepped toward her, his smile growing.

She reached behind her and unfastened the zipper of her dress, watching his eyes heat as she did. She drew her arms from the dress, then held the fabric to her bosom as he sat on the bed beside her. He gazed down at her hands, holding the cloth to her chest. He took one and brushed his lips along the back of it, sending tingles quivering up her arm.

She released the dress and it dropped to her waist. His gaze locked on her breasts, barely covered by her powder-blue, lacy bra, and glided over the swell, sending heat fluttering through her body.

"I knew your breasts would be perfect."

Her cheeks heated at his compliment.

She reached behind her and unhooked the bra. They'd already made love, but they'd been fully clothed. This was the first time he'd see her naked.

She pushed the straps from her shoulders, watching him and the fire blazing in his eyes. Then she slowly slid the bra down. At the first sight of her rigid nipples, his breath caught.

"Ah, fuck, sweetheart. They're so beautiful."

He cupped her breast with his big, warm hand. At the feel of his fingers around her, her nipple cushioned against his palm, she drew in a deep breath.

He knelt down on the floor in front of her and cupped the other one, too. He caressed lightly, then his thumbs glided over the nipples. They swelled, growing harder, sending pleasure spiking right through her body. She ached inside and she felt the dampness forming between her thighs.

He leaned down and when she felt his mouth cover her nipple, she moaned softly. The feel of his hot, wet mouth around her drove her wild. She cupped his head and drew him closer. When he suckled, she moaned louder.

He moved to her other breast and lapped at the nipple, then took it inside.

"Oh, yes. I love that," she murmured. "But I want to see you now."

He laughed against her flesh, then stood up. "Whatever you want."

He unfastened the first button of his shirt. Then the next. She watched as he revealed his chest, broad and muscular. Then his stomach, the abs well-defined and calling to her to stroke them.

She rested her fingertips on his chest, then glided over the tight ridges of muscle.

He undid his belt and pulled it from the loops, then tossed it aside. Then he released the button on his jeans and she licked her lips as he slid down the zipper.

He dropped the pants to the floor and stood in front of her in only his boxers.

"Don't stop there," she said, her voice a husky murmur.

He chuckled, then pushed the remaining garment down his legs. When he stood up again, her gaze locked on his swelling cock. She longed to wrap her hand around it. Feel it pulsing in her grip.

"Now you," he said, holding out his hand to her.

She took it and stood up, then pushed the dress over her hips, letting it flutter to the floor. Then she tucked her thumbs under the elastic of her panties and eased them down, conscious of him watching her, his eyes blazing with heat. Raging hotter as she revealed her intimate flesh.

She glided the panties all the way down to the floor, then stood up.

His intense male gaze gliding over every part of her had goose bumps shimmering over her entire body.

He stepped forward, taking her into his arms. She sucked in a breath at the shock of his hot, hard body against hers. She slid her hands down his back, then over his rock-hard ass, and pulled him closer. His rigid erection pressed hard against her belly.

He walked her backward until she felt the bed against her legs, then he leaned her back until she was lying on the bed, her feet still on the floor. His lips captured hers in a deep kiss, then he eased back.

"Yes. This is the way I want you."

CHAPTER TWELVE

Del knelt down and guided her legs open. Abi felt a little embarrassed at him staring at her folds, but the warm appreciation in his eyes relaxed her. He ran his hand along her inner thigh and she shivered.

"You are so beautiful. I've longed to be with you like this for so long."

His fingertips danced up her naked stomach and he enveloped her breasts in his large hands again. It was so warm and exciting in his grip. She found herself arching to him.

He chuckled. Then he leaned forward and kissed her ribs. Moving upward to the lower swell of her breast, his hand shifted as he kissed up to the peak, then his tongue lapped across her swollen nipple.

"Ohhh, yes," she murmured.

He opened his mouth around her and suckled softly. She arched again, loving his moist warmth around her.

She pushed her hands over her head as he moved to her other breast, his hands around her waist now. Then he glided his raspy cheek against her stomach. And moved downward.

Oh, God, he was going to kiss her there. She murmured as his lips brushed below her navel, then fluttered kisses on a continuing downward path. Then he pressed her legs wider apart.

"Now I'm going to taste you, sweetheart."

She drew in a breath as he glided his fingers along her swollen folds, then opened them to reveal her clit. She could feel his warm breath on it. Then the stubble of his beard brushing against her inner thigh.

"Oh, God." She gasped softly as his mouth covered her. She arched against his heat, delightful sensations fluttering through her.

His tongue glided over her in a slow, steady lick. Then he fluttered it over her clit.

She moaned at the pleasure spiraling through her body. Her fingers twined in his hair as she breathed deeply. He slid his tongue lower and she felt it push inside her. She arched, wanting more.

He laughed against her flesh, then shifted back to her clit. The lightest touch of his tongue sent shivers through her.

His finger stroked her folds, lightly at first, then he pressed one finger to her opening and glided it inside her. The feel of him stroking the inside of her passage took her breath away. When he began to suckle her clit at the same time, she moaned, pleasure quivering through her.

"Del . . . oh, that feels so good."

Another finger slid into her and she trembled with delight. He began to pulse them inside her, his tongue working magic on her sensitive nub. Joy swelled through her in waves, rising higher and higher.

"Oh . . . Del . . . yes. I'm going to come."

"Yes, sweetheart," he murmured against her slickness. "Come for me."

Intense sensations surged through her as his tongue flicked over her clit, his fingers pumping into her. She gasped, then shattered in a mind-blowing orgasm. Her moans filled the room as he kept urging her on and on with his expert attention.

Finally, she slumped back on the bed, out of breath.

He surged onto the bed and lay down beside her, resting on his side with a huge smile on his face.

"Thank you," she whispered, barely able to articulate.

He drew her close to him, his strong arms around her. She loved the feel of being pressed against his solid body. She slid her hand down his chest, enjoying the muscular ridges along the way. Then she found his hot shaft resting against his belly and she curled her fingers around it. She stroked, gliding up and down. He moaned softly.

"I love the feel of your soft hand around me."

She squeezed and his moan turned into a groan.

"Oh, sweetheart, I'm loving that."

She smiled. "That's good."

She flattened her free hand on his chest and pressed until he rolled onto his back. She leaned forward and licked his hard male nipple, then teased it with the tip of her tongue. When she began to suckle, his hand cupped her head, his fingers entwined in her long hair.

"Ah, sweetheart."

She gazed up at his face as she kissed down his ribs, then over his ridged abs. She smiled as she lifted his cock and pressed her lips to the tip. She kissed it lovingly, then swirled her tongue over it. The pleasure on his face sent blood surging through her, setting her heart racing.

She loved knowing she was giving him joy.

She opened, gliding her lips around his wide cockhead, pushing down as she slowly took it into her mouth. When it was all the way in, she curled her tongue under the corona and swept around it, to his soft moans.

She was aching inside, wanting to shift up and press his hard erection to her soft flesh, then slide down on him, taking him deep inside. But she resisted. Instead, she glided her mouth down on him, taking him deep into her throat.

"Ah, fuck, yeah."

She opened and took him deeper, then glided back, squeezing him with her lips as she moved. She began to bob up and down, slowly at first, then speeding up, then slowing again, moving her hand in rhythm with her mouth. His breathing was erratic and she could see the heat in his eyes. The fact she was bringing him so close to orgasm had her yearning to have him inside her again. To feel his big cock stroke her insides, sending heat quivering through her.

She glided her hand over his stomach then down between his thighs. She cupped his balls in her hand and caressed them gently.

"Ah, sweetheart, I'm going to come any second."

She nodded, gazing at his face again. She pumped him faster and he groaned. She felt him stiffen, then his cock pulsed in her mouth. Hot liquid erupted into her, shooting down her throat and filling her mouth. She kept pumping with her hand, sucking his thick cock dry.

When he finally dropped back on the bed, she glided from his cock, then licked it like a lollipop.

He grasped her arms and pulled her up to him, then ravaged her mouth, his tongue pulsing inside.

"Damn, you are so sexy. That was sensational."

"I'm glad you enjoyed it."

"Enjoyed it?" He chuckled. "Fuck, that's an understatement."

He kissed her again, then rolled her on top of him. His hands cupped her behind and he pulled her tight to his body. Although his cock was sagging, she could feel it thicken and rise as he kneaded her ass. She pressed her breasts hard against his chest and undulated. Her hard nipples spiked into him and he groaned.

His cock was now a hard ridge against her belly.

"Damn, it shouldn't be possible for me to be ready again so soon, but you are so fucking sexy."

"That's good," she murmured with a smile, "because I think I'll die if I don't feel your enormous cock inside me soon."

A half grin curled his lips. "Enormous, eh?"

He rolled her onto her back and tucked her under him, his eyes glittering.

"Well, with flattery like that, you get whatever you want."

She felt his hot flesh glide over her slickness, then press against her. He entered her in one deep thrust and her eyes widened as pleasure surged through her.

"Oh . . . my . . . God," she murmured, barely able to speak.

Her channel was stretched around his thick member, his body pressing her tight to the bed.

His lips nuzzled against her collarbone and tingles danced along her skin while her intimate muscles squeezed around him.

Then he drew back. Painfully slowly. His cock caressing her tender passage.

"Ohhh." The word crooned from her in a long, soft moan, resonating through her whole body.

Then he drove deep again, making her gasp. Pleasure trilled through her, setting her nerve endings aflame.

"Ah, sweetheart, I love your body so tight around me."

He began pumping into her as she clung to his broad shoulders. Joyful sensations bombarded her, pleasure spiraling tight in her stomach as he rode her faster and faster. She could feel the rising tide flooding through her, sending her heart pounding.

Her breathing accelerated as she felt the orgasm start to blossom. Euphoria was a whisper away.

"Come for me, sweetheart," he murmured in her ear.

"Yes," she breathed. Then the pleasure swept through her like a flood, surging higher and higher. She hung on tight as he drove her over the edge, catapulting her to a state of pure joy.

She moaned, flying high on the wings of bliss. Her whole body quivering in his arms.

He kept pumping. Deep and fast. Keeping her at the height

of ecstasy for what seemed like forever. She moaned and moaned, until she could barely breathe. He groaned and drove deeper, pinning her to the bed, then erupted inside her. She wailed a final cry of delight and collapsed on the bed.

He slumped on top of her, both of them panting for breath. Finally, he rolled away, a laugh rumbling through his chest.

"I can see I won't get a lot of sleep while you're here with me."

"Oh, my." She giggled. "Well, that's not good."

He gazed at her, a devilish glint in his eyes. "On the contrary. Sleep is highly overrated."

The next morning, Del surprised her with breakfast in bed. Then when she got up and tried to do the dishes, he wouldn't let her.

"You know, I'm pregnant, I'm not an invalid," she pointed out.

"I know, my love, but that means you deserve to be pampered."

She grinned. "Okay. As long as you don't think I'm helpless."

He chuckled. "I would never think that. You are one of the strongest women I know. Do you want some more coffee?"

He'd made decaf for her. She was sure he'd made a special trip to get it while she was in the shower.

"No, thanks."

He sat down across from her with his steaming coffee mug in hand.

"But seriously, we should find out from the doctor if there are any special precautions we need to take, since last time was so difficult."

"I already have an appointment scheduled early next week," she said.

"I'd like to go with you. I want to know everything I can do to help. If the doctor says you should stay flat on your back in bed for the whole term, I want to make sure that happens. I know how much you want this baby. And so do I."

Tears welled in her eyes. He was so protective and wonderful, even though it was another man's baby she carried.

She knew he'd be a great father.

As much as she knew Liam would, too. He would love the child so much, he couldn't do otherwise.

She sighed. But she was with Del now. And that's all that mattered.

"So is it all right?"

At Del's question, she realized her mind had wandered. "Um . . . is what all right?"

He laughed. "So far this morning I've had smiles, tears, and indifference. I see it's going to be an interesting day."

"There were no tears," she said, feeling a little defensive.

"It's okay, love. I want you to be comfortable expressing whatever you're feeling and I promise to take it very seriously. Your changing hormones may cause your emotions to fluctuate, but I know that if you get upset, it's based on real issues you're concerned about. So please promise to talk to me."

She nodded, feeling the tears well again. "I will." She wiped her eyes. "And this time it's because you're being so sweet and understanding."

He took her hand and squeezed, his warm smile lighting her heart.

"And what I was asking about earlier was if you're okay with me going to your doctor's appointment with you."

"Of course. I want you there."

Her phone buzzed. It was sitting on the built-in desk beside the fridge. Del got up and retrieved it for her. She took it, deciding to enjoy his pampering, and glanced at the display.

She frowned at the sight of another text from Liam.

Del leaned toward her. "Is everything okay?"

"It's Liam again."

Del's eyes grew somber. "He still wants to talk about your feelings?"

"It just said to check my email." She tapped at the phone, opening the email from Liam, and read it.

"Yes, he's asking again when I'm willing to meet with him. He said he's going away on business for a few weeks early next month, so we need to work around that."

He also said unless she wanted to join him on his trip, but she didn't tell Del that.

"Why don't you suggest a Skype call?"

"You know he wants to meet in person."

"Of course he does. Because then he can use his charm on you." He took her hand. "And I can't blame him. If I'd had you and lost you, I'd do whatever I could to win you back. I hope he doesn't start sending flowers and expensive gifts again."

"He knows that I'll do like last time and send back the gifts and donate the flowers to the hospital."

She fretted as she thought about the timing.

"You know we don't want to wait until he gets back. I'm really hoping to get the divorce settled before I'm showing."

He raised an eyebrow. "You've decided you're not going to tell him the baby's his?"

She frowned and started at her empty cup.

"No, it's not that. I want him to agree to the divorce—hopefully have it all signed and sealed—before I tell him."

"Okay. So you want to set up a meeting with him next week?"

"Actually, he doesn't just want a meeting. He wants me to come to his country house for a weekend."

"You're not actually considering that, are you?"

"What choice do I have? He's absolutely adamant. And right now, he holds all the cards." She patted her belly. In fact, more cards than he was even aware of.

She took his hand. "Del, I don't want to go, but you know how stubborn he is."

"I also know how persuasive he is. Especially with you."

"I think this is the only way I'll convince him. I *have* to go."

"Then I'll go, too."

Hope sprung inside her, but faded immediately. "Liam will never go for it."

"So don't tell him. I'll just arrive at the door by your side."

"I know you're worried about me being alone with him, but you have to trust me. I want you and me to be together. To make that happen, I need to do this. Alone."

CHAPTER THIRTEEN

The limousine cruised up the long driveway carved out of the thick woods to a large white house standing in a clearing on the shore of a glittering lake. Abi could see sandy beach stretching along the shore past the lovely landscaping, consisting of colorful flower gardens and neatly trimmed shrubs and bushes.

The driver pulled around the circular drive to the end of the tiered stone walkway leading to the entrance, then opened her door. She stood by the car as he retrieved her bag from the trunk, noticing the lovely flowers in different shades of pinks and purples lining the path. She didn't know much about flowers, but those colors were her favorites and she was sure Liam would have considered that when he'd had these gardens planted.

He'd bought this house after things had started to fall apart between them, and he'd tried to convince her to move here. He'd thought starting fresh in a new place would help.

But when he'd surprised her with the idea, she'd already decided to ask him for a divorce. So she'd never even been to the house before today.

"After you, ma'am," the driver said, her small suitcase in his hand.

As she started up the path to the front door of this lovely, sprawling home, she realized she would have fallen in love with it. Surrounded by trees and water, the casual elegance of the classic Cape Cod architecture—white wood finish, teal shutters, steep shingled roof—appealed to her. And in the fading light of the day, the soft glow of the lights from inside was homey and inviting.

The driver opened the front door for her and she stepped inside.

When she walked into the large living room with its high vaulted ceilings and rustic antique beams, her breath caught. The space itself was open and bright, with white built-in shelves and cupboards along one wall, large windows looking out the front, and pairs of French doors opening to the back, where she could see a patio and the lake glittering in the fading sunlight beyond. The neutral furniture, in creams and taupe, gave a very relaxed feel to the airy space.

"Abi, it's good to see you." Liam stepped into view from the kitchen, which was open to the large living room and dining room.

He looked so handsome in his jeans and short-sleeved button-down shirt. She quivered inside at the thought of him touching her. Wrapping his arms around her and claiming her lips.

He walked toward her with a welcoming smile.

"Hello, Liam."

She walked toward one of the French doors, wanting to keep a distance between them, not wanting to give him a chance to kiss her.

He gestured to the driver, who then took her bag into another room and returned a moment later.

"Is that all, sir?" he asked Liam.

"Yes, thanks, Greg."

But as the driver turned, Abi spoke up. "Actually, Liam, why don't you have the driver wait. I really think we can hash this out in about an hour, then he could take me back."

Liam merely chuckled. "Nice try, Abi. But you agreed to stay for the weekend."

The driver disappeared out the door, leaving them alone.

"What do you think of the place?" he asked, gesturing around them.

"It's really lovely."

His eyes turned wistful. "I thought you'd like it." Then he smiled again. "If you'd like to freshen up, the master bedroom is down the hall. You'll see the open doors."

She drew in a deep breath. "I'm not staying in the same bedroom with you."

His gaze caught on hers. "Are you sure?"

She knew he wasn't asking her if she'd made up her mind. He'd used that deep, rumbling tone he had to remind her that she was weak around him. That he could seduce her into doing things she wouldn't have thought she'd do in calmer moments. That is, moments when his masculine aura wasn't playing havoc with her senses.

"I'm quite sure," she said, mustering up her resolve.

He nodded, but his glittering eyes said *we'll see.*

"I hope you're hungry. I have dinner ready." He turned toward the kitchen and she followed.

It was a generous-sized kitchen with one wall totally open to the living room, a breakfast bar with high cushioned stools the only division between the rooms.

He opened the wall oven and the enticing aroma of lasagna filled the room. As he pulled it out, she picked up the salad sitting on the counter and carried it to the dining table. He set the flat pan on a hot pad on the table, then pulled out a chair for her. She sat down and he sat across from her.

The table was already set with china and stem glasses. He picked up the bottle of wine already open on the table.

"No wine, thank you," she said quickly.

He raised an eyebrow. "Really? But you love this wine."

It was true. Liam had introduced her to the delights of fine wine early in their relationship, and she'd particularly liked this one. He was really doing everything he could to win her over.

He started to pour anyway.

"Liam, I'm not having wine," she said through gritted teeth, hoping he wouldn't push it any further.

"That's fine. Leave it if you really don't want it, but the bottle's already open."

She knew what he was doing. Often when she'd turn down dessert, he'd bring her an extra fork, knowing she'd probably wind up indulging in a bite of his. If he filled her glass, he expected she'd probably change her mind and have some anyway.

He cut the lasagna and served her a piece. She loved lasagna, but as the thick aroma filled her nostrils, she felt a wave of nausea.

Oh, God, she didn't think she was going to be able to eat it.

She reached for the salad and filled her bowl.

He sipped his wine, watching her over the glass. When he set it down, he leaned forward.

"I think I know what's going on here."

Her gaze darted to his. "Going on? What do you mean?"

"I mean, I think you're turning down the wine because you want to keep a clear head. You're afraid that wine will make it easier for me to seduce you into my bed." He smiled. "But believe me, I don't need the help of wine. The chemistry between us is all I need."

She sighed, on one hand relieved, because she was worried he'd figured out she was pregnant, which was totally paranoid because there's no way he'd believe that. She still barely believed it herself. On the other hand, her concern rose at his quiet confidence that he'd be able to easily entice her into his bed. Because his confidence was well founded.

"That has nothing to do with it," she responded. "The truth is, I've been a bit off lately and my doctor suggested I drop some things from my diet for a little while. In fact, I don't think I should eat the lasagna. I'm sorry, I should have warned you."

"Is it something serious?" he asked, concern in his chocolate-brown eyes.

"No, I'm perfectly healthy. It's . . . uh . . . food sensitivities. It'll take a little time to figure it out, so for now, I'm being careful what I eat. The salad is fine, though."

She took another bite. Hopefully, that explanation would cover any issues that came up with food. Including the fact she wouldn't be drinking coffee or tea unless it was decaf.

"And what about the banana cream pie I have for dessert?"

"Really?" Her mouth watered at the thought. "Um . . . yeah . . . I think I can handle that." It was her favorite dessert of all time.

"Good."

They continued eating. Her salad was done in no time and she reached for a roll.

"How are your siblings?" he asked.

"They're fine. Jaime's going a bit crazy with the boys out of school for the summer. Kurt's back from his honeymoon and the two of them seem disgustingly happy."

"That's nice. I'm happy for them."

The wistful look in Liam's eyes troubled her. She knew he wanted that happiness with her, but it was a fairy tale he was clinging to.

"And how's your business?" she asked.

She bit into the roll she'd finished buttering. It was fresh and warm and melted in her mouth.

"It's doing very well. I'm considering buying a chain of resort hotels. That's why I'm going away for a few weeks."

"Really? That's different for you."

His current company was more high-tech based. He'd invested in a few good ideas and had picked some winners.

"Diversifying is always good, but mostly, I wanted a change." He pushed his empty plate aside. "But I'm sure you don't really want to talk about business."

"No, that's true. I want to talk about you signing the divorce papers."

He laughed, then stood up. "I'll get dessert. Coffee?"

"Um, no. Herbal tea if you have it. Or decaf."

He returned a few minutes later with a cup of fragrant apple-cinnamon tea and set a plate with a generous portion of pie in front of her.

She picked up her fork and took a bite of the dessert. The creamy feel of it in her mouth and the delightful taste of the banana and custard made her melt.

"Oh, that's so good."

"I'm glad you like it."

The pie was gone all too quickly. She sipped her tea and realized he was only half done.

"I can get you another piece," he offered.

"No, thanks. I'll have more salad."

She filled her bowl, then when they'd both finished the meal, helped him clear the table.

She settled into a chair kitty-corner to the couch. He brought her another cup of tea and set it in front of her, then sat down on the couch with his glass of wine.

The sun was setting over the lake, giving them a stunning view of the rose, mauve, and blue streaked sky reflected in the water.

After a few moments of appreciating the view, Liam turned to her.

"Abi, I really want to have a serious discussion about us. I want us to get back together. I know I was an idiot after . . . what happened. I pulled away and I deeply regret that." He leaned forward, his elbows resting on his knees, and stared into her eyes. "But I really do love you. And I'm going to do everything I can this weekend to prove that I won't let you down again."

The intensity of his voice and his deep, penetrating gaze unsettled her. Her fingers tightened around her cup.

"Liam, I'm in love with Del," she blurted.

He frowned. "I know the two of you are close. You've been friends for a long time, but—"

"Del and I are together now. He even asked me to marry him."

He clasped his hands together, frowning. "I see. That's very odd since at the wedding, the two of you were still just friends." His eyebrow rose. "And, in fact, the last I saw, Del had stormed off."

"Because of you."

He shrugged. "Still, it seems quite a turnaround."

"Yes, well, I went and talked to him. When things are right, they can move quickly."

"I don't think four years is particularly fast." His eyes grew solemn. "Now with you and I . . . that was fast. Because you and I are meant to be together."

She pursed her lips. "No, *Del* and I are meant to be together."

He leaned back. "So Del was perfectly okay with you coming here to spend the weekend with me?"

"He knows I'm here to talk to you about the divorce, and we're both anxious to have you sign the papers so we can move forward with our relationship."

He rested his hands on his long, lean, denim-clad thighs.

"Hmm. So you're telling me your incentive for me to sign the papers is so you can leave me for my best friend?"

She sighed. "Liam, you have to let me go."

He shook his head, his intense gaze locking on hers.

"Not in a million years, kitten. You're mine."

CHAPTER FOURTEEN

Abi stood up, her heart sinking.

"If this is how you're going to be, there's really no point in me staying."

"But you will. Because if you really want to be with Del, you'll do everything you can to convince me. Just as I'll do everything I can to convince you. We're a lot alike in that way. We don't give up on what we want."

"Well, right now I want a break from this conversation."

He stood up, too. "Great idea. How about we go for a swim?"

She glanced out the window.

"It's getting dark. I don't want to go swimming in the lake at night."

"It's a good thing we have a pool then."

The "we" disturbed her. Insinuating this was her house, too. And her pool. Which, since they were still legally married, was true.

"I didn't bring a swimsuit."

"I'd suggest we go skinny dipping, but I know you're not

going to go for that. But no worries. I have a bathing suit here in your size."

A pang of jealousy shot through her at the thought he might have had other women here. But that was ridiculous. Liam should be seeing other women. He should be moving on.

She wrapped her hands around herself, goose bumps quivering across her arms. She loved going in the water, but it hadn't been the warmest of days.

"Now that the sun's gone down, it's probably too cool for me."

"It's seventy-four degrees and the pool's heated, so you'll be fine. And there's a hot tub if you do get cold." He smiled. "Of course, if you'd rather cuddle up with me and watch a movie together, I'm sure I can keep you warm."

The thought made her tremble. The heat of his gaze alone would do the trick. But the thought of being snuggled up beside him, his strong arm around her, holding her tight to his muscular body, made her knees weak.

"No, a swim will be fine."

"Good."

He pressed his hand to her lower back and guided her toward a hallway, then turned at a double doorway and she realized he was taking her into the master bedroom.

Her suitcase sat on a luggage rack by the window.

The room was open and airy, just like the rest of the house, with the high, sloped ceiling, windows on three sides of the room, and French doors leading out to the patio. The walls were painted a lovely soft aqua and there was a love seat and two armchairs in the same neutral tones as the rest of the furniture in the house, and a stone fireplace.

He opened a drawer in the dresser and pulled out a bathing suit in a floral fabric in vibrant pink tones and black, as well as a pair of trunks. He dropped them on the bed. The big, comfortable-looking, inviting bed.

Then he started unbuttoning his shirt.

"I'm not going to change in here with you."

He shrugged. "Suit yourself. You can wait until I'm finished."

He shed his shirt and she found herself mesmerized by his rippling muscles as he unbuckled his belt and pulled it from the loops. Then she realized he was unzipping his pants.

She spun around, her heart pounding, only to meet his reflection in the mirror as he dropped his boxers to the floor. Oh, God, the sight of his heavy cock hanging between his legs made her ache inside. To feel it in her hand. To stroke it and feel it rise up.

Before she could turn her head away, he pulled up his trunks, then walked to the French doors leading outside.

"I'll take towels out with me. Don't take too long, or I'll come back in for you."

Once he closed the doors, she picked up the bathing suit. It was actually a two-piece, and it was pretty tiny.

She walked to the en suite bathroom. When she stepped inside, she paused. It was huge, with a sleek freestanding tub and a large open shower. The floor and walls were done with tiny tiles, but a long area carpet defined a path from the doorway she stood in to yet another set of French doors leading outside. There was even a large oval ottoman that looked luxuriously comfortable near the bathtub. She could imagine sitting in the tub, bubbles all around her, while Liam sat on that ottoman and read to her.

Of course, it would be much more likely he'd climb into the tub with her and wash her back, then other parts of her body, his large hands gliding over her wet skin.

She sucked in a breath, pushing the thought from her head, and dropped the bathing suit on the ottoman, then stripped off her clothes. She pulled on the bikini bottoms, then the tiny top. It cupped her breasts and lifted them high. When she glanced in the mirror and saw how little the bathing suit covered, she shivered at the thought of going out like this.

It wasn't like Liam hadn't seen her in less, but she was trying to keep him at a distance.

She wasn't going to back out of the swim, though. When she walked to the bedroom again and spotted the button-down shirt Liam had been wearing, she picked it up and pulled it on. It draped over her, covering her to mid-thigh.

Now she didn't feel quite so naked.

When she breathed in, she could smell his musky male scent. She wrapped her arms around herself, imagining being enveloped in his arms.

Maybe she didn't feel naked, but she did feel vulnerable. And needy. She wished she could just surrender to her desire for him. Let herself sink into his embrace and give herself to him.

She shook away those thoughts and walked to the French doors Liam had exited through and stepped out into the night. She walked past the cushioned patio furniture, following the stone patio around the corner of the house.

Liam sat by a swimming pool with a lovely curved shape. There was a small waterfall on one side, the trickling water glowing under a soft light. In fact, the whole pool was aglow.

Liam stood up as she approached. The sight of his broad, muscular chest and his tight, sculpted abs took her breath away.

"Here, let me help you with that," he said as he rested his hands on her shoulders, then drew the shirt down her arms.

Her first urge was to protest, but he slipped it all the way off and tossed it on a nearby lounge chair, leaving her practically naked in front of him.

"Mmm. I knew that suit would look great on you." His warm, appreciative tone sent shivers through her.

"You're cold." He ran his hands down her arms, over the waves of goose bumps, and heat washed through her.

"Maybe we should go in the water now," she said, her voice a little hoarse.

He smiled and took her hand. The feel of his fingers around hers was familiar and comforting, but at the same time it made her want things she shouldn't.

He led her to the concrete steps and drew her into the pool with him. The water was delightfully warm and soon she was up to her waist.

She drew her hand from his and swam to the deep end. When she reached the walk-out steps, she sat on the bottom one, up to her waist in water, and gazed around. The moonlight glittered on the lake.

A moment later, Liam's head broke the surface of the water next to her and he treaded water.

"It's a great view, isn't it?" Liam said.

"It is. You picked a lovely spot."

"When we're together again, we can come here as often as you like. Or move in and live here all the time, like I'd intended when I bought it."

"We aren't going to be together, Liam."

"You're not really keeping an open mind about this." He moved closer and grasped the side of the pool right beside her, then slid his arm around her waist.

"Liam . . ."

"Come on, kitten," he murmured, stroking the wet hair behind her ear, his touch singeing her senses. "At least give me a chance to convince you."

"I—"

But his lips captured hers before she'd realized his intent. He pulled her tight to his body, his mouth moving on hers. His tongue nudged her lips then dove inside.

His body was warm and hard against hers and she shivered. It was so good being this close to him. Melting against him as he kissed her with his sensuous lips.

But she couldn't allow it.

She pressed her hand flat to his chest and pushed, but with his arm around her, it did no good. Finally, she tore her lips from his.

"No, Liam," she ground out. "Let me go."

His arm loosened around her and she scurried to her feet and fled up the steps of the pool. He pushed himself up, water sluicing from his body, and followed her.

"Wait, Abi. Don't go in yet. Let's go in the hot tub. It'll relax you."

He caught her arm and slowed her fast pace to the door.

"You know how much you love it. And I set the temperature at a hundred because I know you prefer it not too hot."

She let him guide her to the sunken tub a few yards away and she lowered herself into the water. He turned on the bubbles and settled in beside her.

She sat tensely on the edge of the seat, wondering if he was going to try something again, but he settled back and rested his head against the built-in cushion. The rush of the water and bubbles over her body felt wonderful and she soon sank into the seat to enjoy it.

"I remember how much you used to love coming to my apartment when we first started dating and going in the hot tub. So much so that I had to coax you out of it so you wouldn't overheat. And then you were so disappointed when you were pregnant and . . ."

He paused, his gaze flickering to her. Neither of them liked to talk about the pregnancy. To remind each other of what they'd lost.

". . . the doctor advised against going in the hot water," he continued.

Oh, God, what am I doing? I shouldn't be in here.

She jerked to her feet and moved to the steps.

"I'm sorry, Abi." Liam stood up. "I didn't mean to—"

"No, I just want to go inside."

He wrapped his hands around her waist to steady her as she moved up the steps, then followed her as she fled toward the doors. He caught her arm.

"Here, use this door," he said, as he drew her to a closer one.

He pulled open the door and she realized it led to the large en suite bathroom. She stepped inside.

"You're shivering."

Goose bumps danced across her skin and her teeth chattered, though how much from being cold and how much was anxiety she wasn't sure.

"Here." He drew her toward the shower and turned on the water, adjusting the temperature.

He gestured her toward it, but she shook her head.

"I'm not getting naked with you here."

"So don't."

He pressed her under the water and the warmth of it flowing over her skin was wonderful. He stepped under the water behind her and held her against his body.

"It's okay," he said before she had a chance to protest. "I just want to warm you up."

After a moment, her shivering subsided as the water and the heat of his body warmed her. She should pull away, but it was so comforting being held by him like this.

"Baby, I'm sorry I reminded you of the pregnancy, but maybe it would help if we actually talked about it."

"No," she blurted. "I mean . . . that's not what it was about."

Oh, God, how did she explain why she had actually fled from the tub?

Then sheer panic flooded through her as she felt tears well from her eyes. This was no time for a show of irrational emotion.

She thrust her hands under the water and wiped them across her face to camouflage the tears with fresh water, but she was afraid he'd already seen them.

"Abi, are you okay?"

CHAPTER FIFTEEN

Abi nodded. "I'm just stressed. Being here is stressful for me."

"Okay, I'm sorry. I know this is a difficult situation for you. But right now, let the water relax you."

But she couldn't relax. Not with him so close like this. Not with her hormones spiking the way they were.

"I'm done," she said. "I want to get dressed now."

"All right."

He guided her from the water, then grabbed a large, fluffy towel and wrapped it around her torso. Before she knew what was happening, his fingers had slid under the towel and he'd unfastened the hook of her bikini top and was pulling the halter strap over her head. Then he eased the top from under the towel, leaving her breasts naked under the thick fabric.

He turned and retrieved a robe from a nearby cupboard and wrapped it around her.

"Slide your arms in."

The fabric was thick and soft. She slid her arms into the sleeves and he wrapped it around her.

"Now drop the towel and the rest of your bathing suit to the floor. You don't need to get dressed. This'll keep you warm and cozy."

Her back was turned to him, so she dropped the towel and tied the robe snugly around her waist. Then she shimmied the wet bathing suit bottom down from under the fabric. Liam grabbed another robe, then while facing the cupboard, dropped his trunks to the floor, revealing his muscular ass.

Oh, God, it was as hard and firm as she remembered. She would love to run her fingers over it, then cup it in her hands.

He pulled on the robe and turned around, tying the sash.

He smiled. "A little better now?"

She pulled the robe tighter. "Yes, thank you."

"Good. Now let's go and talk."

Liam held her hand as he led her into the living room, then sat her down on the couch beside him.

"Abi, every time we talk about this, we wind up going around in circles, but this time I'd like you to be open to hearing what I have to say. I know you don't believe I love you, but"—he squeezed her hand—"I really do."

She drew back her hand back and rested it on her knee, not wanting to feel the warmth of his fingers around hers any longer. Not wanting to be affected by the gentleness of his touch.

"I know you've convinced yourself of that," she said, "but you asked me to marry you because of the baby."

"That may have triggered it, but I was already in love with you."

She shook her head. "We hadn't been going out that long." She gazed into his solemn brown eyes. "And you're a good man, Liam. You wanted to do the right thing and you felt that was to marry me. I'm sure you *wanted* to love me. You wanted us to be a family. But once I lost the baby . . ."

She sucked in a deep breath, the pain duller than it used to be, but still intense.

"I think you were clinging to what we might have had," she said. "The family you always wanted to be a part of."

He took her hand again and drew it to his mouth. The brush of his lips made her heart flutter.

"Can you honestly tell me you don't love me?" he asked, his deep voice melting through her. "Because no matter how short the time we had together before we found out you were pregnant, I could see it in your eyes when you looked at me."

He tucked his fingers under her chin and lifted, gazing deeply into her eyes.

"I can see it there now."

She turned her head, pulling from his tender grip, unable to look into those intense brown eyes any longer.

"I thought I was." She still did, but she couldn't admit that to him. Not if she wanted any chance at getting her divorce. "But when you pulled away . . . when you left me thrashing for a life-line in the depths of my sorrow for so long, I had to face the fact that if we were really in love, you would have been there for me. That somehow, we would have found a way to make it work." She gazed at him again, her heart aching. "I tried for over a year, but . . ." She shook her head. "It did no good."

"Baby, you've got to understand how painful it was for me. I didn't know how to deal with it. It was an intense blow right to the gut." His voice grew quiet. "It was like losing my parents all over again. Like when I'd been left all alone."

"But you weren't alone this time. I was there with you. We could have shared the pain."

He drew in a deep, ragged breath and her heart ached at the depth of pain in his eyes.

She rested her hand on his cheek, drawn into the gut-wrenching sorrow in those depths, and the moment his gaze locked on her again, she felt herself falling. Deeper into the mesmerizing emotional chaos.

"Abi . . ." His voice was wracked with pain and need rumbled through her. Then his mouth found hers and the tender brush of their lips touched something deep in her soul.

She leaned into the kiss. Wanting to be closer. Wanting to help soothe his pain.

Needing to feel what they used to share.

Her heart swelled, because no matter what, she'd never stopped loving this man.

His arms swept around her and he held her close, his lips still moving on hers. She felt cocooned in his warmth. Swept away to a sweet, intimate place. She melted against him with a soft murmur.

His tongue glided past her lips and stroked inside. She sighed into the kiss. The ache pulsing from deep within expanded to a need so intense she felt her will slipping away.

"Oh, baby, I love you so much. I want us to be together." Then he took her lips again.

Oh, God, so did she.

Her heart pounded. But she couldn't. She couldn't lose herself in an emotional riptide that could leave her empty and lost. If she lost this baby . . . If he abandoned her again . . .

A wash of agony swept through her.

She flattened her hand on his chest and pressed.

"No, Liam."

She slid a few inches away, putting a little distance between them.

"I'm sorry. I know how hard it was for you," she said. "And I want you to know I'm not blaming you. But the simple fact is that . . . in that desperate, painful time . . . being together wasn't enough. *I* wasn't enough."

His expression tightened.

"The fact that you pulled away . . . when I needed you so desperately . . . I . . ." She shook her head, fighting back tears.

Remembering the agony of being shut out by him. "I know that I can never be safe with you. Emotionally."

Shock washed across his features.

"Abi . . . that's not true."

"It *is* true. You abandoned me. Left me to suffer alone. I needed you and you weren't there for me."

The pain in Abi's eyes tore at Liam's heart. He'd been wrapped up in his own pain back then. Grieving the loss of the baby. Of being a father.

Of losing his family when he was only five years old.

He'd been alone for so long. Until he'd met Abi. She'd made him feel whole again.

And when he'd found out she was pregnant, he had been thrilled. He would finally have his own family. A set of three people—and hopefully more in the future—who loved each other unconditionally. Who cared about each other above all else.

When Abi lost the baby . . . all those dreams had been torn from him.

Not only that one child, but any children. Abi could no longer have children, so that dream of a family had been stolen from him forever.

But in wallowing in that desperate pain . . . somewhere along the way he'd lost Abi, too.

There was nothing he could say . . . nothing he could do . . . to make up for that.

She stood up. "Where's my room?"

His hope of her staying in his bedroom was shattered. He stood up and led her to the room beside his.

"I'll bring your suitcase," he said, as he opened the door to her bedroom.

"Thank you."

He retrieved her bag from the master bedroom and carried it into her room and set it on the love seat.

As soon as he left the room, she closed the door behind him.

Abi couldn't sleep. She'd tossed and turned for hours, but now she just lay there staring at the ceiling. The talk with Liam about losing the baby had her dwelling on her fear of losing this baby, too. She stroked her stomach, thinking of the life growing inside her.

Finally, she pushed back the covers and got out of bed. The soft illumination of moonlight on the carpet drew her to the window and she gazed outside. The water on the lake glittered with the silvery light. The sky was clear and deep, inky blue.

She opened the French doors that led from her bedroom onto the deck and stepped outside, breathing in the fresh, warm summer air. She walked from the wooden deck to the stone patio, then to the pool and sat on the edge, dangling her feet in the water.

She loved the water. She swished her feet around, watching the rippling circles cascading across the surface.

She glanced toward the dark house, turning to the window of the room where Liam was sleeping. She remembered that night so clearly. She'd woken up in the middle of the night to sharp cramps. The pain had caused her to double over. Liam had woken up and called an ambulance, but they were going to take too long, so he'd carried her to the car and had held her hand all the way to the hospital.

But the doctors hadn't been able to do anything. When they'd told her that she'd lost the baby . . .

A sob shuddered from her throat. She drew her legs from the water and hugged her knees tight to her body, tears flooding from her eyes. Her body shivered. She sat there, cocooned in her pain. Letting it wash through her body and soul.

"Abi, are you okay?"

At Liam's words, she lifted her head from her knees. She drew in a deep breath and tried to keep her voice even.

"Yes. I'm just enjoying the view."

The lake, silvery and smooth as glass, lay beyond the pool, and leaves in the tall trees between here and there rustled in the soft breeze.

"Really? It looks to me like you could use someone to talk to."

He held out his hand and she stared at it for a moment, considering whether to tell him she wanted some time to herself.

But he was right. She did want to talk to someone.

Even if that someone was him.

Maybe especially because it was him.

She took his hand and let him pull her to her feet. He didn't release her hand as he led her to the rattan sofa on the patio. He sat down, drawing her beside him, then he turned to her and took her other hand.

She might lose this baby, too, and she didn't know how she'd endure that pain again.

"Liam, you never talk about the fact that if we were to get back together again, you'd never have the family you've always dreamed of. I know how badly you want to have a child of your own."

"Abi, being with you—"

"No, please. Let me get this out." She squeezed his hands, staring into his concerned eyes. "What you really want is for us to be married . . . and for me to get pregnant. That's what you *really* want. Right?"

"Of course. I would love that. But I know we can't have that. That doesn't mean I want you less."

"If we *could* have that, though. If that magically happened for us . . ."

His brown eyes . . . deep and somber . . . seemed to fill with hope. Her chest tightened.

What the hell was she doing? But the words had started tumbling from her and she couldn't stop now.

"Wouldn't you be terrified?"

He shook his head. "Why, Abi?"

Her hands clenched tight, squeezing his fingers.

"Because of what happened last time. Because we'd be terrified that we'd lose the baby again. Would you really be able to go through that a second time?"

"If we were given a miraculous gift like that, I would believe that we were being given a second chance at happiness."

She shook her head and it drooped forward.

"Why are you asking about this? Has your situation changed?"

Oh, God, she'd said too much. She couldn't let him suspect . . . Not yet.

"I've been thinking about the baby . . . *our* baby . . . about how painful it was . . ." Her voice caught and she sucked in a deep breath, tears welling in her eyes again.

"Aw, kitten." He pulled her to him, his arms tightening around her. "I'm so sorry."

His hand cupped her head, holding it tight against his solid chest. She could hear his heartbeat against her ear. Regular. Soothing.

His hand stroked up and down her back. She was a bundle of tight muscles nestled against him. Barely able to catch her breath.

He rocked her back and forth. "I'm so sorry, baby. I'm so sorry."

Oh, God, she needed this.

She'd needed it even more in that long, terrible time after she'd lost the baby.

She wrapped her arms around him tightly and held on. Clinging to him. Soaking in the comfort he was offering her.

His lips brushed the top of her head and he rested his cheek against it. The warmth of him . . . all around her . . . was so sweet . . . so deeply moving . . .

She turned her head and gazed up at him.

His deep, penetrating gaze locked with hers. She could see her pain reflected there. See his struggle to stay strong for her.

Liam's heart ached at the pain tearing at Abi right now. Which dragged forth the pain he'd buried away deep inside.

He should have been there for her like this when it happened . . . and the long months after when instead he'd thrown himself into his work to hide from his own pain.

As he stared into her desolate blue eyes, reeling from their shared emotions, she tipped up her face, her lips parting in invitation.

An invitation he couldn't ignore.

He swooped down and captured her lips. The sweet comfort of her mouth on his filled him with a need so deep he thought he'd lose himself. He pulled her tighter to him, deepening the kiss. His tongue swept inside her mouth, tasting her sweetness. Her delightful womanly comfort curled around him, seeping through to his very bones. Her tongue glided along his and stroked. He groaned and suckled on it.

He tucked his arm under her knees and lifted her in his arms, then carried her toward the house. He pulled open the outside door to his bedroom and carried her inside. Her arms clung to his neck like he was a lifeline.

He laid her on the bed and snuggled in next to her, finding her lips again.

His heart pounded. He wanted her. He *needed* her. She was his everything, and right now she seemed to need him just as much.

Liam grasped the hem of her T-shirt and pulled it over her head. She wore only panties under the shirt. He leaned back and gazed at her body in the moonlight, blown away by how incredible she looked. Her breasts were firm and fuller than he remembered. Her skin smooth and creamy.

His gaze shifted back to her face. And despite her puffy eyes, she almost seemed to glow.

"God, you are more beautiful than ever."

CHAPTER SIXTEEN

Abi lay there, mesmerized by the frank admiration in Liam's eyes. His gentle fingers stroked her cheek, then glided down her neck to her chest.

Then he cupped her breast. She arched against his big, warm hand. Her nipple peaked, pressing into his palm.

Oh, God, she wanted more. She wanted to be close to him. So close there was nothing between them. Their bodies naked and touching from head to toe.

She wanted him inside her. Filling her so deep he became a part of her. The two of them becoming one.

"Liam," she whispered, stroking his raspy cheek.

Seeing the deep need in her eyes, he leaned forward and brushed his lips to hers in a tender kiss. She wrapped her arms around him and pulled him closer. She pressed her tongue to his lips and pushed inside, then stroked, tasting sweet spearmint.

She wanted him to take her. Slowly. Penetrating deeply. Her body was ready for him. Wet with need. Aching for him inside her.

He stroked her face, cupping it between his hands.

"Abi," he murmured softly, then kissed her again.

Then he kissed down her neck to her chest. When his lips found her breast, then wrapped around her hard nipple, she moaned, pulling him tighter to her. He suckled and she moaned. Her fingers coiled in his hair, the thick waves wrapping around them.

He continued downward, his lips brushing against her belly, then lightly past her hips.

When she felt the first stroke of his tongue against her dampness, seeking her hidden button, she arched. It was heaven being with him. Here in his arms, he would help her find release. She would forget her fear . . . her pain . . . for a little while.

His fingers opened her folds and he licked. Pleasure jolted through her and she moaned again.

But a tiny thought nudged through the delightful sensations like a seedling pushing through the soil . . . She'd promised herself . . . A lightning flash of realization careened through her. She'd promised Del . . . that she wouldn't succumb to Liam.

His tongue glided over her and he suckled.

She moaned at the intense pleasure.

"Liam," she cried, then grasped his head and tugged, urging him upward.

His tongue slipped away and he prowled upward until he was facing her again. His lips turned up in a smile.

"I thought you were enjoying that."

"I was but . . . I can't."

The light of amusement seeped from his eyes and he surged forward, covering her mouth with his and consuming it with passion. His insistent tongue found hers and curled around it, urging it into an ardent dance.

When he released her lips, she was breathless. He continued his onslaught, brushing his lips against the base of her neck, sending tingles dancing through her as he found that special spot that weakened her knees and drove her wild.

She clung to him, her heart pounding against his. He slid his hand down her back, drawing her tighter to him as it moved. When his hand reached her ass, she could feel his thick erection against her. She squirmed. Her damp folds were pressed tight against his hard shaft and the movement sent dizzying need through her.

Oh, God, she wanted that big cock inside her. Deep. Thrusting hard and fast.

But she had to cling to sanity and stop this.

"Liam, please," she murmured.

"Yeah, baby." He rolled her under him and pushed her panties down enough to allow his cock to brush against her intimate flesh. His hard shaft stroked against her and she could barely cling to her resolve.

"Liam, no," she begged.

He stopped moving and gazed down at her. He'd clearly thought she was begging for him to fuck her. But she gazed up at him . . . his cock still cradled against her soft, wet flesh . . . and she whimpered. She wanted this so much, but . . . she knew it was a very bad idea.

"Please, Liam. I need you to help me."

"Of course, baby. Anything. What do you need?"

"I need you to stop. I need you to be the strong one." She grasped his shoulders. "We both know if you want to, you can convince me to give myself to you. But I promised myself . . . and I promised Del . . . that I would not have sex with you."

His gaze turned dark.

"We both know you can have me right now if that's what you set your mind to," she continued. "But please . . . if you really care about me . . . help me walk away."

Liam stared at Abi in shock. He thought she'd been begging for him to be inside her. To slide into her depths and take them both to heaven. His cock was still nestled against her soft, wet folds. At the tiniest movement, it would glide inside her.

The fierce need in Liam turned cold in his belly. She'd promised Del she wouldn't be with Liam this weekend. And even though she clearly wanted him . . . even admitted that she would give herself to him . . . she was asking him to stop.

Fuck!

He would do anything for Abi. This was not playing fair. He wanted her and she wanted him. That should be all that mattered.

Even when she denied her need for him, he could always persuade her. He knew that wouldn't work if she didn't really love him. That's why he pushed his edge at every opportunity. Hoping she would finally admit it. To herself. And to him.

But she had turned it back on him.

Asked for his help. .

And, fuck . . . he couldn't refuse her, no matter how potent his need for her was right this moment.

He sucked in a deep breath. Then slowly he drew his cock from the sweetness of her warm flesh and fell back on the bed. He sucked in a few more breaths.

Before he could change his mind, he stood up and scooped her into his arms, then carried her out the door. Moments later, he set her down in her room, just inside the door.

She stared up at him. He kept this gaze on her eyes, not her delectable naked breasts.

"Thank you, Liam."

He gave her a curt nod and turned to go, then stopped and turned back to her.

"Abi, I'm human. I've made mistakes. But the last one cost me you." He tipped up her chin and his solemn gaze locked on hers. "I won't let that happen again."

She nodded, her eyes glistening.

He stepped through the doorway.

"But I *am* human, so lock the fucking door behind me in case I change my mind."

Liam walked into the kitchen to find Abi preparing breakfast.

"Something smells good."

"Probably the coffee," she said, her back turned to him as she stood at the stove, flipping something in one of the two pans in front of her.

She wore a colorful, loose flowing shirt and snug black pants. He would love to wrap his hands around her waist and draw her close to his body, then press his lips to her soft neck. But instead, he turned to the cupboard, grabbed two mugs and set them beside the coffeemaker.

The coffee was still trickling into the pot. He leaned back against the counter, waiting. The pot wasn't very full, so it would be another few minutes.

"Do you want me to set the table?" he asked.

He knew offering to help make breakfast was pointless. She didn't like anyone in the way when she was cooking.

"Nope. Already done."

Liquid stopped flowing into the pot and he glanced at it. It only looked like enough for about two cups.

"That's not very much coffee. I'll put some more on."

"Only if you want it," she said. "I'm having tea."

"Really?"

That wasn't like Abi. She loved her morning coffee. She'd often grumbled in the morning when she'd been pregnant, unhappy at not being able to have her morning kick start.

He poured himself a cup and took a sip.

Abi placed an omelet on one of the plates stacked beside the stove. She handed it to him and placed another omelet on the remaining plate.

"Did you sleep well?" he asked as he followed her to the dining table.

"Um . . . yeah, fine."

When she sat down, she poured herself a cup of fragrant herbal tea. As they ate, they talked about how sunny it was outside, how high the temperature would go today, and various other mundane things. He didn't want to push her by talking about feelings or anything to do with the divorce. Not so soon after what happened last night.

But he didn't intend to let her get away without more discussion this weekend. He intended to convince her they should be together. Last night had been very positive. They'd actually shared their feelings about losing the baby. She'd opened up to him about it more than she ever had before.

And he'd opened up to her, expressing feelings he'd never spoken about before. He was sure this was a good thing.

After the meal, he helped her clear the table and put the dishes in the dishwasher. It felt so good doing these ordinary things together. Like when they'd been living together as husband and wife.

"How about we go for a swim, then relax in the hot tub after?" he asked.

"A swim would be great."

She walked back to the table to scoop up the two empty mugs, then returned to the kitchen. As she walked toward the sink, she tripped, seeming to catch her foot on the side of the island, and tumbled forward. He grabbed her, stopping her from falling, but one of the mugs fell from her hand and landed on the tile floor, shattering.

"Oh, no. I'm so sorry."

"It's okay, Abi. It's just a mug."

But her eyes seemed to be gleaming. She crouched down and started to pick up the larger pieces, then squeaked in pain. He glanced down to see blood dribbling down her hand.

"Here, Abi, let me see."

He drew her up and carefully took the large chunk of broken

mug from her other hand. He guided her around the broken ceramic shards and put her hand under the water. The water ran red, then pink and finally went clear.

The cut wasn't too bad. He turned off the water and pressed a hand towel against the wound.

"You're okay, baby. I'll get a bandage."

But when he glanced at her face, he realized tears were welling from her eyes.

"Abi?"

"I'm sorry. I didn't mean to break the mug. I'm such a klutz." She stared at the towel against her hand. "And now I've gotten blood on your towel."

He glanced down to see a small red stain had formed on the white towel.

"It's okay. I don't care about the towel. Or the mug."

But tears now streamed freely down her cheeks.

"Abi, this isn't like you. Tell me what's wrong."

She shook her head, wiping her eyes. "Nothing. I'm sorry. I'm just feeling a little emotional today."

He frowned, staring at her. A little emotional?

Abi never cried about trivial things like this. Except when she was pregnant. In the first trimester, she used to cry at the drop of a hat. He remembered how she'd hated being so emotional.

He remembered her turning down the lasagna last night and her favorite wine. Then the decaf tea rather than coffee. And she seemed to be avoiding the hot tub.

And . . . last night she'd asked him what-ifs about her being pregnant again. He'd thought it was odd she'd choose a scenario that would never happen, but he'd assumed it was because she'd needed to think about that situation so she could exorcise some of the intense emotions around what had happened.

Now he was beginning to wonder if . . .

His chest constricted.

"Fuck, Abi. You're pregnant, aren't you?"

CHAPTER SEVENTEEN

Abi's gaze jerked to Liam in shock. He frowned, the expression on her face clearly giving him his answer.

"Fuck. When were you going to tell me?" he demanded.

She couldn't hide the guilt from her face and his frown deepened.

"Or weren't you going to tell me at all?"

"Oh, Liam, of course I was."

His eyes narrowed, his gaze boring through her. His teeth gritted and his hands balled into fists. He strode out of the kitchen. She followed him, stepping around the broken ceramic shards still on the floor.

He was pacing around the living room, steam practically shooting out his ears.

"So Del got you pregnant. No wonder he asked you to marry him."

Her stomach tightened. She should tell him that Del wasn't the father, despite the fact it would be so convenient to let him believe it.

And she wanted to tell him Del proposed simply because he

was in love with her. But the pregnancy *had* been the trigger, so she wouldn't go there.

"Fuck. You're still bleeding."

Liam grabbed her wrist and led her to the bathroom down the hall. He pulled out a first-aid kit and swabbed antiseptic on her wound, then applied a bandage. He strode from the bathroom.

"Go sit down in the living room and I'll clean up the broken mug," he said as she followed him down the hall.

She sat in one of the armchairs, listening to the clinking in the kitchen as he swept up the pieces and tossed them in the garbage.

Liam stared at the shards of ceramic lying in the garbage. Like the shattered remnants of his marriage.

His heart pounded. He loved Abi so much and . . . God, he should be happy for her that she was able to conceive after being told it would never happen . . . but all he could feel was the pain of losing her all over again.

Because how could he keep her from marrying Del now that she carried his child? He could never do that. He couldn't keep a father from being with his son or daughter. The three of them should be together as a family.

He put away the broom and walked back to the living room, his feet leaden. He sat down across from Abi, knowing he had to sign the divorce papers so she could marry Del.

It was the right thing to do.

"Liam, there's something you don't understand."

"Really? And what's that?" What new bombshell would she throw at him now?

She stared at her entwined fingers.

"The baby . . . it's not Del's."

"It's not?"

She lifted her gaze, her eyes glittering with anguish.

For the first time, his thoughts shifted to a possibility that he barely dared to consider. Hope flickered in him.

"It's yours," she said.

He froze, his breath caught in his lungs.

Then his heart exploded with joy. This was everything he'd ever wanted. He was going to be a father after all. He was going to be part of a happy, loving family.

Abi was carrying his child.

Abi watched the changing emotions wash across Liam's face. From despair, to awe, to full-blown joy.

"Liam, nothing's changed. I still want the divorce."

His gaze jerked to hers. The sparkle in his eyes dimmed.

"But everything's changed. I'm the baby's father. The three of us should be together."

"I'm sorry, Liam. But I love Del. I want to marry Del. We'll figure something out so you can be part of the baby's life, too, but—"

"I don't want to just be a part of it sometimes. I want to be there all the time. Every day. Not some part-time father on the sidelines." He put on his stubborn face. "Abi, we're married. You're carrying my baby. You'll move back in with me so we can be together. I'll take care of you and ensure you get the best care so this baby is safe."

She locked gazes with him.

"No. That's not going to happen," she said forcefully, knowing she had to show strength. "Liam, I know this is a shock, and I'm sorry this is so difficult for you, but you can't force me to live with you. If you won't give me the divorce, then I'll live with Del without being married." She shook her head. "But no matter how this unfolds, I'm not coming back to you."

Liam watched as she stood up and strode down the hallway and into the guest bedroom, then closed the door behind her.

He ached as a chaotic mélange of emotions—anger, pain, and even sparks of joy—swirled through him.

He and Abi were having a baby and that was the greatest gift he could ever imagine. He would not let his chance at finally having the happiness they both deserved slip away.

Whatever it took, he would find a way to convince her to stay with him.

Liam went out for a walk along the beach to mull things over, trying to settle his raging emotions. If he was feeling this disoriented by the whole thing, how must it be affecting Abi, with her turbulent hormones and all?

But despite everything, joy kept bubbling up through it all.

He was going to be a father!

When he got back, Abi was still in her room.

He made some lunch, then tapped on her door.

"Abi, it's a beautiful day. Come out and let's enjoy it together." At her silence, he tapped again. "Come on, sweetheart. We don't have to talk about the baby. We can have a nice lunch by the pool. Enjoy the sun and the water. You must be getting hungry."

Finally, he heard footsteps, then the door opened.

He smiled. "I made some chicken wraps. I put in walnuts just the way you like them. There's also homemade coleslaw and Waldorf salad. Hopefully, there's something that your stomach will be okay with."

She gazed up at him.

"That's why you didn't eat the lasagna last night, isn't it? Because you were feeling nauseous."

"Yes."

"Okay, go put on the bathing suit you wore last night—it's hanging in the bathroom—and I'll take the food out to the table by the pool."

She sighed, then nodded.

Ten minutes later, they sat down at the teak table by the pool together. He was happy to see that she ate a good amount of lunch. Finally, she pushed her plate away and sipped her lemonade, then sat back and stared out over the lake.

"It really is a beautiful house," she said.

"I always knew you'd like it here."

She drew in a deep breath and turned to him.

"Liam, we need to move forward. Being stuck like this isn't good for either one of us. Will you please sign the papers?"

He frowned. "No," he said simply.

"Okay, I think we both agree that the two of us talking isn't going to get us anywhere. Will you agree to meet with Del and me so the three of us can discuss it?"

"I'm afraid I leave on an extended business trip on Monday. Further discussion will have to wait until I get back."

"How long?" she asked.

"Three weeks."

Abi's heart sank.

"I don't want to wait that long before we settle this."

She wanted to tell her family about the baby, but not until the issue of the divorce was settled. She knew they would pressure her about which man she should be with, each of her family members with their own preference, and she couldn't face that on top of everything else.

"All right. You want to tie this up as soon as possible? Then come on my trip with me. I'll be staying at one of the resorts in the chain I'm buying. It'll be an idyllic setting—clear, blue ocean, sandy beaches—you can relax and de-stress."

"I doubt that."

He sent her a charming half grin that made her knees weak.

"Am I really so hard to get along with?" he asked.

"No, of course not."

He took her hands. "Abi, my hope had been that the two of us being together here at the house would remind you what it was like when we were married. That spending the weekend together, away from the rest of the world—including spending the nights together—would remind you of how happy we'd been."

"Is that why you're suggesting that I accompany you on this trip? Because I'm not going to agree to that."

"What about this? If you agree to spend the three weeks with me truly living as husband and wife, and giving it a real shot . . . then at the end of the three weeks, if you aren't convinced, I'll sign the papers."

CHAPTER EIGHTEEN

Abi's heart stuttered as shock gripped her. "Are you serious?"

"I've never been more serious in my life."

"And by living as husband and wife, you mean sleeping together? Having sex?"

"Of course. I want you to give this a real chance."

Except she wouldn't have a chance in hell of being rational if she was in his bed, with him making love to her.

But she wanted this to be over. "What if I agree to sleep in your bed . . . but no sex?"

"No."

"But a lot of married couples don't—"

"No. Sex is part of the deal."

She frowned. "But I'm pregnant. You remember last time how I felt nauseous for weeks early in the pregnancy?" She hadn't felt well enough to be intimate, even though she'd wanted to. "The morning sickness will probably start kicking in any time now. What if I don't feel up to it?"

His jaw twitched. "Baby, I'm not going to force myself on

you. But if we shut out that side of the relationship, then we're not giving this a real chance."

He ran his fingers along her hair, then stroked it behind her ear, sending tingles through her.

"Abi, this won't work if you're spending all your energy trying to keep me at a distance. If I sense that's what you're doing, then the deal's off. I'm asking you to give this an honest try. I think our future happiness . . . and the baby's . . . is worth it."

He tipped up her chin and she was drawn into the depths of his chocolate-brown eyes.

"So will you go into this with a sincere intent to make it work?"

She drew in a breath.

"I'll need to talk to Del. He understood why I came here to spend the weekend, but he wasn't happy about it. Obviously, he'll be against this idea. I'll talk to him, though. He and I both want this to be settled as soon as possible."

Liam frowned. "And if he demands you don't go?"

She pursed her lips. "I'll tell him how important it is to me."

"I can't believe Liam agreed to let me come along," Del said as he settled into the town car Liam had sent to meet them at the airport. "But I still don't like it."

The thought of Abi in bed with Liam for the next three weeks . . . touching her . . . making love to her . . . drove him crazy.

But it was the only way to end this thing.

When she'd told him about Liam's proposition, he'd tried to talk her out of it, but she was highly stressed and just wanted this to be over. The fact Liam had promised he'd sign the divorce papers if she did this was huge.

So Del had agreed. On one condition.

That he came along, too.

Not that he wanted to be in the next room knowing Abi was

in Liam's bed. It was a horribly awkward and gut-wrenching situation. But if he was there, Abi wouldn't sink totally into a fantasy world and forget what they shared. He knew Abi loved him and he planned to be there to remind her of that every day.

"I know you don't." She snuggled against him and he tucked his arm around her. "But after this is over, we'll be free to get married and we'll have a lifetime of happiness together."

"Abi, you don't know how much I want that."

She gazed up at him and smiled. When she rested her soft hand on his cheek and stroked, his heart swelled with joy.

"Yes, I do. As much as I want it. And that's saying a lot."

He couldn't help himself. He dipped down and kissed her. Her soft lips moved against his, and he tightened his arm around her, pulling her into a deeper kiss. He plundered her mouth with his tongue, driving deep. Exploring. She tasted so sweet.

Her soft sigh drove his need for her higher. She cupped his cheeks as she glided her tongue into his mouth, then her hands glided down his chest. When he felt her hand continue down his stomach, then over his growing cock, he grasped her hand.

"Sweetheart, we can't do this here," he whispered against her ear.

She bit her lip, then nodded, her cheeks blossoming red. He didn't know if it was embarrassment or lingering excitement.

The hormones from the pregnancy seemed to be making her easily aroused.

Liam had suggested they come to the resort a few days after him since he would be tied up in meetings a lot at first. After that, he only had intermittent meetings over the rest of the trip as the business of buying the resort chain progressed. That had given Abi time to tell her family she was going away on vacation for a few weeks, and for both of them to pack. During those few days, her hormones had kicked into high gear and she'd been all over him.

He'd enjoyed every minute of their lovemaking. In bed. On the kitchen table. In the shower. On the stairs. Even in the car.

She'd been insatiable. Which had thrilled him.

Not so much now, though, as they drove to her husband's resort villa where she'd stay in his bed for the next three weeks.

And here he was getting her aroused right before he delivered her to Liam.

She snuggled against him, then gazed out the window.

The car was gliding along a road skirting the ocean, with a beautiful view of palm trees on one side, white sands and aqua-blue ocean on the other.

It was late afternoon and the sun would be setting soon. So Liam would probably offer her a sumptuous dinner in his undoubtedly luxurious villa overlooking the ocean, with a fabulous view of the sunset reflecting on the water. And Del would be sitting in his room, probably on the other side of the resort, going crazy thinking of Liam seducing her into his bed.

Not that he actually had to seduce her, since she'd agreed to sleep with him. And once she was in bed with him, Del had no doubt of what would happen between them.

The driver turned and followed a winding road lined with palm trees. They arrived at a gate and the driver texted something on his phone and the gate opened. After several minutes continuing along the road, now lined with thick flowering bushes, they arrived at a beautiful cleared area with a large white villa set amidst beautiful landscaping of tropical plants with brightly colored, exotic flowers. Large windows overlooked the ocean view and there were large balconies on the second level.

The driver pulled up to the entrance and opened the passenger door. Del followed Abi out of the car while the driver retrieved the luggage from the trunk. As they walked toward the front door, it opened and Liam stepped out into the warm sunshine.

"Welcome," he said with a big smile. "Did you have a nice flight?"

The driver disappeared into the house with the suitcases.

"It was very nice," Abi said. "I've never been on a private jet. Your staff treated us very well."

"Good."

He held out his hand to Del.

Del hesitated briefly, considering ignoring it and heading into the house, but this situation was awkward enough without him being peevish. He wanted to make this as easy on Abi as he could.

He shook Liam's hand with a firm grip.

Then Liam turned and took Abi's hand and drew her in for a kiss. It was a light casual kiss, but it still made Del want to drag him away from her. Especially knowing the effect it was probably having on her, given her natural attraction to Liam, augmented by her pregnancy hormones.

Abi glanced at Del, guilt flashing across her face.

Fuck, these three weeks were going to be excruciating.

"Come in," Liam said. "I think you'll enjoy the villa."

As they stepped in the door, the driver returned. "Anything else, sir?" he asked.

"No, that'll be fine."

As the driver headed out the door, Abi glanced at Del then back to Liam.

"Del probably wants to get settled in, so shouldn't he go with the driver? Or is he staying nearby?" Abi asked.

"Yes, very nearby. Instead of staying at the main resort, I decided Del should stay here with us. There's plenty of room."

"Really?" Abi asked. "I thought you wanted me all to yourself."

"Our suite is huge if we want to spend time alone. You said you wanted Del here for support, so I assumed you'd be happy having him stay here in the villa so you can talk to him anytime.

If it makes either of you uncomfortable, I can get him a room at the resort."

"Here will be fine," Del said. Whatever benefit Liam thought this gave him—and he was sure Liam believed there was one—Del would deal with it.

"Good. Then I suggest you both settle in and we all meet for dinner in an hour. I thought we'd eat on the terrace and watch the sunset."

"That sounds lovely," Abi said. "I'd really like to change."

Del didn't like the smile playing on Liam's lips at Abi's words. Liam turned to Del.

"You have the room at the end of the hallway there. It overlooks the pool and the ocean." Liam rested his hand on the small of Abi's back and guided her to the open spiral stairway. "Abi, the master bedroom is upstairs."

The feel of Liam's hand on her back sent ripples of awareness through Abi. As soon as he'd kissed her at the front door, even though it was only a brief brush of lips, Abi had felt her hormones sparking.

She walked up the stairs, watching Del walk down the hallway, Liam's hand still on her back as he walked right behind her. Abi knew this must be really difficult for Del.

They reached the top of the stairs and Liam guided her down a short hallway to a set of double doors. The doors were open and as they walked into the room, she saw her suitcase set on a stand by the closet.

"I should unpack," she said as she started toward the suitcase, but Liam caught her arm and pulled her back, then drew her against him.

"I've missed you," he said, his deep, silky voice gliding through her in a sweet caress.

She gazed into his chocolate-brown eyes, sparks flaring in the depths as his face moved closer, and she found herself leaning into the kiss. His lips brushed hers, but instead of stopping there, like he had downstairs at the door, he deepened the kiss, gliding his tongue inside her mouth.

She murmured softly. She was stressed and confused and hormonal and . . . His tongue pulsed inside her.

Oh, God, horny as hell.

She cupped his face, loving the feel of his rough stubble against her hands, and pulled him tighter, driving her tongue into his mouth. His hand glided down her back and he pulled her tight to his body. He arched his hips forward and she felt his cock, iron hard, against her belly.

Need careened through her but . . . Oh, God, Del was downstairs. And in an hour she'd have to face him.

She jerked her mouth from Liam's, sucking in a breath. She'd only been in this house for five minutes and she was already throwing herself at him.

Having Del here was good. It was helping her make better decisions already. Helping her from falling completely under Liam's spell.

"I really should unpack."

Liam released her, a smile quirking up his lips.

"I think you said something about changing."

CHAPTER NINETEEN

Abi drew in a breath, trying to ignore the glitter in his eyes. Trying to ignore her own desire to strip down in front of him right now.

"I think I'll take a shower first."

His smile broadened. "Great idea. Let me show you where it is."

He took her hand and led her to a door beside the floor-to-ceiling window revealing a stunning view of the ocean. He guided her outside to the huge balcony, which had a private hot tub sunk into the smooth wooden floor.

"Why are you bringing me out here?" she asked.

"This is where the shower is."

He pointed and she realized there was an open shower stall with three walls: part of the bedroom window forming one wall, a glossy marble wall housing an array of spray nozzles, and another clear glass wall facing the ocean.

Which meant that if she was in that shower, she would be visible to anyone on the deck, or in the bedroom. Possibly even from the ocean.

"I can't shower in there."

"Don't worry," Liam assured. "This stretch of beach is totally private, so no one will see you. And no one can see the shower from the patio downstairs."

"I mean, I'm not going to shower in front of you."

"Why not? I'm your husband."

And she had agreed to live as husband and wife while they were here.

"Please, Liam. I need a little time to settle in."

He smiled and took her hand, then pressed it to his lips. The contact sent a spiral of delight quivering through her.

"Of course, kitten. I'll go down and see how dinner's doing." He nuzzled the back of her hand again. "But I'll be back in thirty minutes, so don't take too long."

He walked into the house and she hurried along behind him. He opened a cupboard and pulled out a large white towel and dropped it on the bed. Then he went to the closet and pulled out a fluffy terry robe and handed it to her.

"Maybe you'll be more comfortable with this near at hand."

"Thank you. Where's the bathroom?"

"That door in the corner."

She watched him walk to the double doors and open one. He winked as he closed the door behind him.

She hurried to the open bathroom door. As soon as she stepped inside, her breath caught. It was huge, with marble floors, a large marble tub in the center of the room, and a chaise longue a few feet away. And one wall was clear glass with the same stunning view of the ocean. Which meant this room was totally visible from the balcony outside, too. The toilet was in the corner with a marble barrier giving privacy from the window.

She stripped off her clothes and pulled on the robe, then grabbed the towel and went outside. She glanced around, assuring herself no one could see her, then she dropped the robe and stepped into the shower. The warm water flowed over her body.

She soaped herself and scrubbed her skin. As she rubbed her soapy hands over her breasts, she couldn't help imagining Liam in the shower with her, his big hands gliding over her body. The familiar ache started inside.

She leaned the top of her head against the glass wall, the water flowing over her back. She had to get a grip on herself.

She rinsed off the soap and slipped from the shower, then dried off with the big towel. Ten minutes later, she was unpacked and dressed in clean clothes, feeling refreshed. She was running a brush through her damp hair when Liam came back into the room.

"Feeling better?" he asked.

"Yes, thank you."

"So what do you think of the villa?"

She glanced around the bedroom, then out the window to the ocean beyond.

The bedroom was very open and airy, with the abundance of glass making the inside feel like it melded with the outside. It was a huge room, with a full sitting area with couches, armchairs, and a large television. The neutral contemporary décor didn't detract from the stunning outside view, and it gave a cozy, yet upscale feel to the room. She remembered the downstairs had the same feel.

"It's very nice. It'll take some getting used to having an outdoor shower, as well as the bathtub being practically outside."

"I thought that was one of the best features of the place."

His devilish smile sent sparks flirting along her nerve endings.

"I'm sure you did," she said. "Why don't we go downstairs so we can see the rest of the place?"

They walked out of the bedroom into the upper hallway.

"There are two more suites on this floor," Liam said, as they passed by two closed doors, "but Del is in the second largest suite in the villa."

They walked down the large, spiral staircase. Del was sitting in the living room gazing out at the view.

"Liam is showing me around the house," Abi said to Del. "Join us."

"Sure." Del got up and followed them.

Abi was amazed at the size and luxury of the place. There was a room with a pool table. Several sitting rooms. Televisions in every room. An office with a high-end desktop computer and huge monitor. Even a small gym.

They stepped out the door to a stone deck with an infinity pool that seemed to blend into the ocean. In the shallow end, there was an area that was only about ten inches deep, where the pool angled back so sunbathers could comfortably lounge right in the water.

There were lots of cushioned lounge chairs around the pool. There were also outdoor couches and chairs in various locations around the huge patio to provide different conversation areas. Liam led them to the railing at the end of the patio where she saw that there were a few steps down to a wooden deck that led right to the white sand of the beach.

"How do you like your room, Del?" Abi asked.

He turned back to the house and pointed. "Look for yourself. You can see the whole thing from here."

As they walked back to the house, she saw that Del's room, like the whole main floor and the master suite, had an entire wall of glass facing the ocean. As they got closer, she could see the inside of his room.

There would be no privacy for Del if anyone was out here on the patio. At least with the master suite, no one would be walking on the second-story balcony to peer into their room. Hopefully, Del's room had drapes.

"It's time for dinner," Liam announced.

She and Del followed him across the patio to stairs leading to a higher level. They passed several large pots filled with greenery and one with a plant with large red blossoms. Then she saw a round teak table set with china place settings and crystal glasses. A couple of staff were setting out food.

When they reached the table, Liam pulled out her chair and she sat down. Del sat on one side of her and Liam on the other.

There was a lovely salad with a vinaigrette dressing and some kind of fish with a fancy sauce. Abi wasn't quite sure what, but it smelled delicious. The staff poured white wine into the stemmed glasses in front of Liam and Del. As a woman poured what looked like white wine into her glass, she started to protest.

"Don't worry, Abi," Liam said. "It's sparkling white grape juice."

The staff finished serving and disappeared into the house.

"Del," Liam said, "this is a difficult situation for all of us, and I know it's put you in a particularly awkward position, but I want you to know that I value your friendship and hope that no matter how this unfolds, that we'll still remain friends. In the end, we both want what's best for Abi, and for the baby."

"I agree with the sentiment," Del said, "but will you feel the same way when Abi still wants the divorce at the end of the three weeks?"

Liam's eyebrows arched. "You seem pretty confident."

"Despite the fact that *you* seem to be holding all the cards."

Abi didn't like where this was going. "Could we put this conversation on hold so we can enjoy our dinner and the lovely sunset?"

She stabbed a piece of lettuce and popped it into her mouth as she gazed at the golden light washing over the ocean. The sky was aflame with purple, rose, and gold.

The men both sat back in their chairs and turned their attention to their meals.

Over dinner, Abi asked Liam about the resort and his plans to buy it. He told them he had most of the details worked out, now it was just a matter of meeting with some of the other current owners, then the lawyers writing up the papers. He had about four more meetings over the rest of the stay, the final one to sign all the legal documents. His next meeting was in a few days.

When they finished the main meal, the staff brought out a platter of fresh fruit and some pastries, along with coffee. Liam had arranged decaf for Abi. Since the sun had set, the light was fading, so the staff lit candles and turned on lanterns that were hung around the patio.

Liam asked Del about the classes he would be teaching in the fall and soon they were talking like they used to, reminiscing about when they'd taken one of those classes when they were still students.

Abi watched them, wishing this strain had never been put on their friendship. Why did she have to have fallen for both of them?

Finally, the staff came and cleared away the dishes.

"I'd suggest we all take a moonlit walk along the beach," Liam said, "but the moon's not cooperating."

Abi glanced up to see the moon was obscured by clouds.

"We could play some pool," Del suggested.

She knew he probably wanted to keep them up as late as possible. Anything to defer her climbing into Liam's bed. But she was tired. The traveling and the pregnancy had taken a lot out of her.

"You two go ahead," she said. "I'm going to turn in."

Liam stood up and drew back her chair as she stood. "I'll join you."

Del rose, too. He did not look happy. She stepped toward him and gave him a hug.

"I'll see you in the morning," she said.

"Yeah, sure. Have a good sleep."

Liam tucked his arm around her as he accompanied her into the house. She glanced back to see Del staring out at the ocean.

Once they got into the bedroom, Liam closed the doors behind them.

"Do you actually want to go to bed right now, or would you like to go in the hot tub? I turned the temperature down low enough so it's safe for the baby." He smiled. "It'll relax you."

"Do I need relaxing?"

He walked behind her and rested his hand on her shoulders. She stiffened.

He laughed. "Yeah, I'd say you do."

He began massaging her shoulders, and she found herself relaxing a little. As the tension melted away, she found that his touch started having other effects. Tingles dancing across her skin. Heat flashing through her body. A hunger started to build in her.

"Maybe the hot tub is a good idea."

She walked to the door and stepped outside, breathing in the fragrant night air. Instead of heading to the hot tub, she walked to the stone railing and gazed over the ocean. Liam stepped behind her and wrapped his arm around her waist, drawing her back against his body. His hard, muscular body.

He was her husband. She was supposed to be spending this time with him as his wife. She shouldn't feel guilty that being in his arms like this excited her. Made her want to strip off her clothes, step into the hot tub, and climb right onto his lap. Facing him. His rigid cock sliding right into her.

Then she'd ride him like a wild stallion. His cock filling her again and again.

His hand glided upward and cupped her breast. His fingers found her hardening nipple and squeezed it. She arched against him.

"Oh, baby, I've missed touching you like this." His lips played along her neck and she whimpered in need.

God, she wanted to lean over the railing and pull up her dress so he could fuck her right here and now. Her hands even crumpled in the cotton of the full skirt, itching to do it.

His hand glided over her hip, then he cupped her behind.

She started to pull up the fabric, lost in the siren call of her hormones.

Then she heard a splash. Her gaze shot to the pool below and she saw Del under the crystal-clear water, then his head break through the surface. He gazed up and saw her leaning against the railing.

Oh, God, could he see that Liam's hand was on her breast? Even if he couldn't, he could see that Liam was standing close behind her. Two lovers staring out at the ocean.

Guilt surged through her.

She pulled away from Liam and strode to the door. Once inside, she turned to him.

"I'm sorry, I changed my mind about the hot tub."

"I figured. You know, you don't have to feel guilty being with me. We are married. And Del knows this is part of the arrangement."

"I know. It's just . . . it's stressful right now. I need a little time . . . before we . . ."

He drew her close and captured her lips. The kiss was sweet and tender.

"Baby, I told you I wouldn't force myself on you. We can just go to sleep."

She nodded. Sleep. That's what she needed.

She pulled her pajamas from her suitcase and turned to the bed. Then stopped cold at the sight of Liam, already bare-chested, dropping his pants to the floor. He stepped out of them, totally naked. Then he walked to the bed.

"You're not going to sleep like that, are you?"

He smiled. "Yeah, I am. Kitten, I said I wouldn't force myself on you. But that doesn't mean I'm going to make it easy for you to ignore me."

He climbed under the covers and folded his hands behind

his head, watching her. She stared down at the pajamas in her hand. Damn, she couldn't strip off her clothes right in front of him.

She turned and walked into the bathroom, then changed into the PJs. When she climbed into bed with him, he moved in behind her and wrapped his arms around her. Being curled up in his embrace was warm and comforting.

It was also crazy sexy and had her body quivering with need. Especially when she could feel his cock swelling against her. But she ignored it as best she could, drawing in deep, slow breaths.

Somehow, after what seemed like an eternity, she finally drifted off to sleep.

Abi awoke to the sound of spraying water nearby. She opened her eyes to the morning sunlight streaming in the bedroom window. She stretched as she enjoyed the stunning view beyond the glass. As she shifted her gaze, the sight of Liam, totally naked on the other side of the window, water washing over his muscular body, took her breath away.

She bit her lip as she watched the water rush over his head, flattening his hair to his scalp, then over his broad shoulders and down his back. His taut buttocks, which she knew were rock hard, were glazed in the moving, sunlit water. Her heart rate increased and she longed to rip off her pajamas and join him right now.

He turned, giving her a profile view. The sight of his long cock, hanging heavy between his legs, sent need thrumming through her. Her fingers ran over her breast, stroking the sensitive nipple, before she realized what she was doing.

He soaped his chest, covering it in white suds, and she licked her lips as she watched the foam wash over his body. Finally, he pumped some shampoo into his hand from a spout on the marble wall and stepped out of the water enough to soap his hair. When he stepped back under the flow to rinse it off, his eyes closed. He was facing her, his long, dripping cock in full view.

Her insides ached with need and she could feel wetness pooling between her legs.

He pushed the water back from his face and opened his eyes.

CHAPTER TWENTY

When Liam opened his eyes, he saw Abi staring at him with such hunger in her eyes, he almost choked. His cock jumped to attention, swelling to a painful level of need.

God, he wanted to stride in there right now and take her.

As soon as she realized he'd seen her, her eyes widened and she scampered from the bed into the bathroom.

He turned off the water and dried off, then walked into the bedroom.

He wanted her. Badly. And if he chose to, he was sure he could easily sweep her into his arms, and into his bed. But right now, it was more important to him that he gain her trust. He needed to give her time.

As he pulled on his boxers, he heard a familiar sound from the bathroom. Abi was throwing up.

He walked to the door and tapped, then stepped inside to see her folded over the toilet.

"Aw, kitten."

He walked to her side and crouched beside her, then gathered her hair in his hand and held it back. When she was finished, he guided her to the chaise and sat her down, then brought her a damp cloth to wipe her face.

He sat down beside her and slid his arm around her.

"I have some packages of crackers in the bedside table," he said, "and I read that peppermint tea can help with the nausea. Want me to get you either of those?"

"No, nothing, thanks."

She leaned against his side, her head resting on his shoulder. It felt so good having her there.

"Okay, let's get you dressed and downstairs."

He half expected her to protest, but instead she turned toward him and hugged him tight. He squeezed her gently, then helped her to her feet and guided her into the bedroom. He sat her on the bed, then opened her suitcase.

"Shorts or a dress?" he asked.

"I think a bathing suit and cover-up."

He pulled out an aqua-and-purple-print bikini and loose flowing top in a matching fabric and handed it to her.

"Thanks." But then she frowned, her hand flattening on her stomach and she looked a little green.

"Are you going to throw up again? Do you want me to help you back to the bathroom?"

She looked doubtful, then finally shook her head.

"No, I think I'm okay." She sighed. "Maybe you could stand behind me and help me with the hook on the top. It can be tricky and I'm not up to struggling with it right now."

He sat down beside her and she pivoted away from him. She slipped off her pajama top, baring her smooth, creamy back to him. The thought of her bare breasts so close made his cock twitch. He longed to stroke her smooth skin, then glide his hands around and cup her breasts. But instead, he waited patiently as she slid her arms into the straps of the small top. He took the sides of the band and fastened the clasp. It took two tries to get it to snap closed.

She slid the shirt over her head, then stood and dropped her

pajama pants, then pulled on her bikini bottoms without him seeing a thing.

If she weren't suffering from morning sickness, he didn't
think he'd be able to stop himself from commanding her to shed
what she was wearing and climb right back into bed . . . and on
top of him.

"You go ahead downstairs, kitten, while I get dressed."

But he was so fucking turned on that getting dressed wasn't
all he'd do.

By late morning, Abi was feeling a lot better and had gone out on
the patio to enjoy the sun. The nausea had caught her off guard
when she'd scurried off the bed right after Liam caught her ogling
him. She'd wanted to hide away and get dressed before he came
back in, but her stomach had had other ideas.

She swished her feet in the pool, sending ripples across the
water. Liam had been so sweet taking care of her this morning.
He'd been like that with the first pregnancy, too. Always there
with her. Seeing her through the tough times.

Oh, God, she didn't want to remember that. This was hard
enough as it was.

In the afternoon, the three of them played badminton, then
went for a late afternoon swim in the ocean. Most of the day, Del
hadn't said much, other than solicitous queries about how she was
feeling.

Liam and Del raced into the waves, then dove in and swam
deeper into the ocean. She was content to walk into the gentle
waves as they rolled onto the sandy beach, then stop when she was
waist deep, loving the feel of her body gently buoying up and
down as the water pushed and pulled past her.

When they returned to the villa, the staff had a wonderful
dinner ready for them. An avocado-lime shrimp salad followed by
mahimahi garnished with an onion topped with a slice of lemon
served on a bed of rice and surrounded by broccoli florets.

They watched the sunset on the patio, then Abi went for a swim in the pool while the men finished off the bottle of wine from dinner.

After a while, she walked out of the pool, conscious of both men watching her. The heat of their gazes as they lingered on her bikini-clad body sent need quivering through her.

She sat on the side of the pool, facing the ocean, and dangled her feet in the water. Liam walked to a lounge chair, and she watched as he shed his shirt, revealing his taut muscles. She couldn't drag her gaze from him. She longed to run her fingers over those ridged abs of his.

Del sat down beside her and lowered his feet into the water, too.

When Liam dove into the water, Del leaned toward her.

"I can't stand the thought that he made love to you last night."

"We haven't. I . . . told him I needed time."

"And he was okay with that?"

"He said he wouldn't push me. Then this morning, with the morning sickness . . ."

For the first time today, she saw a smile spread across Del's face.

"I've got to admit, I'm happy to hear that. It's been driving me crazy knowing you're in his bed."

Liam's head popped through the surface of the water and Del pushed himself to his feet. He stripped off his shirt and dove into the pool, too. The smooth line of his body as he glided through the air and into the water was a delightful sight.

She slid off the edge into the pool and treaded water, enjoying the feel of the warm water around her as she watched the men continue to swim and dive into the water, each trying to outdo the other in an unspoken competition.

She couldn't take her eyes off them when they walked along the diving board, water glazing their hard bodies, and dove into the pool. A craving started deep in her core, aching inside her.

Her nipples hardened as she thought about swimming up to one of them and clinging to his shoulders, then wrapping her legs around his waist and arching against him. Feeling his cock swell against her. Then pulling aside the crotch of her bathing suit and sliding his hard shaft inside her.

Finally, Del walked from the pool and dried off. She watched hungrily as he patted the towel over his chest, then down his ridged stomach.

"You seem to be enjoying the view."

She glanced around to see Liam had swum to her side. Her cheeks flushed.

Del walked into the villa.

Liam laughed. "Relax. If watching Del heats you up before you climb into my bed, I'm not going to complain."

She stared at his handsome face, thrown off balance by his closeness. His intense masculine aura. At the sight of the need in her eyes, now turned to him, his mouth turned up in a smile.

"It's getting late. Maybe it's time to call it a day."

"It's only nine thirty," she said, guessing at the time. "Maybe I'll ask Del to play some cards."

She swam to the steps, then walked out of the pool. Liam was right behind her. She dried off and went inside.

The three of them played cards for about an hour, but then she found herself yawning. It was hard to keep her eyes open. Still, when they finished the current hand, she grabbed the deck to shuffle.

"Abi," Liam said, "you can hardly stay awake. I think that's enough cards for tonight."

"But—"

"Baby, you need your sleep."

She couldn't really argue. She'd have to face heading to bed with Liam at some point. She just knew with her raging hormones that she was bound to throw herself into Liam's arms, and that made her feel guilty.

Del put the cards away as Liam guided her to the staircase.

"Good night, Del," she said as they walked up the stairs.

"Good night," he said, and her heart ached knowing he would be alone in his bed, fretting over her in bed with Liam.

Damn, maybe it would have been kinder if she'd insisted Del not come with them.

Liam closed the door to the bedroom and watched Abi walk to the dresser. The sway of her hips sent heat pulsing through him, and when she leaned over to open the middle drawer, displaying her curvy ass, his cock grew.

From the hunger in her eyes when she'd watched Del strip off his shirt, he knew she was aroused, yet she'd delayed coming to bed. She was still fighting the idea of being with him. He could subtly push it, reminding her that she'd agreed to have sex with him during this trip, but that's not how he wanted this to play out.

He wanted her to *want* to. He wanted her to need him. To crave him as much as he craved her.

She closed the drawer and glanced over her shoulder at him, nibbling her lower lip.

Fuck, he knew she was going to run into the bathroom to change again. Not that he didn't get it. He just wished she was more comfortable with him.

He walked behind her and rested his hands on her shoulders, gazing at her in the dresser mirror. She glanced at his reflection nervously.

"I'll help you with the clasp on your bathing suit top," he said.

"No, I'm okay."

He ran his hand down her back. "Don't be silly, kitten. You said it's tricky."

He lifted the loose flowing shirt that covered her bikini-clad body, exposing her curvy ass wrapped snuggly in her tiny bikini bottom and her smooth back. He fiddled with the clasp until it released. The sight of the strap on her bikini top opening made his cock swell even more.

He wanted to glide his hands around her body, then cup her soft breasts in his hands. Then he'd glide one hand down her smooth stomach and dip under the front of her bikini bottom to find her intimate folds, which he was sure were slick.

He glanced at her face in the mirror and her expression was tight. Their reflected gazes caught and he saw need in her eyes. But also trepidation.

His jaw tightened and he stepped back. Her shirt fell back into place.

She wanted privacy so he'd give it to her. He strode across the room and went into the bathroom, then closed the door. He wanted her to change in the bedroom instead of hiding, and if that meant she needed him to give her privacy at first, then that's what he'd do.

He stripped off his clothes and sat down on the chaise to wait. The thought of her in the other room, pulling off her shirt, then shedding her bikini sent his blood boiling. God, at this rate, as soon as he got into bed and felt her soft body against him, he'd be in danger of losing it.

He wrapped his hand around his cock and stroked. He'd promised he wouldn't force himself on her, but that didn't mean he couldn't fantasize about her. He'd love to walk back into the room and sit in the armchair, then demand she strip off whatever pajamas she'd donned and stand in front of him. He'd tell her to stroke her lovely, round breasts for him. He'd watch her small hands cover her mounds and caress them, then because she knew how much it turned him on, she'd flick her fingertips over her nipples, making them harden and peak. He'd tell her to pinch them and pull until he heard the lovely little gasps she made when she got really turned on.

Then he'd command her to sink to her knees in front of him and grab his cock, then stroke it.

He squeezed then stroked faster at the thought of her hand around him. When she leaned forward in his fantasy and wrapped her lips around him, he groaned, pumping faster. His hand became her mouth moving up and down on him, the thought of her moist warmth encompassing him driving him wild.

He tensed and the tight coil of need in his groin released. Pleasure burned through him, and white liquid pulsed from his cock in a fountain as he groaned his release.

Abi stood at the dresser, staring at her flushed cheeks and anxious expression. Liam had stridden to the bathroom and closed the door behind him.

Was he annoyed that she was holding back so much after agreeing to his terms? He'd said he'd give her time, but she didn't blame him for getting impatient for her to fulfill her promise.

And the truth was, she wanted to. The thought of touching his solid body . . . running her hands along his ridged muscles . . . then wrapping her fingers around his thick, swelling cock had her nearly panting with need.

She was trapped in her own little world of need and guilt.

She quickly stripped off her shirt and bathing suit top and tugged on the oversize T-shirt she'd pulled from the door, then she wiggled out of the bikini bottoms, watching the bathroom door. She slipped into bed and pulled the covers snug around her.

She closed her eyes. Trying to relax. Trying not to think about the awkwardness when Liam climbed into bed with her.

She knew she shouldn't resist her desire to be with him. Del understood the agreement and had given his blessing, since he wanted Liam to sign the divorce papers as much as she did. And she was going to honor the terms of the agreement at some point. So why not tonight?

The bathroom door opened and Liam walked toward the bed. She lay still, her eyes closed as he approached. He pulled back the covers on his side of the bed and sat down.

And then he turned off the light.

She frowned. Liam liked to make love with the light on. Was he turning it off hoping she'd be more relaxed?

He climbed under the covers and snuggled up behind her, wrapping his arm around her waist and drawing her close to him. He nuzzled the back of her neck, sending tingles dancing down her spine. Her insides melted with need.

"Good night, kitten."

Good night? Was he really just going to go to sleep?

A few minutes later, his slow steady breathing gave her the answer.

Liam didn't know why he'd woken up, but he opened his eyes to the darkness and blinked. In the silvery moonlight, he saw Abi, her face only inches away, gazing at him.

"Hi," she murmured softly.

CHAPTER TWENTY-ONE

"Hi." Liam's voice was low and sleep-roughened.

Abi's luminous blue eyes were wide and filled with an emotion he couldn't read.

"Are you all right, baby?" he asked.

She nodded.

"Can't sleep?" he asked. "What time is it?"

"It's after two." She rested her hand on his chest, over his heart. "And yes, I'm having trouble sleeping."

She moved closer, until her lips were a mere breath away.

"Because I can't stop thinking about doing this," she whispered.

Then her soft lips found his, moving on his mouth gently. Heat flooded through his body. Her lips moved more passionately, then she surged closer, pressing her body tight to his, her soft breasts crushing against his chest.

His arms slid around her waist.

She tore her lips away. "Oh, God, I want you so badly."

He could feel her bead-hard nipples driving into his chest,

and her words made his cock swell. She rocked against him, squeezing his cock between their bodies.

She took his hand and glided it over her hip then in front of her. She pulled up the loose T-shirt she was wearing and slid his hand between her legs.

Fuck, she wasn't wearing any panties. And . . .

"Oh, fuck, baby. You're drenched."

The slickness glazed his fingertips.

Her hand found his cock and she squeezed it. It pulsed in her grip.

"Oh, God, I need you," she whimpered.

Then she dragged his tip over her slick folds, glazing him with her slickness.

"Kitten, slow it down. I want to—"

Too late.

She pressed him to her opening and he groaned at the delightful warmth of her surrounding him as she pushed his thick shaft inside her.

She wrapped her leg around his thigh, holding him tight to her body. Then she lay there, staring into his eyes.

"It feels so good." She sounded like she was near tears, but sweet, poignant tears of pleasure.

They lay there for an eternity, staring into each other's eyes, their bodies joined.

She squeezed him with internal muscles, filling him with a gut-wrenching ache. Then she did it again and he groaned.

"Fuck, love. This is incredible. Being inside you like this."

It felt intimate and agonizingly sweet. It was like she'd found his deepest and most powerful longings and fulfilled them with the comfort of her body.

It was like being home.

This was what it felt like to be accepted unconditionally. To be truly loved.

And he saw it in her face.

Her fingertips rested on his cheek and glided slowly over the stubble. Love glowed in her beautiful blue eyes. She squeezed him again and he moaned. His cock throbbed, and he knew that he could easily come any second. One stroke would probably do it.

But he didn't want this to end.

He tightened his arm around her waist, keeping her tight to him, almost losing it as that small movement pushed his cock a little deeper inside her.

"I'm so close, Liam. Please make me come."

Oh, fuck, her words slammed straight through him. His cock twitched, needing to move inside her so badly he thought he'd die.

She squeezed him again and . . .

"Oh, fuck!" His groin tightened and heat blasted through him.

She moaned and contracted tighter around his shaft, her face contorting into that familiar expression of blissful abandon.

"Oh, God, Liam," she gasped. "I'm . . . coming."

He rolled her onto her back and pumped into her as his cock exploded inside her, filling her with his seed. He found her clit and stroked it. Her moans grew louder as she rocketed to another orgasm.

He ground deep into her, pinning her to the bed as he continued to stroke her clit.

She sucked in a breath, then moaned again, finding her third orgasm.

He kept her at the crest for a long, long time, reveling in her sweet moans of pleasure, but finally he relented and let her fade back to earth.

She sucked in air, trying to catch her breath. But when he tried to roll away, she held tight. "Don't leave me. Not yet."

Those words bore through him, making his heart ache.

"Never, kitten. I'll never leave you."

His mouth found hers and he kissed her passionately. Then he stroked her hair back.

"God, baby, I love you so much."

Her eyes filled with uncertainty, but then she cupped his face and pulled him into another kiss.

He grasped her hips and rolled onto his back, taking her with him. Now she lay on top of him, his cock still deep inside her. Impossibly, it was still hard.

She rested her head on his shoulder and sighed contentedly.

This was heaven. Holding her like this. Loving her like this.

Her breathing settled into a steady rhythm, deep and even, and soon he realized she was asleep.

He held her close, not wanting to fall asleep himself. Not wanting to miss a single second of her in his arms like this.

Abi woke up to find herself draped over Liam, her ear against his heart, the steady sound of his heartbeat soothing.

Last night, when he'd turned out the light and cuddled her close, she'd been surprised. She'd known she should be relieved she could just go to sleep without any worry of disappointing him, but she'd been aroused all evening, her hormones not giving her any peace. Lying in his arms, with his warmth and heady masculine scent surrounding her, she couldn't fall asleep.

Couldn't think straight.

After hours of struggling with her conflicting desires, she'd finally turned to face him, needing to see his face. In the soft light of the moon, his face had had an ethereal glow, making him look almost godlike.

She'd stared at those perfect features, unable to tear her gaze away.

Then he'd opened his eyes.

What had followed had been dreamlike. Perfect.

Intensely moving.

Then, when he'd said he loved her, doubt had quivered through her, as it always did. She wanted him to love her so badly. But she knew he didn't.

He couldn't.

But for the first time in a very long time she wondered . . .

Was it possible he actually could?

Liam awoke as he felt Abi move from his body and slip out of bed. He blinked his eyes open to see her hurrying to the bathroom. He pushed himself to his feet and walked to the door she closed behind herself. Then he heard her retching.

He tapped and walked in, then like yesterday, he pulled back her hair and sat with her through her ordeal. Once she was settled on the chaise, he fetched her a glass of water and gave her a packet of saltines. He sat beside her, his arm around her waist as she nibbled the crackers.

"Thanks," she murmured.

He smiled and kissed her forehead. "Anytime, baby."

When she felt well enough to stand up and walk back to the bedroom, he took her hand and walked by her side, but before she sat on the bed, he pulled her into his arms and held her close.

"Last night was incredible," he murmured against the crown of her head, then kissed her, her hair soft against his lips.

"Liam." She drew back and gazed up at him. "Last night . . . when you said you loved me, I . . ."

His heartbeat stalled and he tipped up her chin, searching her blue eyes.

"Yes, kitten?"

She sucked in a breath. "I think I started to believe it."

His heart swelled as joy swept through him.

But then he realized it wasn't happiness reflected in her eyes, but caution.

"I suppose I always knew you loved me but I . . . just didn't want to believe it."

Shock jolted through him. "Why, baby?"

She bit her lip. "Because it was easier to believe that you never really loved me. Because if you did love me . . . *really* love me . . ."

She drew in a slow, quivering breath. "How could you have left me all alone to deal with the pain?"

Her lip trembled and she gazed at him with such intense sadness his breath locked in his lungs.

She shook her head. "Maybe love isn't enough."

Oh, God, Abi was right. Liam realized he'd been fooling himself all this time.

And being incredibly selfish. He loved her, yet he'd abandoned her in her time of need. Only worrying about himself and his pain.

So despite the fact he loved her, and she loved him . . . Maybe love wasn't enough. Maybe he'd blown it so completely they could never turn things around.

His heart ached at the thought.

She drew away from his embrace and, heedless of his presence, stripped off her pajamas and donned a sundress, then left the room. He showered and dressed, and then he went downstairs and poured himself a coffee. Del walked into the kitchen.

"Something happen between the two of you last night?" Del asked. "Abi looked pretty upset when she came down and she went straight out for a walk along the ocean."

"I didn't push her into anything if that's what you're asking," Liam said tersely.

Del rested his hand on Liam's shoulder and squeezed. "I know."

Liam's gaze shot to Del's.

"Don't look so surprised," Del said. "Despite the fact we're competing for the same woman, you're my friend and I know what kind of man you are. And despite the fact I want to be the one who wins her, I hate that that means you have to lose her."

Abi walked back to the villa, dreading seeing Liam again. When she'd told him that maybe love wasn't enough, his eyes had filled with a pain so deep and devastating, it tore at her heart.

She stepped onto the wooden deck, then went up the steps to the stone patio. Del was lying on one of the lounge chairs facing the pool.

"Have a nice walk?" he asked.

"Yes, thanks." She glanced at the house. "Where's Liam?"

"He's out. He changed tomorrow's meeting to today." He sat up and pushed down his sunglasses, gazing at her over the rims. "Abi, you know if you want to talk, I'm happy to listen."

She slumped down on the lounger beside him.

"Did you two have a fight?" Del asked.

"No. In fact . . ." She gazed at him, chewing on her lower lip. "I've finally come to believe that Liam really does love me."

She saw Del's expression crumple. The anguish in his eyes almost rivaled the pain in Liam's eyes earlier.

Almost.

"I seem to be taking quite a toll on the two men in my life this morning," she said.

"I assume that means you'll go back to Liam, because we both know you're totally in love with him." Del's hands tightened into fists. "I don't know why I ever thought I had a chance. Especially now that you're carrying his child."

"Well, you see, that's the thing. Even if he does really love me, and that means he has all along . . . that didn't stop him from withdrawing when I needed him most. What if I lose this baby, too?" She sucked in a breath at the pain digging through her. "That in itself would be hard enough. On me . . . and on Liam. But if Liam were to abandon me emotionally again . . ." She shook her head.

Del took her hand, cradling it in his bigger one.

"I need the man I love to be someone I can depend on. Especially in the most difficult moments." She turned her head and lost herself in his warm, olive-green eyes. "Like you." She squeezed his hand. "You've always been there for me."

He pushed himself forward and knelt beside her, drawing her into his arms.

"And I always will, sweetheart. No matter what happens."

Liam had said not to expect him back until after dinner, so Del did his best to entertain Abi all afternoon. They had a nice lunch, then had the chauffeur drive them around the island.

"The island really is gorgeous," Abi said as she gazed out the window at the tall palm trees sprouting from flat, grassy terrain, with white sandy beach and the beautiful aquamarine ocean beyond. The sunlight glittered on the water as they passed luxurious resorts on the beach and beautiful luxury homes. As the road curved around a large bay, white boats with brightly colored sails dotted the water.

Abi rested her head on Del's shoulder, and all Del wanted to do was go back to the villa and spend time with her alone.

She smiled at him. "Why don't we tell the driver we're done and want to go back?"

He grinned. "Are you reading my mind?"

She laughed. "No. Your eyes. It's clear as day what you want."

"And what's that?"

She shifted a little closer and took his hand, then brought it to her mouth. The soft brush of her lips against his skin filled him with intense need.

She smiled wider and rested her hand on his chest. Then she slowly ran it downward. Traveling down his ribs, over his stomach then . . .

"Oh, God, Abi," he choked as she caressed his swelling cock over his shorts.

She stroked it, then squeezed lightly.

He grabbed her hand and held it still.

"Do you really think we should be doing this here? The

chauffeur and the others believe you're Liam's wife. Fuck, what the hell am I saying? You *are* his wife."

"But the driver is on *that* side of the dark glass divider and we're on *this* side."

She tightened her hand around him and stroked. Fuck, he was so hard.

CHAPTER TWENTY-TWO

Del pushed the button on the console beside his seat and told he driver to take them back to the villa. Then he dragged Abi into his arms and kissed her with such passion, her hand drifted from his cock to his shoulder, clinging to him as he swept his tongue into her mouth and devoured her.

When they arrived at the villa, the driver opened their door and Del followed Abi from the car, hoping the driver didn't notice his state.

"Are there many staff in the villa now?" Abi asked the driver.

"No, ma'am. They won't be back until later this afternoon to prepare dinner. Would you like me to call someone in?"

"No, thank you. In fact, tell them not to bother with dinner this evening. We'll eat something light."

"Yes, ma'am. If you need me again, just text." He got in the car and drove away.

Abi watched the car until it disappeared around the bend, then she grabbed Del's hand and, giggling, tugged him toward the villa. She dropped her bag inside the front door, then continued through the main floor to the patio, Del on her heels, their hands still joined.

"Where are we going?"

"Just follow me."

She let go of his hand and raced down the stairs to the wooden deck, then across the sand. She kicked off her sandals, then his eyes widened as her shirt fluttered to the ground behind her. Next, she flung her wrap skirt aside, now in only her bra and panties.

"Abi, do you think you should be doing that?"

She turned suddenly and grinned. "Why not? Liam said it's a private beach. Don't you want to feel the warm ocean water on your naked skin?" Her gaze fell to his growing cock. "*Every* part of it?"

Her hands were working behind her back as she talked, then she dropped the straps and eased her bra forward. As it fell away, his gaze locked on her perfect breasts, the tips rosy pink. And peaking to hard nubs.

She stroked them, then pushed down her panties in a swift motion.

Now as she stood in front of him totally naked, he sucked in a breath. The glow of her pregnancy enhanced her already natural beauty. She wasn't showing yet, but he could hardly wait to see her naked body when it began to swell with the child. It would be so incredibly moving to see her like that.

He hoped beyond hope that he'd get the chance. That she would still be his.

"Now you," she said, her gaze simmering as she watched him.

He stripped off his clothes, then left them in a heap as they ran toward the water, the warm sand squishing between his toes.

They frolicked in the water, diving into the waves and laughing. He couldn't drag his gaze from her breasts as the water splashed over them, then sluiced away. She raced toward him and surged into his arms, then he kissed her, his tongue driving into her mouth. She stroked his cock under the water and he was so hard he was trembling with need. She grasped his shoulders and wrapped her legs around his waist, his aching cock snug between their warm bodies.

"I think you want to fuck me right here in the water," she murmured against his ear.

He kissed her, then pressed his forehead to hers.

"Do you now? What makes you think that?"

She pushed her hand between their bodies and stroked the side of his cock.

"There's one big reason." Her hand wrapped tightly around him. "One very *big* . . . *hard* . . . reason." She started stroking him.

"Oh, fuck, baby." He tried to stop her movement, but she kept pumping him. "I'm so close, I'm not going to be able to hold back."

"Mmm." She nuzzled his neck. "Then don't."

He felt her slickness against his tip, then she eased him inside her. His cock glided right into her, all the way. He held her tight to him, trying not to move. Knowing he could explode inside her at any second.

She wrapped her legs tighter around him. "Oh, God, you feel so good inside me."

Her nipples, hard as pearls, spiked into his chest. He cupped one of her breasts, the nub drilling into his palm.

She nipped his neck, then moaned softly. "Oh, God, Del. I'm so turned on. Please fuck me."

He cupped her ass and drew her back, then drove in deep again. She gasped, her eyes widening.

"Oh, yes. Like that," she breathed.

He pumped again and she moaned.

Fuck, she was already close to orgasm. He could see it in her eyes. Feel it in the way her pussy clenched around him.

He guided her back, then pulled her tight again. His cock throbbed with the need to release.

She nipped his neck. "Please, Del," she whimpered. "Make me come."

He pumped into her, driving his cock deep again and again. Her fingers clenched around his shoulders, digging into his flesh. Faster and faster he filled her until that first moan erupted from her lips. He pumped in slower, deeper strokes now, keeping a steady rhythm.

"Oh, yes, Del. Yes. Just like that."

Then she moaned, her voice echoing across the water, the sweetness driving him over the edge.

"Ah, fuck." His aching cock drove deep, then erupted inside her, intense pleasure washing through him in waves.

Her moans continued and he found her clit and teased it, sending her into another orgasm. Her face glowed with blissful abandon.

Finally, her moans subsided and she dropped her head against his shoulder. She sighed contentedly.

"Oh, God, you're beautiful when you come," he said.

She giggled and kissed his shoulder. "Coming is beautiful. Like finding a little pocket of heaven."

He laughed and kissed her cheek. "*You're* a little pocket of heaven."

Abi walked with Del across the beach toward the villa, his arm snug around her. It felt good being this close to him. Knowing he loved her. Knowing he'd always be there for her.

Making love in the ocean, totally naked, so open and free, had been exhilarating. When they got back to the patio, they grabbed some terry robes from the guest bathroom and Del insisted she sit on the patio and relax while he prepared dinner. He returned a few minutes later with a platter of cold cuts, cheese, crackers, freshly cut veggies and dip, and fresh fruit for dessert.

They ate dinner and sipped lemonade, watching the sun sink low on the horizon.

"So now that you've had this revelation about Liam, what happens next?" Del asked.

"I don't know. I promised to give these three weeks a real chance. We'll take it a day at a time."

She found she was twisting her fingers around each other, so she dropped them to rest flat on her thighs. She knew her feelings toward Liam were colored by old wounds. Was she really being fair to him? This was his child and she had to seriously consider the option of staying with him. He had grown . . . they both had. And she really did love him. Could they make it work?

But she loved Del, too. It didn't seem right somehow. Loving two men. If she loved Liam, was what she felt for Del just infatuation? But if so, would it really have lasted all these years? Maybe being with Del was the right choice.

"Abi, this is obviously upsetting you. Why don't you talk about it?"

"What is there to say? I don't want to hurt Liam. And I don't want to hurt you." She sighed. "But no matter what I do, I'll be hurting one of you."

And that thought hurt her.

He rested his hand on hers and stroked it. The feel of his thumb brushing her thigh sent a tingling awareness rippling through her. She didn't want to think about any of this anymore. Liam would be home in a few hours and right now, she wanted to enjoy as much intimate time with Del as possible.

She stood up and took his hand.

"After that swim in the ocean, I could use a shower."

"Okay. I'll clear up the dishes."

A wicked grin spread across her face.

"I don't want to take it alone," she said and tugged him toward the outdoor shower stall.

"Oh," he said, his lips turning up in a grin.

She turned to him and untied her robe, then dropped it to the ground. She felt warm in the glow of his appreciative masculine gaze.

He dropped his robe to the ground, too, and she stroked

down his flat stomach to his rising cock, then wrapped her hand around it. She knelt in front of him and licked him. He hardened under her tongue.

"Mmm. Salty."

He laughed and pulled her to her feet, then kissed her passionately. Moments later, they were under the warm water, soaping each other's bodies.

Liam got out of the car and went into the villa. He didn't see Abi and Del inside, so he walked out onto the patio. They weren't in the pool or the hot tub, so he walked to the railing to see if they were on the beach.

He turned around and—*Fuck!*

The sight of their two naked bodies under the shower, their hands gliding over each other's skin . . . white suds washing down their limbs . . .

Abi's hand squeezed around Del's thick cock and she began stroking him while Del soaped her breasts. Swirling his hands round and round her soft mounds.

Jealousy burned through Liam at seeing Del touch his wife like that, but at the same time, watching Abi's hand glide up and down Del's cock had his own stirring painfully in his pants.

Del's hand glided down her stomach, then between her legs. Seeing Del's fingers stroking Abi's soft pussy mesmerized Liam. Abi moaned and turned around. She leaned against the glass wall of the shower as Del moved close behind her.

Her eyes widened when she saw Liam. Their gazes locked and they were both frozen . . . captured in an enthralling, erotic spell.

Del didn't see Liam, his attention on Abi's ear as he nuzzled.

Then Abi's mouth formed an O as her body pushed tight against the glass.

Fuck, Del had pushed his hard cock inside her. How could the sight of another man fucking his wife turn him on?

Liam stepped close to the shower, Abi's wide eyes locked on him.

Del began to move, his lips gliding along Abi's neck, his face buried in her hair. Her body pressed against the glass with each thrust, her breasts bouncing softly. She flattened her hands on the glass, biting her lip as she stared at Liam, both of them transfixed.

Liam pressed one hand against hers, the clear wall a rigid barrier between them. Del thrust in quick, short strokes now. He was still kissing her neck as he held her body tight against the glass, her breasts crushed flat, the nipples like dusky rose flowers. Liam flattened his hand over one of them, wishing he could feel the soft flesh molding to his palm.

Her gaze was locked with his as Del pounded into her. Liam watching her seemed to excite her even more.

God, he wanted to rip off his clothes and push into the shower stall. He wanted to push his cock inside her, too. To fuck her at the same time as Del.

He could see her pleasure build . . . feel her intense excitement. He was sure having him there was ramping up her arousal.

Then she sucked in a breath and threw back her head. She wailed her release, her face glowing with blissful abandon.

Fuck, his need to be inside her surged through him. He was surprised he didn't come just watching her.

There was something about seeing Del fuck her that excited him, more than he would have thought possible.

Del groaned, driving Abi's whole body tighter against the glass. As Del erupted into Liam's wife, his gaze lifted for the first time. Del's eyes widened. Then he shuddered against Abi and crumpled against her.

As Del lifted his head, Liam's hands clenched into fists and he strode into the villa then up the stairs, putting as much distance between him and them as he could.

CHAPTER TWENTY-THREE

A moment later, a tap sounded on the door, then Abi stepped into the bedroom. She'd pulled on a white terry robe.

"Liam, I'm so sorry."

He turned to her, barely holding back a snarl. Now out of the heat of the moment, conflicting emotions were seething through him.

"What should I expect? I knew he'd been fucking you."

Her gaze dropped to the ground, and she looked so morose he felt a twinge of guilt.

"Liam, I didn't mean to disrespect this time with you. I have feelings for Del . . . but I should have waited."

He sighed, knowing he shouldn't be taking out his anger on her. He was the one who'd been a fool and screwed up their marriage.

"After this morning's talk, what the hell should I expect? You obviously don't believe the two of us will ever work out."

"Liam, I'm sorry about this morning. I didn't mean to hurt you." She sank onto the edge of the bed. "I'm confused. I don't know what to think. I don't know what to feel." She pushed her wet hair behind her ear. "The worst is that no matter what I do, one of you will be hurt."

His heart ached.

"Fuck, baby. I know this is hard on you, too."

He pulled her to her feet and into his arms. She rested her head on his shoulder and he stroked her hair, trying not to remember that she had been aroused and naked with Del only moments ago.

But at the memory, his cock swelled, pressing hard against her stomach.

Then he felt her hand glide over his pants. Her fingers tightened around him, sending pleasure spiking through him and making him ache for more.

"Hell, baby. You were just in the shower with Del."

She tipped up her head, and the hunger in her eyes knocked him off balance.

"Yes, and despite the fact it upset you, it's clear it also turned you on seeing me with him."

"Abi, let's not go there." He started to draw away, but she grasped his cock tighter, stroking it now.

The wicked pleasure of her moving hand rendered him immobile.

"Why not?" Her wide eyes were filled with desire. "The thought of you watching us turns me on." She squeezed him tighter, making him throb. "A lot."

She released him and eased the robe down her shoulders, baring a lot of skin. His gaze dropped to the swell of her bosom, wondering if she was going to drop it all the way.

It fell to the ground and he sucked in a breath at the sight of her naked breasts, the nipples hard as pearls. Then his gaze dropped to her pussy. His cock throbbed.

"I think we should explore this a little more," she said.

"What exactly are you suggesting?"

"Well . . ." She bit her lip as she ran her fingers over her erect nipple. "You watched Del and me. Why don't we invite Del to watch us?" She squeezed the hard nipple between her fingertips, driving him wild. "Just think about it. Him sitting in the chair right there, while you prowl over me and push that big, hard cock of yours inside me."

Fuck. His cock ached at the thought.

She took his hand and kissed his palm, her delicate lips sending tingles dancing through him. Then she knelt down in front of him, pressing his hand to her cheek.

"Or maybe you want me as your slave so he can see how you command me. You can order me to suck your cock while you watch him getting turned on at the sight."

He stroked her hair, still cupping her soft cheek in his other hand.

The thought of being her Master while Del looked on . . . showing that in the bedroom, Abi totally belonged to him . . . appealed to the primal male in him.

"And if you decide you want to watch me with Del again . . . you would have total control. Instructing me exactly what to do. Where to touch. What to kiss." She pressed her cheek tighter against his hand. "When to come."

Her hand glided along his inseam, then her fingers slid over his balls and up his rigid shaft.

"Maybe you'll want me to suck both your cocks at the same time." When she squeezed him, he had to suppress a groan. "Switching from one to the other as you both stroke my breasts. Or just sit back and relax. You know I'll do whatever you command me to do."

The thought of commanding Abi to do things to Del and him was a powerful aphrodisiac. He could imagine ordering her to sink to her knees in front of Del and stroke her hand over his jeans, then unzip and pull out Del's hard cock. Then feel her hand wrap around his swollen cock, too.

"Fuck, woman. You're driving me crazy."

She unzipped his pants and her fingers wrapped around his hot shaft. She pulled him out and pressed her lips to his cockhead.

His hand stroked over her head as pleasure surged though him.

"Ah, fuck, kitten."

Her lips glided down, then drew back up again, tight around him. An urgent need gripped him. To be fully immersed in her soft body.

He pulled her to her feet and guided her backward until she was pressed against the wall.

"I'm going to fuck you so hard, you won't remember ever being with another man."

He found her mouth and drove his tongue deep. Her arms flung around his neck and she arched against him, her soft breasts crushing against his chest.

His fingers glided down her smooth stomach, then between her legs until he found her hot, wet folds. Then he grasped his cock and pushed it to her opening. Pulling his mouth from hers, he stared into her blue eyes as he drove forward. The slick warmth of her surrounding him took his breath away. Her mouth opened into an O and her eyelids fell half closed.

She was pinned against the wall by his body, the two of them sucking in deep breaths.

She leaned closer and her lips wrapped around his earlobe. Then she nipped.

"Fuck me, Liam."

Her breathy tone was his undoing. He drew back, loving the tight embrace of her pussy as his cock slid out of her body. Then he drove inside again, pushing her against the wall. He pulled back and thrust again.

"Oh, Liam."

The need in her voice turned his blood to liquid fire. He thrust deeper and faster. Driving into her again and again.

His cock ached with the need to fill her with his seed.

"I'm so close," she moaned.

He found her clit and stroked it as he continued to jackhammer into her. Her voice rose to a high trill, then he saw it. The bliss on her face as an orgasm washed over her.

She moaned continuously as he pumped into her, her face glowing with ethereal beauty.

"You are so fucking beautiful," he grated, his own pleasure rising to a crest.

He nipped her neck and her waning pleasure spiked again.

Then the tension that was coiled deep in his groin released and an intense, exhilarating pulse of pure delight surged through him. He groaned, erupting into her, shuddering as he shot to ecstatic heights.

Liam drew Abi close to him, listening to her soft breathing as they lay in bed together.

After their spectacular lovemaking where he'd taken her against the wall in a wild burst of carnal need, Abi had gone out for a walk.

That was her excuse to leave, but he knew she wanted to go down and talk to Del, who had been left wondering and worrying about Liam's reaction. He didn't know what she'd told him.

Probably nothing but reassuring comments that things were fine between them. She probably didn't want to tell her lover that her husband had just fucked her hard against the wall after they'd both gotten turned on thinking about him watching her get fucked by another man. Maybe even sharing her with him.

He kissed the top of her head, breathing in the delicate floral scent of her hair.

God, he loved this woman.

His cock swelled as he remembered watching Del fucking her in the shower. Her gaze on Liam the whole time.

The glass had been a barrier between him. He'd been on the

outside looking in. Just like he was in the relationship between the three of them now. Abi had agreed to spend this time with him, but after her comments this morning . . . about love not being enough . . . he knew in his heart he'd probably lost her for good.

So the question was, did he spend the next few weeks relishing his time with her, keeping Del at as much of a distance as he could, because he knew that his relationship with Abi would be over after this?

Or was there a way he could show Abi that the three of them together made some kind of sense?

Liam opened his eyes to sunlight streaming across the bed. He was flat on his back and Abi was nowhere to be seen.

He gazed at the large window to see nature's masterpiece beyond. Vibrant golden-washed clouds streaking low across a sky of pink, mauve, and blue. The sun a blazing yellow fireball gently kissing the horizon, its golden light reflected in a glittering band across the ocean from horizon to shore. The white sand of the beach bathed in the wondrous colors.

His heart ached. This was exactly the kind of thing he wanted with Abi. To wake up and hold her in his arms while they enjoyed a beautiful morning in paradise. Whether that paradise was a gorgeous sunrise at a tropical resort, waking up to sweet lovemaking in their own bed in the home they shared, or getting up to change diapers and calm their crying child before they started the day together.

Being with Abi was his paradise.

And he'd be damned if he'd give up on it yet.

He pushed back the covers and got out of bed, then showered and dressed in swim trunks and a casual shirt in soft white cotton. He went downstairs and headed out to the patio. Abi and Del were sitting on lounge chairs gazing at the spectacular sky. The sun was higher now and the brilliant-colored clouds were fading to a soft white.

The two of them looked so comfortable and relaxed. His jaw twitched. Like a happy couple.

Abi glanced around and saw him. When she smiled at him, it felt like the sun was rising all over again.

"Good morning," she said. "Breakfast is ready to be served if you're hungry."

"Sounds good." He headed for the patio table, already set with plates, stemmed glasses for juice, and coffee cups. He sat down as Abi and Del walked to the table to join him.

Abi was stunning in her bikini top and the long, flowing skirt wrapped around her waist. When she reached the table, she rested her hand on his shoulder, then leaned in and kissed his cheek. His heart thumped at the casual yet sweetly intimate gesture.

She picked up the coffee thermos from the table and poured him a cup, then turned to Del.

"Coffee?" she asked.

"That would be great," Del said.

Liam couldn't help noticing the way Del looked at her. A light glowed in his eyes that left no doubt about his feelings for her.

Fuck, why did this whole thing have to be so complicated?

Abi sat in the chair between Liam and Del as a staff member brought out a tray with cinnamon French toast and set a plate in front of each of them, then set a platter of fresh fruit on the table.

"Did your meeting go well yesterday?" Abi asked.

He engaged in small talk with her about the progress of the deal. Del asked some polite questions, too, but clearly he was uncomfortable after yesterday's incident.

Once breakfast was done and the staff had cleared away the dishes, Liam stood up and took Abi's hand.

"Come in the pool with me," he said. At her hesitation, he laughed. "Don't worry. I'm not suggesting a strenuous swim right after eating. We can relax in the shallow area."

The pool had a Baja shelf, where the bottom of the pool

formed a shallow shelf with water about ten inches deep, which curved in a smooth S-shape at the edge, forming a contoured reclining bench in the water to lounge on.

"Okay." She followed him with a quick glance at Del as Liam led her to the poolside.

She unfastened her skirt and unwrapped it, then tossed it on a lounge chair. The sight of her lovely body, covered in only the underwire top and skimpy bikini bottoms set his pulse pounding.

Del sat down on a lounge chair facing the side of the pool and Liam could see the desire in Del's eyes, too.

She followed Liam into the pool and he sat down on the curved bottom, the shallow water warm and welcoming. She sat beside him, but he drew her in front of him, between his thighs and wrapped his arm around her waist. Her sun-kissed skin was like warm silk against his hand.

He swept her hair to one side and drew her closer to his body. Taking in the sight of her round breasts, and the feel of her almost naked body as she leaned back against him, made his cock swell. She shifted her hips, causing more pressure against his rising shaft.

He tried to relax in the sunshine and water in this tropical paradise, but all he could think of was the image of her and Del fucking yesterday in the shower. And how hot it had made him. Followed by Abi telling him how much it had turned her on that he'd been watching.

Then her suggestion that they invite Del to watch them.

Fuck, he was so turned on he wanted to cup her breasts right now. Then pull the fabric aside, baring them to Del, and stroke them until her nipples thrust forward. Especially knowing how much it would excite Abi.

As if sensing his mood, Abi shifted again, making his cock ache with need. God, he wanted to tug the crotch of her bathing suit aside and pull her onto his lap, then slide his throbbing cock right into her.

"Del, would you get me a cold bottle of water?" Abi asked.

Del tipped his sunglasses forward. "Of course. What about you, Liam?"

"Sure. Thanks."

Del stood up and disappeared into the house. As soon as the patio door closed, Abi grabbed Liam's hand from her stomach and . . . pushed it downward. She guided his fingers under the fabric and . . .

"Oh, fuck, Abi. You're so wet." The feel of her slick folds sent his heart racing.

She turned in his arms and surged against him, capturing his lips in a passionate kiss. Her hand glided down his stomach and she found his cock . . . and squeezed. He groaned at the exciting pressure of her hand and pulled her deeper into the kiss.

"Uh . . . Should I leave you two alone?"

CHAPTER TWENTY-FOUR

At Del's voice, Abi jerked around then settled between Liam's legs again. But her hand slid behind her back and her fingers gripped Liam's twitching cock and squeezed.

"No, please stay," Abi said.

Abi turned her head to Liam, chewing on her lower lip, clearly wondering if he wanted to go ahead with what they'd talked about last night. Having Del watch them.

Then she turned back to Del.

"I told you last night that Liam wasn't angry about seeing us in the shower. He wasn't happy about it, but when I told him that . . ." She sucked in a breath. "Um . . . that him watching us had really"—her cheeks flushed a deep rose—"turned me on . . ."

Her sentence faded off. She'd clearly started talking before she really knew where she was going with this.

"So are you saying you want me to watch the two of you?" Del's eyes glinted as he frowned. "Is that payback?"

But Liam saw the ridge forming in Del's trunks. The thought was turning him on, too.

"No," Liam said firmly.

"No?" Abi turned to gaze at him again, her eyes wide.

"I mean, it's not payback. I don't want to punish you for what happened. Either of you."

Then he cupped Abi's breast in his hand. Her nipple immediately peaked into his palm.

"But, Del. It's clear that Abi is very turned on by the idea of one of us watching her with the other."

He pulled back the fabric of her bikini top to bare one breast. The nipple thrust forward.

Del's gaze dropped to her naked breast.

"I don't know about you," Liam said, "but I'd like to give her what she wants so badly."

He plucked at Abi's hard nipple lightly. His groin tightened at the feel of it against his fingertips.

Del's green eyes darkened and he heard Abi's breathing accelerate. Liam felt his own excitement rise at this illicit sharing between the three of them. He unfastened her top, then peeled it from her body.

"I'm happy to be the one watching," Liam continued. "But as her husband, while we're on this island, I will be in charge."

"You mean like setting rules?" Del asked.

"Abi and I enjoy an interesting relationship in the bedroom. Sometimes she likes to submit to my authority."

Del's gaze jerked to Liam.

"You have a fucking *Fifty Shades of Grey* thing going on?"

"She likes it when I take control of the situation," Liam said. "And I do discipline her when it's warranted. But believe me. She enjoys it."

Del's eyebrows rose. "Abi?"

She bit her lip and nodded.

"Del," Liam said, "why don't you come into the pool and sit with us? Then I can show you what I mean."

Abi was tense in front of him. She was afraid Del was shocked and might reject her now. Fuck, even though that would be to Liam's advantage, he didn't want Abi hurt like that.

From everything he knew of Del, and they'd been friends for a long time, he believed Del was open-minded enough to accept this about Abi.

Fuck, it would be a pity if he didn't learn to satisfy that side of her. He would be missing a lot. And so would Abi.

Del pursed his lips. Then he nodded. "All right."

He stepped into the pool and walked toward them, then sat down beside them on the contoured bench.

"Abi," Liam said. "Take off the rest of your bathing suit."

Obediently, she stood up and faced him and Del, then slipped her fingers under her bottoms and eased them down slowly. Del's eyes darkened even more as she revealed her neatly trimmed pussy. She continued pushing them down her slender thighs, then let them drop to the water. She stepped out of them and let them drift away.

"Now kneel down in front of Del."

Del watched Abi follow Liam's command. As she knelt in front of him, totally naked, his cock swelled even more. It was already rock hard from watching Liam strip off her top and stroke her nipple, then at the sight of her exposed pussy.

And the fact she was following Liam's commands was exciting him. He wasn't sure why.

"Show me how you kiss him, Abi," Liam commanded.

Abi's eyes were wide as she gazed into Del's. He could tell she was excited . . . and a little nervous. She rested her soft hands on his shoulders then leaned in close. Her lips brushed his in a delicate kiss. Her tongue glided along the seam of his mouth as she leaned in a little closer.

He groaned and slid his arms around her, then pulled her into a deeper kiss. Her soft breasts against his chest drove up his need.

He opened to her tongue and greeted it with his own as hers slid inside. Then he suckled.

"Nice." Liam's eyes were ablaze as he watched them. After a moment, he said, "That's enough for now."

She drew back, her gaze still locked on Del's, need raging through her eyes.

"Now, baby," Liam said, "I want you to free his cock and stroke it for me."

Abi turned her focus to Del's bathing suit and she pulled open the front and reached inside. Her fingers curled around his hard cock and she drew it out.

It was weird sitting here with Abi holding his cock in her hand, Liam watching beside them, but as she started to stroke him, the awkwardness melted away, replaced by a growing need to be inside her.

"Do you like the feel of his rigid cock in your hand, kitten?"

"Yes, Sir," Abi said.

A shiver of excitement raced down Del's spine when she called Liam "Sir." He loved it, and hated it, at the same time.

"Describe it for me," Liam said.

Abi licked her lips. "It's really hard. And thick. It's pulsing in my hand."

Fuck, he swelled even more hearing her describe his cock out loud.

"Do you want to feel it in your mouth?" Liam asked.

"Oh, yes, Sir." Her luminous blue eyes were locked on Del's face, filled with hunger.

"Then do it. Take him in your mouth. Show me how you suck his cock."

Del's breath caught as she bobbed down and swallowed his cockhead whole. Seeing her lips encircling his shaft . . . feeling them squeezing around him . . . made him ache for more.

Then her tongue swirled around the tip. He moaned softly.

She dipped down more, her lips tight around his shaft as she moved. His blood rushed through him as she went down farther and farther. And she kept going until she was at his root, his whole cock inside her.

"Goddamn, sweetheart," Del rasped. "That feels so good."

She slowly glided up again. Her hand wrapped around him, then she stroked his shaft as she sucked his tip.

The water around them rippled as Liam shifted to see them better. Del could see Liam's cock straining at his bathing suit.

"Abi," Del said. "I want to see you stroke Liam's cock while you're sucking me."

Abi slid off his cock, her hand continuing to stroke him, and she turned her gaze to Liam. Liam nodded and pulled open his bathing suit and slipped it off, freeing his cock.

Fuck, the man was massive.

Abi wrapped one delicate hand around the thick shaft and Del couldn't help watching, fascinated, as she stroked, her fingers barely fitting around his girth.

She leaned down and Del groaned as she immersed his cock in her mouth again, gliding her lovely lips along the length of him. His gaze was locked on her fingers moving up and down Liam's rigid cock at the same time.

Fuck, he never would have believed he'd enjoy having the woman he loved jacking off another man while sucking him.

Oh, God, Abi was so turned on. Her intimate muscles clenched in need.

She squeezed Del's cock in her mouth as she moved, feeling it pulse. She could feel Liam's hot gaze on her as he watched her lips moving on Del. Del's gaze was locked on her hand as she stroked Liam's cock, which was thick and hard in her grip.

She loved giving both of them such intimate attention at the same time. Loved that they were both watching her hungrily.

"Abi, you like Del's cock in your mouth while you pump my cock?"

She nodded, turning her gaze to him while she continued to bob up and down on Del.

"Glide off his cock and suck on his balls," Liam commanded.

She let Del's cock slip from her lips and Del pushed his bathing suit off. She dragged her tongue down the column, then lapped at his shaven balls, her hand still around his erection.

She dragged her tongue over the soft sacs, now stroking both men. Gently, she wrapped her lips around one ball and drew it into her mouth. She cradled it, then gently suckled.

"Ah, fuck, sweetheart." Del's voice was hoarse with need.

She sucked a little more, then let it slip from her lips and she licked the other one. She took it into her mouth and gave it the same tender attention.

Liam stroked her hair back from her face, smiling at her.

"I love watching you do that, baby."

She lapped and sucked on Del, beaming in the glow of her Master's attention.

She licked both his balls thoroughly, then drew one deep and sucked. Del moaned.

He forked his fingers through her hair, then twined them in her tresses and drew her head back. His ball dropped from her mouth.

"Liam, I want to see her suck your cock now."

"All right. Come here, kitten."

She released Liam's cock and nuzzled Del's soft flesh one more time before she turned to Liam and knelt in front of him. But he wrapped his hands around her upper arms as he moved his feet to the seat of the curved bench and pushed himself up to sit on the edge of the pool, drawing Abi forward until her torso was bent over the curve of the bench, her ass in the air. She rested her elbows on the sloped back of the bench, then grasped Liam's cock in her hand.

CHAPTER TWENTY-FIVE

Abi stroked him, the solid thickness of Liam stretching her fingers as she tried to wrap them all the way around his shaft. She kissed his broad cockhead, the flesh hot against her lips, then swirled her tongue over him, tasting the salty drops oozing from the small opening.

"Take it in your mouth, baby." The need in Liam's voice thrilled her.

She opened wide, taking the large plum-shaped crown into her mouth. She squeezed as she glided downward.

"Ah, fuck, baby."

Del sat watching as Liam's cock filled her mouth.

"Del, kneel behind Abi and lick her pussy."

Heat pulsed through her as Del shifted to his knees behind her. He ran his hands up the backs of her thighs, then cupped her ass. Seconds later, she felt his warm tongue flick over her slick folds.

She moaned around the meaty cock in her mouth. Liam coiled his hand in her hair and drew her upward . . . until her mouth almost slipped off the end of his cock . . . then he pressed her back down again.

Del's tongue brushed over her, sending exhilarating sensations rippling through her body.

"You like that, don't you, kitten? Del licking your sweet pussy."

She nodded, squeezing his cock tighter in her mouth. Del slid his tongue inside her and swirled. She moaned again, her body melting inside.

Del pressed her thighs apart and his tongue found her clit. She arched against him at the delightful sensation as he teased her sensitive nub. Then his fingers slid inside her. She squeezed Liam's cock with her hand as she drew it from her mouth to suck in a deep breath, opening her legs to give Del better access. Del pumped his fingers into her and she moaned.

Liam chuckled. "That's right, Del. She loves you finger fucking her like that."

She sucked in another breath, then dove down on Liam's cock again. She cupped his balls as she took him deep, nearly gagging in her haste to take him all the way down her throat.

She moved on him in the same steady rhythm as Del filling her with his fingers. Del's tongue teased her clit, then he began suckling it.

Ohhh, it felt so good.

At the same time, she moved up and down on Liam's thick cock, watching his brown eyes turn to burning embers.

Pleasure built up in her at the wild sensations shimmering through her body. She felt it coil tight inside her as it rose . . . higher . . . and higher.

Liam pulled her from his cock.

"Del, drive your cock into her," he said in a gruff voice.

Del sucked deeper on her clit, then his mouth moved away. She felt his hard cock brush against her opening and—

"Ohhh, God," she moaned as his thick shaft drove deep into her, filling her in one hard thrust.

"That's right." Liam said. "That is so fucking hot."

Liam pulled her mouth down onto his cock again. She stroked his thick shaft as she moved her lips up and down on him.

"Goddamn, you are so wet and hot," Del groaned.

He pumped into her, picking up speed. She followed his pace on Liam's cock. Liam stroked her head, his eyes glazing.

"I'm going to fucking come any second, baby," Liam said.

"Are you going to come in her mouth?" Del asked.

"Fucking right," Liam groaned.

Both cocks pumped into her and she squeezed Del inside her passage as she ran her hand under Liam's balls and cradled them, her other hand moving with her mouth.

"Ah, fuck, baby. Ah, fuck. Ahhh, fuuuck!" Liam cried.

He jerked forward and hot, salty semen spurted into her mouth.

She sucked and squeezed, then swallowed it all as Del continued gliding into her, his thick shaft stroking her passage.

Liam pulled free and slid down in front of her. She rested her head on his chest as Del thrust and groaned. She felt Liam's hand slide along her stomach and then his fingers found her clit. He flicked over it and she moaned. Pleasure pulsed through her as the feel of his teasing fingers, combined with Del's pumping cock, swelled through her. Filling her with trembling delight.

"Fuck her harder, Del. You're going to make her come." Liam's eyes blazed with heat as he watched her face.

"Yes! Fucking . . . come . . . for me . . . sweetheart," Del grated, his words punctuating each thrust as his cock drove deeper and harder into her.

"Ohhh, Del. Yes." A wave of blissful sensations rippled through her and she quivered.

"Do it, baby," Liam urged. "Come for us."

One more deep thrust of Del's cock and pleasure exploded inside her, catapulting her over the edge. She moaned, lost in the abyss as ecstasy ravaged her senses, stunning in its intensity.

Del groaned, and she felt him erupt inside her, his arm tight around her waist, as he shuddered against her. The feel of him filling her with his hot seed shattered her senses as she plunged to yet another orgasm. She sucked in air, then moaned again and again.

Finally, they both collapsed on Liam, panting for air.

"That was fucking incredible," Del breathed against her ear.

After a few moments, Del drew back, his cock slipping from her. He slumped down on the bench beside Liam.

Liam hugged her, then kissed her tenderly. He helped her roll sideways to slip between him and Del on the bench. She tucked one leg over Del's knee and one over Liam's as she rested back. Then she realized Liam was staring at her hungrily . . . or rather, her open legs, exposing her intimate flesh.

Was he going to fuck her now, too?

He slid to his knees in front of her and leaned forward. When she felt his tongue on her, she twined her fingers in his glossy, dark brown hair. His tongue moved over her lazily . . . exploring her folds with slow, attentive strokes. Thorough and . . . arousing.

Her insides quivered. His tongue thrust into her slit, swirling deep inside her. Heat pulsed through her, quickly rising again. He licked her with intense concentration, watching her face.

His finger found her clit and he teased it mercilessly as her breathing became more labored.

"Oh, God, Liam." Pleasure surged through her. "Yes, oh . . . I'm going to . . . come."

A third orgasm rocked through her. She wailed, riding the wave until she shattered in pure joy.

Once she finally slumped back on the bench again, Liam smiled.

He leaned in and kissed her, gliding his tongue into her. After he thoroughly devoured her mouth, he pressed his lips to her ear.

"I could taste Del inside you. I've never been so fucking turned on in my life."

She glanced down and saw his cock fully erect again and ready to go.

"Are you going to fuck me now, while Del watches?" she asked eagerly.

Liam laughed. He kissed her again then drew her to her feet.

"I think that's a great idea. And I think doing it in the shower would be perfect, so Del can see your perfect breasts pressed tight against the glass like I did yesterday."

He led her from the pool, Del following, his dangling cock already rising again.

God, what was Del thinking? What was Liam thinking?

This was all so sexy and she was so excited they were doing it . . . but what about later? After the heat of the moment, would Del be disappointed in her, thinking her submission to Liam made her weak? Would Liam be upset and jealous? Would it make it harder to get him to sign the papers?

Her heart clenched. The thought of him actually signing the papers made her ache with sadness. She didn't want to lose him. But she didn't want to lose Del, either.

She stumbled, nausea washing over her. Liam slid his arm around her waist, steadying her.

"You okay, Abi?" Del asked.

She ran her hand though her hair, nodding.

"Yeah, just a little dizzy for a second."

"You want to go lie down?" Liam asked.

She smiled. "No. You said something about a shower."

Liam glanced at Del, then back to her. Del walked ahead and turned on the water in the large glass shower stall. Liam led her under the spray.

The warm, soothing water washed over her body and she smiled. Liam's soapy hands started moving over her. Then Del's did, too.

Del stood behind her, soaping her breasts, and Liam washed down her stomach then crouched in front of her and washed between her legs. His fingers stroked her outer folds, then worked inside until he was stroking over her slit thoroughly. Del's hands stroked under her breasts, then over the tips until her nipples were hard beads aching for more.

When she could barely stand it anymore, her entire body having been tenderly stroked and aroused by their big hands . . . Liam positioned her under the spray of water, letting it wash the suds from her skin.

Then Liam turned off the water and led her from the stall.

"Aren't you going to—?"

"No," Liam said.

"But I thought . . ."

"Kitten, you're a bit wobbly. You're pregnant. It's important we don't tax you."

She rested her hand on his flat stomach and glided down to his still erect cock, hoping to convince him otherwise, but he grasped her wrist and pressed her hand to his lips.

"I said no sex now, and that's an order."

"An order that would be so much easier to follow if we weren't all naked, and your two cocks weren't both standing at attention all ready and willing."

Both Del and Liam laughed.

Del grabbed a towel from a stack near the shower and tossed it to Liam, who wrapped it around his hips. Del did the same.

"What about me?" she asked.

"We *like* seeing you naked," Del said, his eyes glittering with amusement.

Liam took her hand again and drew her toward the patio doors.

"Okay," Liam said, "I'm going to take you upstairs so you can lie down for an hour. Then if you're feeling up to it, we can take a boat tour around the island. After that, we'll all go out for a nice dinner."

He led her up the stairs, then tucked her into bed. But before he drew away she took his hand.

"Liam, why don't you stay and talk for a few minutes?"

He sat on the side of the bed. "About what, baby?"

"Well, about what just happened."

He smiled reassuringly. "It was great."

"Yes, it was sexy and amazing. But how do you feel now?" she asked.

His chocolate-brown eyes grew guarded.

"Did it bother you watching me with Del?" she continued. "Seeing him touch me? Seeing him . . . make me happy?"

"I like to see you happy, kitten."

"I know but . . . I think we should talk about any issues this is bringing up. Bring them out into the open."

He sighed and squeezed her hand.

"Look, Abi. I don't want to analyze this or talk about deeper feelings. We all enjoyed it. That's all that matters. Let's just keep it at that."

She wanted to push him more. She didn't want resentment and jealousy to seethe below the surface. But she knew that look. She wasn't going to get anywhere.

"And keep on enjoying it?" she asked.

His eyes darkened. "I look forward to it. We have a rare opportunity here, with the three of us together . . . feeling so open and comfortable with each other." He shrugged. "Why wouldn't we keep enjoying it?"

After Abi's nap, they enjoyed a tour of the island in a huge yacht. The scenery was spectacular and they disembarked at a local market to do some shopping. Abi bought some souvenirs for her sisters and brother, and a few things for her nephews. Liam bought her a lovely coral necklace. A little later, the yacht anchored for a while so they could swim in the crystal-blue water.

They returned to the villa long enough to change for dinner, then the driver took them to an elegant restaurant where they sat at a table on the terrace with a stunning ocean view. They watched the sun sink below the horizon over appetizers and by dessert a full moon hung over the ocean, the water glittering in its brilliant white light.

Soft music played and she found herself swept first into Liam's arms for a dance, then Del's. The two men shared, one dancing with her for a few songs then turning her over to the other. Reminding her how they had shared her this morning.

When they returned to the villa, she was ready for oh, so much more. She sat down on the couch and held out her hand to invite them to sit beside her. Del sat down.

"I'll get us something to drink," Liam said and walked toward the kitchen.

She rested her hand on Del's thigh, unable to resist touching him. She stroked upward, until she reached the crotch of his suit pants, then she glided over the growing bulge there.

"Starting without me?" Liam asked as he set a tray down on the table.

CHAPTER TWENTY-SIX

Abi's stomach clenched, but then Liam smiled and handed her a lemonade, the ice tinkling against the frosty glass. She took a sip as Liam sat down beside her, too. She set down the glass.

"It's okay," Liam said. "Carry on."

She turned back to Del and rested her hand on his swollen cock again. The feel of it ramped up the need already simmering inside her. She leaned forward and swiveled around to climb onto his lap, pulling the flowing fabric of her dress out of the way as she settled on his thighs. She stroked his face as she glided close to his body, feeling his hard cock tight against her panties, only the thin fabric a barrier between his rigid shaft and her needy flesh.

Liam moved closer and rested his hand on her back, then as she nuzzled Del's neck, Liam drew back her hair.

Intense need flooded through her and she pivoted her hips forward, stroking herself with Del's rock-hard column. Sparks ignited inside her aching core.

Liam settled on the floor behind her and his hands cupped

her ass. The delightful pressure ramped up her desire. He guided her to rock her hips forward and back.

She moaned softly as she moved on Del's thick cock.

Her breasts seemed to swell and her nipples tingled.

"Oh, God," she sighed softly.

It must have been the pregnancy hormones because need surged through her like a tsunami. Liam kept rocking her and Del leaned in and captured her lips. His hand cupped her breast and her breath caught.

It was so intense.

"This is so . . . ohhh . . ." she moaned softly. "So sexy. I'm . . ."

His fingers brushed her nipple. That and the continuous building delight of gliding over his cock, sent her head spinning. Pleasure surged through her.

"Oh, God, I'm going to . . . come."

Liam's lips brushed against her ear. "Fuck, baby. Really?"

She arched her hips forward, her body resting back against Liam's chest. He moved forward, supporting her, rocking with her now, his hands still firmly on her ass.

Del cupped both her breasts, caressing them gently, his thumbs teasing over the nubs.

Then it happened. Euphoria exploded inside her in a tumultuous blast of sheer joy, plummeting her over the edge. She wailed as she rocketed to ecstasy.

After a long, glorious ride on the waves of bliss, she finally slumped against Liam.

She was sleepy and the world felt a bit blurry.

She was sure that stress due to the difficult decisions to come, combined with the intense excitement of this illicit sexual situation and the physical demands of the pregnancy were throwing her off. At the thought of the pregnancy, a worry niggled at her, but she thrust it aside, refusing to go there.

She was vaguely aware of Liam sweeping her up in his

arms . . . then floating through the air . . . until he laid her on the bed. Del had already pulled the covers back.

Del's and Liam's hands moved over her as they undressed her, but then she felt one of them sliding a nightgown over her head and guiding her hands through the sleeves.

"What's happening?" she asked. "I thought the three of us were going to be together again."

Del sat on the bed beside her. "We will. But we think you need to rest right now."

"And if it makes you feel better," Liam said, "we can all sleep together tonight. Would you like that?"

She smiled at the thought of snuggling between the two of them.

"Yes. Very much."

Abi's eyes blinked open and she found herself staring at Liam's naked, muscular back. Her arm was around his waist. Then she realized that there was another body behind her. Del was in bed with them, too.

She rolled onto her back and sucked in a breath when she realized Del was propped up on one elbow watching her. In the moonlight, his eyes glowed softly.

"Oh, hi," she whispered, not wanting to wake Liam. "Have you been awake long?"

"Not too long." He stroked her hair back from her face and tingles danced along her neck. "I've just been watching you sleep. Your face is so angelic."

She ran her hand along his cheek, enjoying the feel of his coarse whiskers. He leaned down and kissed her, his lips moving on hers with tenderness. She slid her arms around his neck and deepened the kiss, gliding her tongue between his lips.

God, she wanted to run her hands down his chest . . . suck on his small male nipples . . . wrap her hand around his cock and stroke it to full arousal. But they were lying here literally behind her husband's back.

Del drew back and his gaze fell to hers.

"What's wrong?"

"It's just strange. The three of us in bed together." She drew in a breath. "I want to be with you . . . feel you inside me . . . but . . . Liam is right there."

Del leaned in and nuzzled her neck.

"I think the very fact that the three of us *are* in bed together proves it's not a problem."

The tingles dancing along her skin from the attention of his lips made it hard to think straight, so she gently pressed him back.

"I tried to talk to Liam about this earlier. To find out what he thought of what the three of us did by the pool, but he just said he enjoyed it."

Del smiled. "What did you expect? It was very . . . enjoyable."

"Yes, of course," she said distractedly. "But I meant more than that. I wanted to know his feelings about it."

"Well, there you go," he said with a grin. "You don't really expect a man to talk about feelings, do you?"

She ran her hand down his hard chest.

"Del, this is serious. I think it's important to talk about it. To deal with any issues any of us might be having before someone gets hurt."

"Sweetheart, I understand why you're concerned, but this is just something we're doing while we're on this island. After that . . . well, I assume whatever happens, things will be strained between Liam and me, given that you're going to choose one of us over the other, so I don't see the friendship between Liam and me continuing. Not that we've really been very close ever since you two separated anyway."

She frowned, her heart aching at the thought of hurting one of them. In fact, she would be hurting both of them no matter which one she chose, because it meant the loss of their friendship.

"I hate that I've come between the two of you."

"It's not your fault we both fell in love with you."

He stroked her hair back from her face. The glow of love in his eyes sent heat rippling through her, turning to need.

She pulled him in for another kiss, her hand gliding down his chest. When she found his growing cock in his pajama bottoms, she fumbled with the buttons of the opening, then slid her hand inside. He groaned softly against her temple as she wrapped her fingers around him.

Abi stiffened when she felt Liam roll onto his back, and she glanced at his face. Del peered in Liam's direction, too. He was still asleep.

"It's okay. Liam's already shown he's okay with us sharing you," Del whispered.

Liam awoke to the sound of soft murmurs beside him. His eyes opened, greeted by the sight of the soft white ceiling above him, washed in the light of the full moon.

Then he turned his head.

Abi was lying flat on the bed and Del was suckling her breast while he caressed the other with his hand. Abi's head was arched back on the pillow and her soft, breathy moans rippled through him.

Del was giving her so much pleasure and . . . Liam was just lying there. Outside.

Del kissed down her stomach and Abi widened her thighs as his mouth moved over her glistening folds. Mesmerized, Liam watched Del's tongue lap at her tender flesh, then his mouth pressed tight against her, to Abi's whimpers of delight. She arched against him as he moved on her as if devouring her. She moaned, but it was clear she was holding back her exuberance, probably not wanting to wake him.

Did she feel guilty?

He wasn't quite sure how he felt. Seeing Del giving Abi so

much pleasure made him jealous. But it was also making his cock as hard as rock.

She arched again and threw her head back. His groin tightened as he realized she was coming.

Ah, fuck. It was such a beautiful sight.

And he wanted to be inside her so fucking badly.

But right now, Del was prowling over her. He pressed his cock to her slick opening and, in total fascination, Liam watched Del's rigid, pulsing cock slide into her.

Liam had to stop himself from stroking his own growing cock, not wanting to alert them that he was awake.

The length of Del's shaft disappeared inside Abi's body, then when he was all the way in, he leaned down and kissed her. The glow in her eyes as she gazed up at him tore at Liam's heart. It was so clear how much she loved Del.

Del drew back, his cock slowly becoming visible, then he glided forward again in a smooth stroke.

Abi moaned softly, then her eyes widened and she glanced in Liam's direction.

Her small gasp was followed by her pressing her hand to Del's chest to stop his movement.

"Liam, I—"

"No, don't apologize, baby," he said. "Keep going." He smiled. "You said you like it when I watch."

She bit her lip, then turned her gaze back to Del.

Del leaned in and kissed her. "All right, sweetheart?"

With another tentative glance at Liam, she nodded. Del glided in and out again. Then again.

But it was clear Abi was too tense.

"It's really okay, kitten." Liam drew out his throbbing cock and took her hand, then pressed it to his hard flesh.

"You see what watching you is doing to me?"

Her fingers curled around him. He groaned softly.

Del started fucking her again, in slow, smooth strokes. She

moaned softly. Her hand moved on Liam's cock to the same pace as Del's movements.

"Wait, Del," Abi said, her hand on his chest again, this time pressing him back. Her fingers were still tight around Liam's cock.

Del's cock slipped from her body as he rolled to his side, his expression uncertain.

"I want to be with both of you." She nibbled her lip, watching them with wide, confused eyes.

"You can, baby," Liam assured. He fully intended to fuck her right after Del was done. "Once you two are finished—"

"No, I mean *at the same time.*"

Liam smiled. "I'm okay with that."

"Me, too," Del echoed.

Now Liam understood why she'd stopped Del.

He and Abi had tried anal in the past, but with his girth it had been a problem. The first time they tried it, it was clear she wouldn't enjoy it. They had continued by experimenting with sex toys, because she really had wanted to share the experience with him. They'd progressed from small vibrators to full-sized penis shapes, but still not anything as large as Liam. Then with the pregnancy, followed by the separation, they'd never gotten any further.

Abi rolled toward him and he welcomed her into his arms. The sweetness of her lips on his as she kissed him made his blood simmer. She arched her leg over him and pushed herself up on her knees, her hands stroking his chest.

She wrapped her hand around his cock again and pressed it to her slickness. The feel of it was like heaven.

Then she slowly lowered herself onto him, sheathing him in her velvety warmth.

"Ah, fuck, baby, that feels so good," he rumbled.

Once she was all the way down, sitting on him, blinking, her eyes glazing with pleasure, she squeezed him. He groaned. She leaned forward, her naked breasts resting against his chest, her hard nipples pressing into him.

She trembled in his arms. The thought that she'd already come once by Del's mouth, and was probably still close from when Del was fucking her, had his groin tightening. He twitched inside her and she groaned.

He slid his hands down her sides, then cupped her ass and pulled it up higher. Del sat beside them, still looking uncertain.

"Del, you're a lucky man," Liam said. "You'll be the first to take Abi anally. So . . . you're the one taking her virginity."

"Fuck. Yeah?"

Liam gestured toward the nightstand.

With his gaze locked on Abi's delightfully displayed ass, Del opened the nightstand drawer and pulled out a bottle of lube. Within seconds, his cock was glistening with it, as well as Abi's slickness.

Abi waited with anticipation as Del moved behind her. The feel of Liam's big cock inside her, pulsing with need, kept her aroused and needy.

Del stroked her back, then over her ass.

"I'm going to go slow, sweetheart," Del said. "I'll stop at any time. Just say so."

She nodded, just wanting to feel him inside her, too.

His hard, slick cock pressed against her ass, then she felt the pressure as he pushed forward. Slowly, her opening stretched around him. She sucked in a breath, then released it. Her gaze fell to Liam's and he nodded.

"Relax, kitten. Is he pressing into you?"

She nodded. Del stopped, giving her a moment.

"You want me to keep going, Abi?" Del asked.

She nodded. He slowly pressed forward again.

His cockhead stretched her. Wider and wider. But it was

nothing like the times Liam had tried. Liam was so big. But she had taken dildos as big as Del several times.

Del paused again.

"Keep going. All the way," she urged, her gaze still locked with Liam's. "I'm okay."

Del started moving again, his cockhead almost all the way in now. Liam's brown eyes crackled with hunger as he watched her face.

Then Del's cockhead was inside her. Del wrapped his hands around her hips as he continued forward, filling her with his shaft.

"Is he all the way in?" Liam asked.

"Almost," she breathed.

Del continued forward, and she moaned softly. Then she felt his body bump against her ass.

"Ohhh, he is now." She drew in a deep breath. "God, I can't believe you're both inside me."

"How does it feel?" Liam's eyes were filled with heat.

"It's incredible. I feel so . . . full."

"How do you feel, Del?" Liam asked.

"Fucking amazing."

Abi stroked Liam's cheek. "What about you?"

He captured her lips, sliding his tongue inside in a quick, possessive sweep, then released her mouth.

"Are you kidding? This is the hottest fucking thing ever."

Abi laughed. "You two keep talking about fucking this and fucking that. But I don't see . . . or feel . . . any fucking going on."

Both men broke out laughing. Then with a wicked gleam in his eyes, Liam surged forward, driving his cock deep into her. That pushed her against Del, forcing his cock a little deeper into her, making her groan.

Both men started moving and the feel of two cocks sliding in and out of her, stroking both her passages, took her breath away. Sparks flared along her inner flesh, triggering quivers throughout her body. Pleasure coiled deep inside her, tightening more and more as their smooth, even strokes continued.

She gripped Liam's shoulders, her eyes widening at the maelstrom of delight shimmering through her. Her pleasure built higher and higher and then every nerve ending seemed to burst into flame. She sucked in a breath as the first throes of passion engulfed her.

"You're both making me come," she cried, then began to moan.

They pumped deeper and faster into her, their hot bodies pulsing against her.

The tight coil inside her released and she spun into a realm of pure joy. She could feel their bodies moving against her, their big cocks filling her deeply. Hear their labored breathing as their hot breaths washed over her.

She trembled between them, catapulting to ecstasy.

Both men groaned, and she felt liquid heat fill her body as they erupted inside her, driving her further into bliss. She wailed, clinging to Liam, her head resting against Del's shoulder.

Her world shattered as a final rush of euphoria burst through her, expanding to dizzying heights.

Then she blacked out.

CHAPTER TWENTY-SEVEN

"Really, Liam, I'm fine," Abi said.

Liam drained the last of his coffee and shook his head, concern pulsing through him.

"Abi, you fainted."

"Yes, well, that can happen to a woman sometimes when things are really"—her lips turned up in broad grin—"*really* good."

Del chuckled. "Come on, man. You've never had that happen before?"

Liam stared at Del and his carefree smile.

"Yeah, like you have."

"Yup, I have." Del laughed again at Liam's frown. "Don't worry. You don't have to get all competitive because I'm talking about last night and that's a score for both of us."

Liam sat back in his chair and nodded, his own lips turning up in a smile.

"It was pretty great." Then he chuckled. "I can't believe we made you faint."

He glanced at his watch. It was almost time to leave.

"So are you sure you can't join me?" Liam asked Abi. "I'd love your opinion on the other resort. Both of you."

Liam was flying to a nearby island to check out another of the resorts in the chain he was buying. He'd hoped to take Abi on a tour of the island while they were there. And he really did want her input on the resort. From the research he'd done, the place would impress on all levels and maybe a part of him wanted to remind Abi of what she, and their child, would have if she stayed with him.

He'd invited Del, too, of course, because Abi wouldn't want to leave him behind. But also because what the three of them were sharing right now was exciting and he wanted to give them as many opportunities to be together as he could.

"I don't think it would be a good idea," Abi said. "My nausea is worse today and I'm feeling a little wobbly. And, no, it has nothing to do with me fainting," she added quickly when she saw his expression tighten in concern.

"Maybe I should cancel," Liam said.

"No, Liam. It's just morning sickness," Abi insisted. "It's worse some days than others, but it's nothing to be concerned about. And, Del, I think you should go with Liam. You don't have to stay here to babysit me."

"Nope. Not going to happen," Del said. "Liam needs to go for business, but I'm sure he'll be happier knowing I'm here in case you need something."

Liam nodded. In fact, he was. He wouldn't leave Abi here all alone. Period.

Liam stood up. "Okay, I need to get going. I'll be back tomorrow."

Abi stood up, too, and wrapped her arms around him. He kissed her, the feel of her soft lips and the delicate floral scent of her making him want what he couldn't have right now. Though convincing his rising cock might be a challenge.

"Have a good trip," she murmured against his ear.

"I'll do my best, but without you . . ."

He stroked her hair back from her face, soaking in the sight of her luminous blue eyes and her lovely heart-shaped face.

Fuck, he missed her already.

"I'll Skype you tonight," he said.

She grinned. "Skype so you can see me?" She giggled. "I can think of ways we can make this threesome thing work even if you're not actually here."

His cock shot straight up. Fuck, so could he. And it involved him taking charge.

The whole time during his trip and the tour of the resort, all Liam could think about was the Skype call that evening. He could be in total control as he commanded Abi to do things for Del . . . touching herself to arouse him . . . touching him . . . and all the time they'd both know he was watching them . . . jacking off to what they were doing . . .

Fuck, he had to get himself under control.

The resort manager and head chef led him through the kitchen, telling him about their award-winning menu with great pride. They entered the main dining room where there was a huge brunch set up for the guests at the resort and it was a luxurious feast including lobster and prime rib, as well as local delicacies and a huge array of delectable desserts.

As the chef described the fare, a staff member hurried to the manager and spoke with him briefly.

"Mr. Perry, I'm sorry to interrupt," the manager said, "but a Mr. Del MacLean called. He's been trying to reach you. He said it's urgent."

Liam pulled his cell from his pocket and turned off airplane mode. Immediately, he saw that he had five voice messages waiting and Del had sent him repeated text messages asking that he call.

His chest tightened. Had something happened to Abi?

"Excuse me, gentlemen," Liam said, and strode to the door as he dialed Del's cell. It rang as he stepped outside into the warm air and sunshine.

"Liam, thank God you got back to me. Abi's in the hospital."

Liam's chest tightened. "What the hell happened?"

"We were out for a walk on the beach and she said she felt dizzy. We headed back to the villa, but she fainted. I got her to the hospital right away."

"What's wrong? Is the baby all right?"

"They don't know yet. They've got her stabilized, but . . . there was a lot of bleeding."

"Fuck." Liam remembered last time. She hadn't fainted, but she'd had pain. And then had bled. Then she'd lost the baby.

God, he didn't want to go through that again. More importantly, he didn't want Abi to go through it again.

"I contacted her doctor in Maryville and she suggests we get her to a hospital back home as soon as possible. She spoke to the doctor here and they said she can travel right away."

"All right. I can be back in about two hours, then we'll fly back together."

He'd used a local airline, wanting to experience what resort guests would on the trip from the bigger island where they'd fly in to the international airport then hop a small plane to the smaller island.

"Liam, the doctor says she should go *now*."

Liam paced. "Fine. Okay. Have the driver take you to the airport now. I'll ensure the jet's ready to go when you get there."

After Liam hung up, he made the necessary calls. His heart pounded in his chest and he hoped to heaven that Abi, and the baby, would be all right.

The elevator doors opened on the fifth floor of the hospital and Liam strode down the hallway to the nurses' station, carrying a large arrangement of flowers in pinks, purples, and accents of yellow.

He'd phoned Del as soon as his flight had arrived and texted once he'd arrived at the hospital, so Del stood at the desk waiting for him.

"Where's Abi? I want to see her," Liam said.

"They've taken her for some tests, so you won't be able to see her until she gets back. Right now her doctor wants to talk to us."

Del led him down a short hallway to an office.

"She said to wait in here and she'll be in as soon as she can." Del sat down in one of the two guest chairs facing the desk.

Liam set the flowers on the desk and sat beside him, his heart pounding.

"How was your flight?" Del asked.

Liam had flown commercial since Abi and Del had flown back on his private jet, but being in first class had made it no hardship.

"Fine. How is Abi? Is she in pain?" Liam knew the doctor would give him the whole story, but he wanted something. The thought of her in discomfort made his heart ache.

"No. She's nauseous and a bit dizzy."

Liam's chest tightened. He had to ask the question he most feared knowing the answer to.

"Do they know if she's going to . . . lose the baby?"

The doctor briskly stepped into the office and closed the door behind her.

"Hello, I'm Dr. McCallister, Abi's family doctor."

She offered her hand to Liam and he shook it.

"I'm Liam Perry."

She sat down behind the desk. "There's a team working to take care of Abi and they've advised me what's going on. Since Abi's been seeing me for years and is comfortable with me, she asked if I'd talk to you and answer any of your questions."

Liam nodded.

"The good news is that mom and baby are doing fine right now," Dr. McCallister explained. "She came close to losing the baby and"—she frowned—"depending on how things went, mom was in some danger, too."

Liam's heart clenched at the thought that they could have lost Abi.

"Should we have known?" Liam asked. "She had some dizziness and nausea and . . ."

Ah, fuck. And Abi had fainted during sex. What the hell was wrong with him that he didn't insist she go to the doctor?

"And . . . ?" the doctor prompted.

"Last night . . . when we had sex . . . she fainted," Liam answered.

The doctor's brown eyes rested on Liam. "All of those things are normal things a woman might experience during pregnancy." Her lips turned up in a smile. "That last one at any time, given the right circumstances. Don't beat yourselves up about it." She leaned forward. "You're her husband, right?"

"Yes," Liam answered.

She turned to Del. "And you're her fiancé?"

"Yes. The divorce isn't final yet," Del said.

"I see. And who's the father?"

"I am," Liam said.

The doctor nodded. "I see things are complicated. Abi told me you're hoping to change her mind about the divorce," Dr. McCallister said to Liam.

"Yes, that's right," Liam said.

She sat back in her chair. "I know this is a difficult time for all of you. But I need you to understand that stress . . . and this situation you find yourselves in is a huge source of stress for Abi . . . is dangerous for her and the baby. Mr. Perry, have you considered the fact that Abi might be worried that you're going to sue for custody?"

His gaze jerked to her face, then shifted to Del who was staring at a paperweight on the desktop.

He *hadn't* considered that.

God, if Abi thought that, she would feel trapped.

"It's important that the two of you figure out what you can do to minimize Abi's stress and make her and her well-being a priority throughout the pregnancy. She'll need both your support."

"Of course," Liam said and Del nodded his agreement.

A knock sounded on the door.

"Excuse me," the doctor said as she stood up to answer it. She spoke with a nurse, then turned back to them.

"The test results look good, but I'd still like to keep her here for a few days. When she leaves the hospital, she should stay with someone who can be with her during the day. She should rest as much as possible."

"We'll figure something out," Del said.

The doctor stayed a little longer and answered their questions, then she excused herself, leaving Liam and Del in the office.

Liam stared at the flowers. Ones he'd picked out with Abi in mind. Because he knew her so well. Because he knew what she liked.

And yet he'd had no clue that she would believe he might take her child from her.

"A lot to think about," Del said.

Liam nodded distractedly, still reeling from the tumultuous emotions roiling through him from everything he'd just learned.

"Yes."

Del stared at him, then stood up and rested his hand on Liam's shoulder.

"We can probably go see Abi now," Del said. "From everything the doctor said, it probably wouldn't be wise for both of us to see her right now, so I'll go grab a coffee while you go in."

Liam drew in a deep breath and nodded, then pushed himself to his feet.

He loved Abi more deeply than he could ever have imagined was possible to love another person. Yet he had caused her so much pain.

He didn't deserve her.

CHAPTER TWENTY-EIGHT

Abi opened her eyes at the feel of a hand on her arm. Liam stared at her, his warm brown eyes filled with sadness. He was sitting in a chair beside her hospital bed.

"Hi." She was so tired. Keeping her eyes open was an effort.

Liam took her hand. "I'm so sorry, kitten."

Alarm spiked through her.

"The doctor told me the baby was okay." Her voice was tight with anxiety.

Had she misunderstood? Had they been waiting to break it to her gently?

He squeezed her hand. "Yes, the baby's fine."

She sucked in a breath, the tension easing from her.

"Thank God." She tightened her fingers around his. "So why did you say you're sorry?"

"Because I wasn't there for you." He leaned back in the chair, pain rippling in the depths of his brown eyes. "Because I'm the one who caused this. I'm the one who put you under so much stress that you almost lost the baby."

She tried to sit up but her head started spinning and she settled back on the pillow.

"Liam, it's not your fault."

He stroked her hair from her face. At the gentleness of his touch, the aching sadness in his eyes, her heart compressed.

"I love you, baby," he murmured. "And I never meant to hurt you."

The depth of feeling in his words tore at her heart.

Oh, God, she loved this man.

But she loved Del, too.

Confusion coiled through her, snaking around her heart and tightening until she could barely breathe.

She couldn't see her life without either one of them.

Tears welled in her eyes. What was she going to do?

Over the next few days, Del and Liam visited her every day. Liam was always there when she woke up in the morning and sat with her while she ate breakfast. Del showed up shortly after and chatted with her, while Liam was a silent presence, his thoughts and feelings hidden from her. Except for the ghost of sadness in his eyes.

She didn't know where things were going from here and neither Del nor Liam seemed inclined to talk about it. Until the third day when the doctor informed her she'd be released the next day. Del and Liam agreed with her that staying in Maryville near her family and Dr. McCallister would be the best.

Del said he could arrange with the university to work from home and that way he could move into her place to stay with her. When September came and he had to go back to teach classes again, the three of them would reevaluate the situation.

During the conversation, she glanced at Liam, but he avoided her gaze. She was surprised he wasn't fighting to be the one to take care of her.

Was the fear of their close call triggering old grief? Causing him to withdraw from her again?

But Liam was there with her. He talked to the doctor every day, keeping tabs on her progress. And he often held her hand and reassured her that everything would be okay. That the baby would be okay. And when she felt the fear well up again, he would hold her hand and prompt her to talk about it.

This was not the old Liam. Last time . . . when they'd actually lost the baby . . . he'd shut the subject down if she tried to talk about it.

She was confused. About her feelings for these two men. About what would happen.

About what she *wanted* to happen.

A knock sounded on Abi's apartment door and she opened it to see a deliveryman holding a gift-wrapped box with a big bow and an arrangement of flowers. She signed the paper on his clipboard, then he handed her the gifts.

She walked to the kitchen and set the flowers on the counter, then pulled away the paper around it. The flowers were in a lovely crystal vase. There was no card, but she was sure these were from Liam.

She walked back into the living room and set the vase on the coffee table, then sat down to open the flat box. She tugged on the wide cloth ribbon, unfastening the bow. She pulled the ribbon from the box, then lifted off the lid. She peeled back the pink tissue inside, revealing a document.

She stared at it in disbelief. It was the divorce papers. A bright pink sticky note stuck out on one side and she flipped to the marked page.

There, right beside the X, was Liam's signature.

He was granting her the divorce.

There was a folded note sitting on the page and she opened it.

Abi,

I know you want to be with Del and I know he'll take good care of you. Better than I seem capable of doing. I don't want to stand in the way of your happiness, so I'm stepping aside. Please know that I will always love you, and if you, or the baby, ever need anything, just call and I'll be there for you.

Liam

Her heart clenched.

Having Liam sign the divorce papers is what she'd wanted for such a long time. What she'd hoped for. What she'd thought she'd needed to find her true happiness.

She burst into tears.

Del walked into the apartment with two bags of groceries.

"Hi, Abi. How are you feeling?"

She was sitting on the couch and as soon as she gazed his way, he realized her eyes were red and swollen. He plunked the bags on the floor and strode to the couch. As he sat down beside her, he noticed the flowers and an open gift box with tissue and wide fabric ribbon trailing from it.

"A gift from Liam?" he guessed. He couldn't believe they hadn't heard from him in two days.

She nodded.

He stroked her hair back from her face. "So what's happened? Why are you upset?"

She handed him a document she was clinging to. He opened it to the marked page and saw Liam's signature.

"It looks like he's granting you the divorce," Del said.

A chaotic whirl of emotions coiled through him. This would mean he would have Abi all to himself. It was what they'd both been hoping for.

But he knew how much Abi loved Liam and a part of him

wondered if this was the worst thing that could happen to Abi. She loved her husband and he was sure that deep inside, she wanted to raise her child with Liam. Even though she loved Del, too.

Abi nodded. "And he's also included an addendum that guarantees he won't take custody of the baby."

"But this isn't good news, is it? It's not what you want anymore."

She stared at him, her gaze laced with guilt.

"It's okay, Abi. We need to be honest with each other."

She drew in a deep, shaky breath.

"I love him," she said. "And I want to be with him." She rested her hand on her stomach. "I want him to be with his baby . . . helping to raise it. Being a father to his child."

Her eyes shimmered.

"But I also want to be with you. I love you, too."

Del sat down beside her and drew her into his arms. She rested her head against his chest.

"Abi, I love you, too. And I want you to be happy. That's the most important thing in the world to me." He stroked her hair. "And I think I know how to fix this."

The knock on the door surprised Liam. Usually, no one bothered him at the quiet country house. He'd come here after sending the papers to Abi several days ago. He needed to ground himself. To think about what his future would be without the woman he loved.

Hopefully, she would still let him be a part of their child's life, but he wouldn't force her to. He definitely wouldn't pursue a custody claim, and he'd put that in writing.

He would do anything to protect Abi, and if that meant stepping out of her life entirely, then that's what he'd do.

He walked to the door and pulled it open. He was shocked to see Abi standing on the other side.

"Abi, what are you doing here?"

"May I come in?" she asked.

"Of course."

He didn't know how she'd gotten here. There wasn't a car in the driveway and he didn't see any sign of Del.

"How did you know I was here?" he asked as he led her to the living room.

"I called your secretary and told her I'm your wife and that I needed to meet with you."

"You could have just called me."

She shook her head. "I needed to talk to you in person."

He gestured to the couch and then moved to the chair, but she grasped his hand. The shock of the contact sent tingles shivering through his entire body.

"No, please. Sit next to me," she said.

He sat down beside her, trying to ignore the urge to pull her into his arms and hold her.

"I want to thank you for your gift," she said.

He nodded. "I want you to be happy."

She squeezed his hand. "I know you do. But I've come here to return it to you."

"The flowers?" he said in surprise, a little confused. "Surely they're dead by now."

"Actually, they're holding up quite well. But, no, I mean the other gift."

She turned to her bag, which she'd set on the floor, and pulled out the flat box he'd wrapped and sent to her. She handed it to him and he opened it, not sure what she was doing.

Inside were the papers, neatly torn in two.

"It was a very thoughtful gift," she said softly, "but it's not what I want anymore."

His heart stuttered. "Abi, what are you saying? Exactly?"

He didn't want to assume anything.

She leaned a little closer, her luminous eyes locked on him.

"I'm saying that I don't want to divorce you."

She raised her hand and glided it along his cheek. The tenderness of her touch moved him deeply.

"I believe that you love me," she said. "And I believe we can work out any emotional issues still between us. Because I know now that we both want this marriage to work more than anything." She drew his face to hers and kissed him lightly, the brush of her soft lips igniting the need in his soul. "And I want you and me to raise our child together."

Disbelief quickly turned to joy surging through him. He pulled her into his arms, holding her tight to him, and captured her mouth in a tender, heartrending kiss.

"Oh, God, Abi. I love you so much."

But he hadn't forgotten the love he'd seen in her eyes when she'd looked at Del. When the two of them had made love.

"What about Del?" he asked.

She leaned back, anxiety washing through her eyes. "Yes, about Del. You know how I feel about him."

His joyful mood waned a little. "You're in love with him."

God, was she only saying this because she felt she owed Liam? Or because she felt stronger about her baby being raised by his real father than being with the man she truly loved?

"Yes, I love him." She took his hand. "And I love you."

"So on some level, you're going to be unhappy no matter which of us you choose."

"I've chosen you, Liam. You're the baby's father. And my husband."

"Fuck. So it's not really that you love me. At least, not more than Del."

"Liam, I love you with all my heart. I always have. And when you signed the divorce papers . . . and promised you wouldn't take the baby from me . . . I knew that you would never emotionally abandon me again. So you are my first choice. Always."

She sighed.

"But in a perfect world, I wouldn't have to choose between you and Del. Because what the three of us have together is very special. You love him just as much as I do. He loves both of us. And I know he'll love the baby, too."

"What are you getting at, Abi?"

He stared into her big, blue eyes, so filled with hope.

"I'm wondering why we can't make ours a perfect world." She squeezed his hand. "Del and I talked about this, and we both agreed. I want to know if all three of us can be together. All of us live together and raise the baby together."

Liam frowned. The three of them certainly had a spectacular sexual relationship. But could it be more than that?

"Why would he possibly agree to that? Won't he resent that he can't marry you? And what about having a child of his own? He'll surely want that at some point."

She gazed at him uncertainly. "If we do this, then I could have another child by him, too."

She stroked his cheek. "Liam, I know you have a certain idea of what a family is. I know you've craved that your whole life. But this could be even better. What child wouldn't love to have three parents to love them?"

She patted her stomach. "I know this child will be dearly loved by all three of us. Wouldn't you still love a child I carried by Del?"

Liam frowned as he stared at her stomach. Thinking of another baby inside her later. Del's child.

Thinking of Del making love to her.

"Where is Del? He drove you here, didn't he?"

"Yes, he's in the park down the street. He didn't want to interfere with us talking, so he's waiting for me to text him."

"Tell him to come in."

Abi grabbed her phone and tapped in a message, glancing at Liam uncertainly.

A few moments later, Del knocked on the door. Liam strode

to the entrance and let him in. Del followed Liam into the living room.

"Abi tells me you want to move in with us," Liam said. "That you think we can make it work with you being her second husband."

"You'd be her husband," Del said. "I wouldn't have a legal status like that."

"But you do agree that you'd essentially be her husband?"

Del shrugged. "Yes."

"And you want to have children with her, too?"

"Is that a deal breaker?" Del asked, staring at Liam's stony expression.

Liam frowned, but then his mouth turned up in a slow smile.

"I think it's the best solution possible and I kick myself for not suggesting it. I know how much you love Abi, and together I believe the three of us will build a very strong foundation for our growing family."

"So you're okay with Abi having children with me, too?"

"I wasn't sure at first, but I realize that any child Abi has, or that you have, I'll love as my own, so of course I'm okay with it."

He tugged Del into a big hug. When he released him, he patted his back.

"We're going to have a house full of love, and that's all I've ever really wanted."

Abi surged into his arms and kissed him.

His heart soared. He knew he'd found heaven on earth. He would spend the rest of his life with the woman he loved. And with his best friend. Together they would create a most unusual family, but one raised with love, caring, and mutual respect.

EPILOGUE

Abi blinked at the sunshine then her eyelids fluttered open. Panic surged through her.

"The baby!" Her hand slid to her stomach.

Liam wasn't in bed, but Del opened his eyes.

"It's okay, sweetheart," he said in a sleep-roughed voice, sitting up and sliding his arm around her. "Jenny's with your sister. Remember, you wanted this weekend with just the three of us?"

She glanced around, her breathing slowly returning to normal. They were at the summer house. She had suggested this weekend away because Liam had been traveling a lot lately and she really wanted the three of them to have some romantic time together.

But also, she had something important to discuss with both of them. Something she wasn't sure Liam was going to be happy about.

"Oh, that's right. It's just she always cries—"

"By eight. I know." He kissed her forehead. "And even when Liam or I get up to feed her, you still wake up."

She laughed. "Well, all those mornings breast-feeding when

you guys couldn't take her have me well trained. Thank heavens my breasts have stopped producing milk now so I don't wake up leaking."

He laughed as his hand slid to her breast and cupped it.

"Ah, good times. Believe me, Liam and I enjoyed those days of mommy breasts."

She turned and snuggled against him, making sure to push her breasts tight against his big, hard chest.

"Am I too small for you now?"

"Hmm, let me check," he said with a laugh as he leaned her back on the bed then cupped both her breasts.

"Good morning. You two look as if you're having fun." Liam set a tray down on the table by the window.

"I'm checking to see if Abi's breasts are too small now that she's no longer breast-feeding."

Liam's eyebrow arched up as he walked to the bed and sat down beside her.

"Good question. Let's check that out a little more closely." Liam grasped the hem of her nightshirt and drew it up, baring her thighs, then Del drew her forward while Liam pulled the shirt over her head and tossed it aside.

Both men now stared at her naked breasts hungrily.

"Mmm." Liam's gaze circled each breast, then lingered on the tips, her nipples rising to tight buds. "I think that at any size . . ." His warm, brown eyes turned to her face. "They're perfect."

They both leaned in and she sucked in a breath as their warm mouths covered her nipples, then she moaned as they suckled.

"Ohhh, as nice as this is, I'd like to have some of that breakfast Liam brought in here before it's cold."

Liam nipped her hard nub, then swirled his tongue over it.

"I can make you a new breakfast," he said hoarsely.

It would be so delightful to go with the flow right now, but she had promised herself she would tell them first thing this morning. If she let sex distract her, she'd never have the conversation this weekend.

She laughed and pressed against their shoulders. "I'm hungry now. And those eggs smell delicious."

The guys drew back and when Liam stood up, she saw that his swollen cock was barely contained in his pajamas. She grabbed her nightshirt and pulled it on again, then scampered to the table.

"The idea was that I was bringing you breakfast in bed," Liam said as she sat down at the round table, a fabulous view of the lake outside the window.

"And I appreciate that, but I feel like sitting."

Del joined them and Liam poured them each a cup of coffee. Abi stared at the steaming cup, longing for a sip, but picked up her fork instead and took a bite of the omelet Liam had made. Mushrooms, onions, peppers, and a delightful combination of herbs. Liam really was a good cook.

Her cell phone chimed and she picked it up and checked her messages. Claire had texted a picture of Kurt holding Jenny while she waved at the camera. A laugh bubbled up in Abi at the sight of her baby girl's adorable face and her brother's huge grin.

"Kurt really enjoys being an uncle," she said as she showed Liam and Del the photo.

Seeing Kurt holding Jenny warmed her heart.

Her family had been taken aback at her announcement that she was going to be with Liam *and* Del. Kurt had been the most resistant, falling into his usual role of protective older brother. But he was slowly coming around.

Her sisters' attitudes had been harder to gauge. Jaime had half-kiddingly said she didn't understand how Abi could want to take care of two men. Claire had jumped to her defense saying it was clear their baby sister had these men trained right because they would do anything for her. Either way, they had both been supportive all the way.

Abi had been most surprised at her dad, who'd simply asked if she was happy.

She smiled and put her phone down, then continued eating.

"You've been traveling so much lately, Liam," she said. "Do you know how long you'll have to keep doing that?"

He'd been gone more than two weeks at a time each month for the past three months.

Liam glanced at her. "I'm not sure."

"Okay. I mean, I know you have to do it for your business, and I'm not complaining, but we all miss you."

The gaze she sent him was intended to let him know how much *she* missed him when he was gone.

He smiled and took her hand. "Don't worry, kitten. I don't think it'll be too much longer."

She sent him a small smile, then ate some more eggs, buoying up her courage to make the announcement.

"What's on your mind, Abi?" Del asked.

She glanced his way. "What do you mean?"

"You've been distracted for days, and now you have this tense aura about you."

Liam raised an eyebrow. "And it's not because of coffee, since you haven't had any yet. And we all know how much you love your morning coffee. Do you have something you want to tell us, Abi?"

She bit her lip. Then she nodded.

"I do. It seems I'm pregnant again."

She watched as both men's eyes lit up, then they whooped in joy. Liam stood up and dragged her into his arms and twirled her around, then Del took her and squeezed her tight.

Finally, she sat back on her chair, her head spinning.

"Why the hell were you so nervous telling us?" Liam asked. "You know we all want more children."

She reached out and took his hand, then took Del's, too. She drew in a deep breath, then glanced from Liam's chocolate-brown eyes to Del's warm, olive-green ones.

"I know, it's just . . ." Her stomach quaked. "It's Del's baby."

Del's face lit up and he surged to his feet and pulled her into his arms again. She was so glad to give Del this.

She loved that she was carrying Del's baby. It made her so happy. But it also stressed her because Liam was her husband, and as much as he'd said he'd be okay with her having Del's baby, she wasn't sure how he'd handle it when faced with the reality.

"Well, it's about fucking time," Liam said. He patted Del on the back, then pulled Abi into a tight embrace.

Her eyes widened. "What do you mean?"

He chuckled, a rumbling from deep in his chest. "Now I don't have to keep going away for weeks on end."

She frowned. "I don't understand."

Del laughed. "Really, man? You did that for me?"

Liam squeezed Del's shoulder. "Of course."

Abi glanced from one to the other. "You guys want to explain it to me?"

"Liam was giving us time alone together," Del said, "while you were most fertile so my sperm wouldn't have any competition."

Abi's jaw dropped as she stared at Liam.

"You wanted me to get pregnant by Del?"

Liam smiled. "I wanted our second child to be fathered by Del, yes. I wanted him to know the joy I've had at seeing my first child born. To know I was responsible for that life being created."

Liam drew her into his arms and kissed her tenderly, then he drew back and stroked her hair from her face.

"Now you can expect me to be home all the time. I'm not leaving the three of you again." His hand slid to her stomach. "Or should I say four?" He laughed. "Especially remembering how horny you were during your last pregnancy."

"Well, considering how much you've been away from us . . .

and how considerate you were to Del . . ." Suddenly, the sweetness of his gesture tugged at her heart and tears welled in her eyes despite her light tone.

"Oh, there are the hormones in action," Del observed with a chuckle.

"As I was saying," she continued, blinking back the tears, "considering those things, I think you should have total say in what we do next, Liam."

"You mean like me ordering you to strip off all your clothes and lie down on the bed with your legs open?"

She sucked in a breath as heat shimmered through her. "Yeah, just like that."

His eyes darkened. "Good. Then do it."

She pulled her nightshirt up and over her head. Their gazes lingered on her naked breasts and she ran her fingers underneath them and lifted. The sparks in their eyes ignited her desire. She glided her fingertips down her stomach, then pushed her panties downward. Slowly. Watching the hunger in their eyes.

She dropped the panties to the floor then sauntered to the bed and lay down across it. She opened her legs wide.

"Oh, yeah, baby, that's nice," Liam said. "I love seeing your pussy exposed like that. Now stroke it for me."

She ran her fingers down her belly, then lingered just above her intimate flesh, teasing them. Then she slid over the slick flesh. She stroked the length of the folds, then dipped a finger inside.

"Oh, I'm so wet." She sighed and arched her breasts upward.

"I think those perfect breasts need some attention," Liam said.

"I'll do it," Del said eagerly, heading around the bed behind her.

He knelt on the floor, then gathered her long hair together and spread it in a mass beside her head, stroking it gently. He kissed her cheek, then his large hands covered her breasts. His gentle caresses had her moaning softly.

Liam walked toward her, then knelt on the floor facing her.

"That leaves me to tend to this." He dipped his head down and licked her pussy.

She whimpered and arched to his mouth. He chuckled against her flesh, then he drove his tongue into her. It swirled and lapped inside her. She curled her fingers in his glossy, dark brown hair, holding him to her.

His tongue found her clit and he flicked over it, sending vibrations of pure delight through her.

"Oh, yes. That's so good."

Del leaned in and captured her lips, kissing her while Liam drove her need higher with strokes and flicks of his tongue on her sensitive bud.

She drove her tongue deep into Del's mouth, undulating against his tongue. Del's fingers rippled over her hard nipples in strumming motions, then he squeezed them and she moaned into his mouth.

Heat boiled inside her as the pleasure built within her.

She tugged her mouth from Del's, sucking in a deep breath as she felt a wave of bliss surging through her.

"Oh, God, I'm going to come."

As Liam suckled her clit, he pushed his fingers inside her and began thrusting. She sucked in a breath, and Del watched her, a smile on his face as the pleasure expanded inside her.

She gasped and exploded on a firestorm of ecstasy.

Liam kept on suckling and thrusting as she rode the wave of pure bliss.

When she finally collapsed on the bed, he lifted his head and smiled at her.

"That's one," Liam said. "I wonder how many today will bring."

He stood up and his cock pushed out of the flap in his pajama bottoms. Long. Hard. And pulsing.

She rolled over and presented her ass to him, anxious to feel him inside her. He chuckled.

"First, baby, I want to see you suck Del's cock."

Del stood up and pulled out his rigid cock and offered it to her. She wrapped her lips around him and swallowed his cockhead into her mouth. She squeezed his shaft with her hand and lapped her tongue around the bulbous, mushroom-shaped head, swirling round and round.

"Oh, yeah, sweetheart. I *love* that," Del said.

"And I fucking love watching your mouth moving on Del's cock," Liam said behind her, his hands wrapped around her hips. She knew any second now, he could drive his mammoth cock right into her.

"Take it deeper, baby," Liam instructed.

She started moving down Del's cock. Slowly. Gripping him tightly in her lips. Del groaned.

"Is she squeezing you tight, Del?" Liam asked.

"Oh, fuck, yeah."

She opened her throat and took Del all the way in. His guttural sounds of pleasure encouraged her. She began moving up and down his hard member, the feel of it sliding between her lips delighting her.

"Fuck, baby, I want to be inside you, too." Liam's voice was coarse with need.

She pulled back, letting Del fall from her lips, and glanced over her shoulder.

"I want that, too," she said.

She watched him wrap his hand around his thick shaft and press it to her slickness. The feel of the hot, hard head against her made her moan.

Slowly, he slid his enormous cock into her, his wide cockhead stretching her vagina as it glided deep inside.

"Oh, yes, you feel so good inside me."

She squeezed him, making him groan.

She gazed up at Del.

"I want both of you inside me. And I don't mean in my mouth." She smiled. "Though I'm quite happy to finish this for you."

Del took her hands and guided her up so she was facing him, still on her knees. Liam held her hips, keeping her firmly against him.

Del kissed her, his lips moving tenderly on hers. Then he smiled.

"I'm quite happy to move to the main event."

Liam slid back, his cock causing a riot of intense sensations in her as it glided down her passage. Then it slipped away.

"Come sit on my lap in the chair," Liam said, taking her hand and guiding her to her feet.

She turned to him and ran her hand over his chest.

"Actually, why don't I sit on Del's lap this time?" She found Liam's nipple and squeezed as she gave him an impish grin. "I was thinking that maybe this time, you could be behind me."

A light flared in Liam's eyes. He had yet to experience that with her. But she'd been practicing every time Liam was away by having Del use larger penis-shaped vibrators in her back passage so she could surprise Liam.

"I would fucking love that, kitten," Liam said, his eyes blazing.

Del grabbed her hand and guided her to the big armchair facing the fireplace, then he sat down. She settled herself on his lap, her knees cradling his thighs between them.

Liam stood by the arm of the chair, watching as Del pressed his cockhead to her wet flesh, and as she lowered herself onto him.

"Oh, God, Del's cock feels so good filling me, Liam."

"And her pussy feels so warm and wet around me," Del said.

Liam dropped his pajama pants to the floor, now totally naked, and she watched hungrily as he slathered lube on his cock. Watching Liam's hand move over it, spreading the shiny gel over the whole thing, made her heart stammer.

He smiled, then leaned in and kissed her. Then he moved behind her and knelt on the floor.

Oh, God, the thought of that massive shaft pushing inside her ass was both intimidating and exciting. The head nudged against her and she moaned in anticipation.

"Okay, kitten?" Liam asked.

"Oh, yeah. I can hardly wait."

He chuckled, then she felt the pressure as he eased forward. Del grasped her ass and drew her cheeks apart as Liam's cockhead pressed inside her. Stretching her.

He kept moving. Slowly. Her channel widening around his flesh.

She grasped Del's shoulders as Liam continued. She started to feel a little pain.

"Do you want me to stop, kitten?" Liam asked. "We can try this again another day."

She realized she'd tensed up, her fingers digging into Del's shoulders.

"No. I really want you inside me there."

She drew in a deep breath and relaxed her body, resting her head on Del's shoulder.

"Okay. Here we go," Liam said.

He moved forward again and she focused on keeping her body relaxed, despite the huge shaft pushing into her. His cockhead was halfway in now, but there was so much more to go. She drew in another deep breath as he continued moving slowly.

His cockhead was almost all the way in now.

He stopped and his hand glided along her back.

"You okay?"

She squeezed around him. Del twitched inside her.

She giggled. "Yeah. I think you should keep going."

Liam grasped her hips again and she felt his cock pushing deeper into her. Filling her more and more.

Finally, she felt his groin against her.

Both men were totally embedded inside her.

"How does it feel, Liam?" she asked.

"Fucking incredible, baby. You're gripping me so tightly."

He drew back slowly, with a soft groan, then glided deep again.

"Fuck, baby, thank you so much for this."

She took his hands and guided them to her breasts, beaming at his appreciation. He cupped her and she turned her head. He captured her lips in a sweet kiss. Then she turned to Del and he kissed her, too, his eyes glittering.

She lifted her body, feeling Del's hard cock sliding along her passage, then she moved down again. Liam groaned and glided back slowly, then forward again. His hands slid back to her hips and he guided her body up and down on Del, while he moved his cock in her ass.

"Oh, God. That feels so good." She sighed, following the guidance of his hands. Moving her up and down on Del.

Del groaned. Pleasure quivered through her. Then drew tighter and tighter. Coiling deep in her core.

Their bodies moved faster now, gliding into her in the same rhythm. The thrusts faster. She felt so intensely full. Two cocks deep inside her. Gliding in and out. Her vaginal muscles tightened around Del, making him groan. Liam nuzzled her neck as he plunged deep inside her, making her moan.

"Oh, God, I'm so close." Her whole body seemed to tingle in anticipation. Ready to explode any second.

"Oh, fuck, baby. You like both our cocks inside you?" Liam asked. "Thrusting deep and hard?"

His cock pulsed deep into her ass again as Del filled her, too.

"Yes," she whimpered. "Oh, God."

"I'm going to fucking come," Liam groaned in her ear.

Then she felt him pulse inside her. Heat filled her.

"Ohhh," she wailed, pleasure pummeling her insides. "I'm . . . ohhh . . ." Then it burst inside her. A primal pleasure exploding deep in her core.

She moaned, riding the wave of bliss.

Del groaned, then pulsed forward, holding her tight to him as he erupted inside her, driving her pleasure even higher.

Her thin wail filled the room. Her world shattered around her as she shot straight to ecstasy. Her two men kept moving inside her, keeping her at the height of bliss.

Finally, she collapsed against Del. He wrapped his arms tight around her.

Liam pulled out and sat on the arm of the chair.

"That was truly spectacular," he murmured.

She squeezed around Del's cock, still partly rigid inside her. She rested her head on his chest and gazed up at Liam.

"I'm glad you're happy about the baby," she said.

"I'm thrilled," Liam said.

She turned her gaze to Del. "And what about you, Daddy?"

He laughed, a sound so filled with joy her heart soared. He tightened his arms around her.

"I am one of the two happiest men in the world."

She laughed as Liam slid his arm around her, too.

"And I've got to be the luckiest woman in the world."

She sighed, enjoying the warmth of her two men close to her. Never would she have believed she could be so happy.